1/08 Ingram 05"

# Hell Hole

# CHRIS GRABENSTEIN

ST. MARTIN'S MINOTAUR
NEW YORK

This is a work of fiction. All of the characters, organizations, and events portrayed in this novel are either products of the author's imagination or are used fictitiously.

www.minotaurbooks.com

Library of Congress Cataloging-in-Publication Data

Grabenstein, Chris.
    Hell hole / Chris Grabenstein.—1st ed.
        p.   cm.
    ISBN-13: 978-0-312-38230-8
    ISBN-10: 0-312-38230-8
    1. Police—New Jersey—Fiction.   2. Soldiers—Crimes against—Fiction.   3. Conspiracies—
Fiction.   I. Title.
    PS3607.R27H46   2008
    813'.6—dc22

                                                                    2008018093

First Edition: August 2008

10   9   8   7   6   5   4   3   2   1

For Captain Dave and Kathy and all
the firefighters of FDNY Engine Company 23
and those who wait for them to come home

# Acknowledgments

I'd like to thank . . .

Chief Michael Bradley of the Long Beach Island Police for telling me so many interesting stories about pirates and police work down the Jersey Shore.

Bruce Springsteen for allowing me to borrow his words.

My agent, Eric Myers, for finding Danny and Ceepak their wonderful new home.

My editor Michael Homler, plus Andrew Martin, Jason Pinter, Kelly Ragland, Hector DeJean, Kenneth J. Silver, and all the other folks at that wonderful new house, St. Martin's Minotaur.

Captain Dave Morkal of the FDNY for teaching me how to get out of a blazing Hell Hole alive.

My four amazing brothers and all my incredible sisters-in-law for their never-ending support.

The three cats who keep me company in the writer's room and Fred, the dog, who takes me on long contemplative walks so I can work out plot twists.

And, of course, my beautiful, beloved first reader (and wife) J.J. I couldn't write without her.

Scrawled on a wall in Baghdad:

*And when he gets to heaven*
*To Saint Peter he will tell*
*"Just another soldier reporting, sir.*
*I've served my time in Hell."*

# Hell Hole

# 1

*It's almost* 1:00 AM on a Saturday and the partiers inside the rental house at the corner of Kipper Street and Beach Lane are chanting like drunken sailors chasing a runaway keg of beer.

*"Two old ladies lying in bed,*
*One rolled over to the other and said,*
*'I wanna be an Airborne Ranger.'"*

Airborne. That's army. Soldiers, not sailors. Sounds like half a beer-blasted battalion.

*"Live a life of guts and danger!"*

No wonder the neighbors called the cops. This is definitely a 10-43. That's what we call a disturbance. Since Sea Haven Township is basically an eighteen-mile-long summer paradise where people buy their beer in suitcase-sized cardboard containers, we get a lot of 10-43s every Friday and Saturday all summer long.

Judging by the heap of bottles and cans in both recyclables bins at the curb, the guys renting 22 Kipper are also on their way to a 10-24.

Intoxicated. I'd say they've been going at it all night long. I see Bud and Heineken and Foster's with a couple Corona Lights tossed in for good measure. Guess one of the guys is counting his carbs.

"What's our play, sir?" asks my partner for the night. Her name is Samantha Starky. She's a part-time summer cop, which is what I used to be. A Jersey Shore town like ours needs auxiliary cops every summer because, for two and a half months, our population swells from twenty thousand to a quarter million and lots of them spend their entire vacations knocking back malt-based beverages.

My usual partner, John Ceepak, isn't working tonight. Apparently, he doesn't need the overtime pay as desperately as I do. Apparently, he also doesn't need a 52-inch plasma-screen TV before *Monday Night Football* kicks off in a couple months.

"Should we radio for backup, sir?"

"No," I say. "We'll just knock on the door and ask them to knock it off."

"Ten-four. I've got your six, sir."

Sam Starky? She's twenty-one. Five years younger than me. Watches a lot of cop shows on TV. Rents too many Tom Cruise movies. *Top Gun* must be a particular favorite if she wants to take my "six."

We weave our way through the jumble of cars parked at all kinds of screwy angles in the street. The house, which I'm sure these guys rented for the week like most of our visitors, looks the same as all the other two-story Colonials standing shoulder-to-shoulder on the streets leading down to the beach.

But most of our visitors drive minivans, not tanks like these guys. Every one of their cars is huge. I count a Suburban, a pickup truck with an extended cab, one Chevy Tahoe, and a couple other SUVs that resemble Darth Vader's helmet on wheels. Their license plates are all from out of state. Pennsylvania. North Carolina. Illinois. Tennessee. Michigan.

*"Saw on old lady marching down the road . . ."*

Great. They've marched on to the second verse.

*"Had a knife in her hand and a ninety-pound load . . ."*

"Should you draw your weapon, sir?" Starky whispers behind me. I carry a gun. She doesn't. I chase bad guys. She writes parking tickets.

"Nah," I say, reflexively checking my Glock to make sure it's strapped to my hip. "They're just drunk."

"They sound like military. They may be armed."

Great. Thanks for pointing that out.

"Come on," I say and lead the way through the bumpers and chrome until we hit the gate that swings open into the postage stamp–size backyard. It's basically a patio with a picnic table and propane grill. I count five pairs of sandals scattered near the door.

Five drunken soldiers against me and Officer Starky. I like our odds. Starky is scrappy. Studies martial arts. Tae Kwon Do, which is different from Karate or Tai Chi. I know this because she's been yammering about it all night while we cruised the sleepy streets of Sea Haven and she made me even drowsier.

Inside, the guys are still screaming and chanting about "ranger school."

*"Whatcha gonna do when you get there?"* hollers the leader.

*"Jump and swim and kill without care,"* comes the reply.

I rap my knuckles against the sliding glass door.

"Police."

Inside all I hear is rowdy laughter.

I'm assuming these guys are soldiers. We also get a lot of vacationing cops and firefighters from up in the city who come down here every summer to blow off a little steam. Usually, we just have to ask once and they blow a little quieter.

"Police!" I call out again.

They answer with a blast of hard-core heavy metal: "Cum on Feel the Noize" recorded by a hair group from the eighties called Quiet Riot. If only this riot were.

"I don't think they heard us, sir," says Starky.

Actually, I think they did. The hard rock anthem is simply their subtle way of telling us to go away.

Now the whole aluminum door frame is shimmying. It's like they've got another car parked inside the living room—one of those pimped-out rides with the giant sub-woofers packed in the trunk. I figure this is what an earthquake must sound like—only with better lyrics. This is why my full-time partner John Ceepak and I only dig eighties music as done by the poet laureate of the Jersey Shore, Mr. Bruce Springsteen.

I knock again. This time I use my whole fist and pound on the glass. "Sea Haven police!"

Suddenly, this huge mountain of a man appears on the other side of the door. A camouflage cap shades his eyes.

I suck in some air. Try to make my chest look one-third as big as his. The bug light overhead illuminates my badge. I really hope I look like a cop, even though I know I look more like a customer-service rep at Best Buy since I'm wearing the uniform polo shirt up top and cargo shorts down below. What can I say? It's the middle of July.

"Sir, can you please turn it down." I make a big knob-twisting gesture. "The music?"

The guy glares at me some more.

He's like a side of beef squeezed tight inside an army green T-shirt. His jaw is as squared-off as the creases in his cap. I think he has head muscles. I can see the scalp flex above his ears.

Wait. He just smiled. Check that. It's a sneer.

He brings a pint can of Foster's lager up to his lips. Drains it. Brings it down. Crushes the can so I can watch his forearm tendons ripple. Then he marches out of view.

"Crank it up!" I hear him shout to somebody in the living room.

"What's our next move, sir?"

I look at Starky. Her eyes are big and blue—like one of those oil paintings of waifish children on the walls of some of our township's finer motels.

"Should I radio for backup?"

Again with the backup.

"No," I say. "There's not much more we *can* do. We'll write them up. Slip a summons under the door."

"Sir, I think we should go in there and *make* them dial it down a notch," suggests Starky. "They're ruining everyone else's vacation!"

"True," I say, "but most courts consider making noise a low-level offense when measured against the high respect they historically hold for the sanctity of the home."

I think I got that right.

Ceepak taught it to me. He's usually the senior partner when we're on patrol. He's memorized the whole Constitution.

"But—" Starky sputters.

Then I remember this other Ceepak trick.

"You have your ticket book?"

"Yes, sir."

I point at all the vehicles parked higgledy-piggledy in the street. "Some of these cars appear to be parked illegally. For instance, that black Suburban is currently blocking an active driveway."

"Yes, sir!"

*"We may need to call the tow truck!"* I say it loud enough to be heard over the "Noize."

Starky scampers back to our patrol car. I think I just made her night. I reach for my radio. If a tow truck shows up, these guys will definitely stop disturbing the peace long enough to come outside to protest their vehicles' imminent impoundment.

Now a van makes the turn off Beach Lane and pulls up in front of the party house. Headlights glint off the FOR RENT sign jammed into the pea pebble front lawn. I hope next week's tenants are quieter. I hope they're monks.

"Excuse me, Officer," says the woman behind the wheel. Her red hair resembles a wiry copper scrub brush. "Is this twenty-two Kipper?"

"Yeah."

"Great."

She opens up her door. I see latex. A bikini made out of stretchy rubber—the stuff they use in bungee chords. She's also wearing spiked high heels. Red. The rear door slides open. Four other women stumble out. Now I see lingerie. A nurse's outfit with an impractically short skirt. A bathing suit made out of yellow caution tape.

Great. The strippers have arrived from Atlantic City.

"Officer Starky?"

I turn around to see my young partner gawking at the five exotic dancers. Her jaw is somewhere near her collarbone.

"Sir?"

"Write 'em up."

"What?" Red protests.

"You're parked illegally."

"Come on," pleads the last girl out of the van. I see she's wearing an American flag. Stars up top. Stripes down below. "We're here to entertain the troops!"

The music behind me suddenly stops.

"Officer?"

I turn around.

It's meaty man from the other side of the patio door. He is currently standing, hands on hips, three feet behind me. Guess he studied "stealth" in Ranger school.

"Is there a problem?" he asks.

"Yeah," I say. "She can not park her vehicle in the middle of a residential street."

"Agreed." He does a series of hand signals to indicate that the lead stripper should return to her van, proceed down the block, and park in an empty spot near the sand dunes.

"Hunh?" Apparently, Ms. Rubber Bands doesn't read military sign language.

"Move your vehicle," snaps lantern jaw. "Now." He turns to the other strippers adjusting their straps and heels and God-only-knows-what-else. "The rest of you? Inside. Move."

The women wiggle and giggle, then squeeze their way around the vehicles and scamper into the house.

"I'm Sergeant Dale Dixon," he suddenly thrusts his hand out toward me. I take it.

"Danny Boyle."

He sniffs. Grunts. Releases his grip. "Boyle."

I nod.

He seems a little wobbly. Those Hawaiian Punch–size tins of Foster's will do that to you. Trust me. I know. There's nothing like Australia's amber nectar to make you forget how to operate your feet.

"I apologize for the noise."

"Yeah, well, your neighbors are complaining."

"Again, I apologize. I'm afraid our homecoming celebration got a little out of hand. I hope you will extend us the professional courtesy of ignoring this minor infraction."

I think about that for a second. Remember how he sneered at me.

"You guys just back from Iraq?"

"Affirmative."

I look up at him. I have to. He's even taller than Ceepak.

Ah, what the hell.

I've been known to party hardy in my day. This one time, a bunch of us made so much noise, the cops came knocking three different times. We didn't let them in, either.

"You'll keep it down?"

He nods.

I nod toward Starky. She folds up her summons book. I clip the radio back to my belt. No need to bother the boys over at Undertow Auto Towing.

"But you guys gotta move these vehicles," I say. "I don't want the neighbors calling again tomorrow to complain about that."

"Roger. Will do."

"And you need to keep the . . . you know . . ." I search for the right word. "The *dancers* away from the windows."

"Right. We're good to go?"

I nod. "Yeah." I gesture toward the house. "You guys all Airborne?"

"Roger that."

"So was my partner."

He looks at Starky.

"Not her. My regular partner. John Ceepak. He was with the 101st Airborne. Military police. You ever run into him over in Iraq?"

"Negative. Never heard of a Ceepak. Then again—it's a big war."

"Yeah."

"We were with the three-one-three out of the Eighty-second. Echo Company."

I nod like I know what the numbers mean, which I don't.

"Sergeant Dixon?" It's one of the other partiers—a tall, lanky guy in baggy shorts and flip-flops. He's on the patio waving a cell phone.

"What?"

"It's Smith."

"Really?" Dixon takes a step toward the house. Pea pebbles crunch under his boots. "Kindly inform Corporal Smith that he is seriously late. This party began at nineteen hundred hours."

The guy with the phone shakes his head. Looks upset.

"Corporal Smith is dead. Suicide."

# 2

*Show's over.*

The strippers climb back into their van. Dixon pulls out a thick wad of bills, peels off several, and hands them to Ms. Rubber Bands behind the wheel.

"Thank you for being punctual," he says.

The stripper shakes her head. "No—thank *you*." The curls in her hair bounce like coils in a rusty bed frame. "Thank you for everything you guys, you know, did for America. You sure you don't want us to hang out? No charge."

"Thank you, ma'am. But we have pressing company business to attend to."

"Okay," she says. "If you change your mind, you know how to reach us."

Dixon chops her a salute. "Yes, ma'am. Thank you, ma'am."

She giggles and salutes back. I'm reminded of Mariah Carey and a USO show. The van pulls away.

"Lieutenant Worthless?" Dixon calls to the lanky guy, the one who came out to the porch with the Nextel phone and the bad news.

"Yes?" Lanky limps across the patio. I'm thinking Lieutenant Worthless came home from Iraq with some souvenirs in his shin. Shrapnel.

"I need to go ID Smith's body."

"I'll go, sir," says this other guy who just came into the backyard. He's enormous—heftier than Dixon.

"Send me, chief!" Another one stumbles out the door. Italian nose. Hawaiian shirt.

"I'll go!" This one's a short, tough-looking dude, maybe Mexican. He has a khaki bandanna wrapped around his noggin.

There are now four juiced-up guys packed on the patio. All of them look like soldiers. All of them also look tanked.

Dixon addresses the one who volunteered first.

"Are you the squad leader of this unit, Mr. Rutledge?"

"Negative, sir."

"Then stand down. Toss me your car keys."

"Yes, sir."

"And Butt Lips?"

"Sir?"

"Go inside and grab me a couple cold beers for the ride."

"Whoa," I say. "Hold up." I raise my hand. The guy Rutledge, the one with the extremely unfortunate nickname of Butt Lips, freezes.

Dixon doesn't like that. He eyeballs me like I'm an insect that just crawled out of his sleeping bag.

"Is there some problem, Officer Boyle?"

"Yeah. You're drunk. No way am I allowing you behind the wheel of any one of these vehicles. You'll kill somebody."

"Duty calls," he says. "The state police insist that one of us come down to their location and identify Corporal Smith's remains. His family, apparently, cannot perform that unwelcome task because they live in Baltimore."

"I understand all that, okay? But you are not driving. Not tonight."

Dixon inches closer. We're nearly nose to nose. Actually, it's more nose to sternum. I feel hot air seep through the vent holes in my cop cap as it steams out of the taller man's snout.

"Shall I call for backup, sir?"

Starky. Ms. One-Track-Mind. I believe she doubts my ability to de-fuse our current situation without heavily armed assistance. Maybe a full SWAT team.

I shake my head.

"Look, Sergeant Dixon," I say, "you're drunk. Okay? You can not and will not drive a vehicle this evening."

"One of my men needs me! I can't leave him like that. Jesus—dead in a stinking shithouse?"

"I understand. You need to be there. Fine. I'll radio in and get per-mission to drive you wherever you need to go." I gesture toward our cop car. "We'll give you an official police escort. Flashing lights, siren, the works."

Dixon gives me the slit eyes again.

"You ever see a dead body, son?"

"Yeah," I answer.

One on a Tilt-A-Whirl. Number two came courtesy of the mad mouse. Then there was the guy I personally made dead. Yeah. I've seen a dead body or three. However, I see no need to rehash any of that with Sergeant Dixon.

But my "yeah" doesn't seem to suffice. He keeps at it.

"You ever see a man after he's jammed a pistol inside his mouth and blown the roof off his brain?"

I shake my head. No. That one I have not seen.

This seems to make Dixon ease up. Soften.

"Me, neither," he says. "Fortunately, I've never had one of my men take the coward's way out before. Fucking Smith. Fucking chickenshit. This was supposed to be a party. . . ."

He reaches into a hip pocket on his cargo pants. Pulls out a leather cigar case. Pops it open, finds a plump stogie. Fires it up with the snap-click of his Zippo.

"Let's roll," he says.

Starky and I follow him to our car. Hoo-ah. We're all off to see another dead body.

———

The desk sergeant gives me and Starky permission to escort Sergeant Dale Dixon down to the rest stop off exit 52 of the Garden State Parkway.

According to the state police, a janitor working the late shift discovered Corporal Shareef Smith's dead body locked inside a toilet stall in the men's room a little after 11:30 PM. The police also found a MapQuest map tucked inside Smith's shirt pocket. It indicated that he was on his way to 22 Kipper Street in Sea Haven, New Jersey. A cell phone number was scrawled in the margins of the map. So the state troopers called; Lieutenant "Worthless" answered.

The state police reported that Mr. Smith had jammed a pistol inside his mouth and blown a hole through the back of his skull. One shot. It's all you usually get when you take the do-it-yourself route.

Exit 52 on the GSP is ten miles south of the Sea Haven exit. But first you have to take the causeway off the island and head west on Route 22 to the entrance ramp. All told, we'll be chauffeuring Sergeant Dixon about fifteen miles.

Now we're crossing the bridge to the mainland, leaving behind the happy tourist world of miniature golf and soft serve ice cream and clam chowder and never-ending surf and fudge. Heading into the other New Jersey. The one where it isn't vacation every day all summer long.

I smell burning leaves.

Or fried dog poop.

"Sergeant?" Samantha Starky is sitting up front with me. I'm driving. Dixon is in the back, flicking his Zippo, firing up his cigar again. Frying the dog poop.

"What?"

"You can not smoke in this vehicle."

Dixon makes like the refineries up near Newark and exhales an acrid cloud of stench. "Says who?"

Starky taps on a little *no smoking* sticker taped to our dashboard.

"Municipal ordinance fourteen fifty-two."

I grin. I think she just made that up.

"Fucking civilian pussies . . ."

Reluctantly, Dixon raises his leg to grind the glowing tip of his relit cigar into the heel of his boot. It's hard for him to maneuver in the backseat. The guy's so immense he had to fold himself up to sit sidesaddle across the transmission hump.

"You ever serve, miss?" Dixon asks.

"In what capacity?" replies Starky.

"Military. Army? Navy? Air Force? Marines?"

"Negative. I felt I could best serve my country by assisting in homeland security."

"What? Back there in Sea Haven? Tough duty, ma'am. Patrolling the beach. Hell, come low tide, you could cut your foot on a fucking seashell."

"Yeah," I say. "That'll hurt. Seashell. Or a crab bite. Crabs always go for the toes."

Hey, I don't mind sounding stupid. Especially if it means Dixon will lay off my partner-for-the-night and redirect his nicotine-deprived wrath at me.

"I did three tours in three years," he says to me.

"Really? They kept rotating you back?"

"Negative. I volunteered. Wanted to earn a few more oak leaves."

Oak leaves are what the Army gives you for being heroic in combat. I know because Ceepak has all sorts of medals and decorations. A whole forest of oak leaves. The difference? He never talks about his.

Dixon keeps going: "The silver oak leaf is the same as receiving the Distinguished Service Cross five different times," he says proudly. "'Given for extraordinary heroism in connection with a military operation against an opposing armed force.' You have to fight somebody to get it. Can't pick it up patrolling a beach in Jersey."

Ceepak has the DSC too. Plus the Silver Star. That one they give for gallantry in a military operation. I asked him if I could look at it once. He said he'd shipped it home to Ohio. Gave it to his mom. Guess she keeps a scrapbook.

Dixon squirms around in the backseat some more. "Over there, you're presented with opportunities to be heroic on a daily basis because every-fucking-body who's not in your unit is your fucking enemy. Hell, the fucking Hajis blew up half of my men with chickenshit roadside bombs. They even got Sully. John Sullivan. One of my best. So now, I tell my guys, 'you see some Ali Baba with a cell phone, put a bullet in his skull because, chances are, he's using that phone to trigger another fucking bomb.' "

Now I wish Sergeant Dixon was smoking that cigar. Might not be able to talk so much with a tobacco stump corking his piehole.

"Sheriff Smith was a good man. Tough as they come. Definitely brought some noise to the sandbox."

"I thought his name was Shareef. Shareef Smith."

"I called him 'Sheriff.' "

Sheriff Smith. Butt Lips. Worthless.

"You give all your guys a nickname, Sergeant Dixon?"

"Roger that."

"So, what do they call you?" I ask, figuring "Dixon" is prime material for a humiliating handle.

"Stone."

"How come?"

"Short for Stone Cold Killer."

Oh-kay.

The tires hum. We glide west on Route 22. Pass the Home Depot. It's closed. A Pathmark grocery store. Closed too. A gigantic Beer Depot where I'm guessing "Stone Cold" Dixon and his squad filled up a couple shopping carts with crates of liquid refreshment. Up ahead, I can see the green-and-yellow sign pointing the way to the entrance ramp for the Garden State Parkway South.

"You ever see a dead body, ma'am?"

Here we go again.

"We'll be there soon," I say, hoping to avoid another grisly lecture. I hear Dixon clicking open and shut the lid on his Zippo.

"Death never smells pretty," he says. "Not like that perfume you're wearing. Jesus. You always wear perfume while helping to secure the fucking homeland?"

Starky keeps her back ramrod stiff, eyes tightly focused on the road ahead.

"Cigar helps cuts the stench of death," says Dixon. "If you'd ever smelled it, you'd know. Hell, you'd be lighting up with me."

"Gum works too," I say.

"Come again?"

"Chewing gum. Or Vicks VapoRub. Smear it under you nose. Or, you can just breathe through your mouth."

I sound stupid enough to shut Dixon up.

He sighs. Disgusted to be riding in the same car with two pukes such as Starky and myself. Good. Maybe he'll remain silent for the short haul down the Parkway.

I ease into the left-hand lane as we near the overpass. My entrance is on the other side. We wait at the traffic light.

I glance up into my rearview mirror. Dixon is staring out the window. Probably looking for someone with a cell phone he can kill.

Then I see something else. To my left.

A junky white Toyota heading home to Sea Haven.

I know he's heading home because I recognize the car.

It's my regular partner. John Ceepak. A man who never stays up past 10:00 PM because he wakes up every morning at five.

I check out the dashboard digital.

One thirty-two AM.

3

The Garden State Parkway is a wide ribbon of concrete stretching the whole length of New Jersey, 175 miles from Montvale to Cape May.

Every now and then they make you stop and toss 35 cents or a token into a plastic basket so you can drive down to the next tollbooth and plunk in another 35 cents. If you have E-ZPass, you can pay without stopping—in some spots you can even pay while doing 50 MPH, which is very difficult to do the old-fashioned, non–E-ZPass way—chucking change at basketball buckets strapped to the sides of tollbooths. Trust me on this one. Me and my buddy Jess tried it once.

Yes, this is the kind of crap I think about when I'd rather not think about where I'm going and why I'm going there.

I slide into the left-hand exit lane. The rest area sits in the wooded center of the roadway so you can access it from either the northbound or southbound sides. Buses are welcome.

These GSP rest areas are like pit stops set up every thirty miles or so. Of course the gas costs more than it does back in the real world. Rest areas are like airports. Independent countries cut off from reality and manufacturer-suggested retail prices.

Okay.

That's all I've got. Time to face what comes next: a dead soldier sitting atop a toilet with the lid to his brain blown open. As I said, it won't be my first dead body. But it will be my young partner's. I know Starky's never seen anybody dead who wasn't dressed up in their best suit and laid out in a padded box at a funeral home. I glance over at her.

She's working her jaw hard. Now she puts a fist to her lips. She looks a little green around the gills. Puke green.

We see the state police vehicles and an ambulance parked near the south side entrance to the main building.

We climb out of the patrol car. Dixon jabs his cigar stub back into his mouth. Rolls it around until it's good and wet.

"I'm sorry for your loss," Starky says as we try to keep pace with the hard-charging sergeant in the parking lot.

What else can she say?

Dixon ignores her. Keeps marching. We're going into the rest stop where, according to the plastic translights, we'll find a Burger King, Cinnabon, TCBY, Sbarro, Starbucks, and a Commerce Bank ATM. No sign announcing the presence of Corporal Shareef Smith, deceased.

"Where the fuck is the men's room?" Dixon asks as we push our way through the first set of glass doors.

"Over there." I point to the sign. Restrooms.

The big building is pretty empty, except for a gaggle of state troopers guarding the men's room, because it's nearly 2:00 AM. During the day, about a thousand travelers zip in and out of here every ten minutes. They hit the head or grab a snack in the shop where everything hangs in bags on pegs. They look at the giant wall map or stand in cafeteria lines so they can guzzle jumbo-sized sodas to refill their bladders and be primed to hit the next head, which, according to that wall map, is thirty-six miles down the road.

Most of the plastic-scooped seats in the food court are empty. I see some sleepy kids in Burger King uniforms scraping down the grills. A few cold slices of pizza sit under infrared lamps at Sbarro. Tables clustered near the Cinnabon outpost are occupied by what looks like a busload of losers on their way home from Atlantic City.

The troopers at the entrance to the men's room see my badge and give us the nod that says it's okay to head in.

"Where is he?" Dixon's voice echoes off the tiled walls in the bathroom entryway.

"Shit," shouts somebody around the corner up ahead. "Who the fuck is it now? Tell 'em to go take a leak in the ladies' room."

I recognize the voice. Can't figure out why.

"This is Sergeant Dale Dixon," he barks.

"Who?"

"One of the Army guys," says some other voice up ahead.

"About fucking time he showed up." Again, I can't see who's talking. Just tiles and a mirror and one of those hand-blower deals mounted to the wall near a barrel of crumpled hand towels. "You think I got all night to stand around in a shitty crapper scraping your buddy's brains off the fucking walls?"

Up ahead, the corridor hits a *T*. There are urinals, stalls, and sinks to either side. We turn right, step into the side where all the men are. Some women too. State police. Burlington County CSI. They're clustered in front of an open toilet stall and block our view at whoever is inside. A state trooper raises his hand, suggests we wait where we are. He also shakes his head in a way that tells me he can't believe his bad luck in catching this call.

I look back toward the toilet stall and see feet under the partition: one pair of scuffed black shoes facing in, one pair of high-tech sneakers facing out. The sneakers are spotted with paint. Brown paint. No. Blood.

That would be the dead man.

Someone in a backwards Jersey Devils cap hauling a boxy camera steps toward the open door and triggers a lightning storm of fa-whomping flashes.

"Jesus!" says the guy standing inside the stall. "You want to fucking blind me? Enough with the pictures, already. We don't need 'em! This thing is open-and-shut. Mr. Smith here stuck a pistol in his mouth, pulled the trigger, and sprayed his brains against the back wall. End of story. Now move out of the way. I'm fucking starving."

The photographer retreats. Starts breaking down his gear.

A fat man steps out, pulls the stall door shut behind him.

Saul Slobbinsky.

Actually, his real name is Saul Slominsky but everybody calls him Slobbinsky because he's the sloppiest crime scene investigator in the state of New Jersey, maybe the world. Once he blew a county prosecutor's whole case by smearing chocolate from a Snickers bar on the lift tape of the only fingerprint found at the scene of a pretty heinous crime.

"It's summer," Slobbinsky told his bosses. "It melted." It became known as the Snickers bar defense: you screw up on the job, it's not your fault. Blame it on the nearest candy bar.

I met Slominsky a couple summers ago on the Tilt-A-Whirl in Sea Haven. At the time, he was with the state's major crime unit. Usually worked a desk job but we were lucky enough to have him come out into the field that particular Saturday and muck up our evidence.

"Anybody know if that Burger King out there is still open?" he asks the room, wiping his hands on his pants.

He's even fatter than I remember. Still has a floppy mustache. Looks like a walrus working on his winter coat of blubber.

"I need one of those angus steak burgers," he says to his crew. "That fucking yogurt cone isn't going to hold me, you know what I'm say-ing?"

Chocolate yogurt. Explains the brown crud clumped in his whiskers.

Rumor has it Saul Slominsky only kept his cushy MCU job with the state because he had a well-connected friend in the governor's office. However, that particular governor gave the New Jersey homeland security job to his boyfriend, got caught, resigned, wrote a book, and told the world about it on *Oprah*.

Slobbinsky lost his "friend" when New Jersey lost its first officially gay governor. Now he works with the Burlington County prosecutor's office. Seeing how he's here in a men's room at 1:00 in the morning, I gotta figure they gave him the graveyard shift. It's where they always put their best and brightest: in the dark where nobody can see them. This particular GSP rest stop is, of course, in the middle of Burlington County. Slobbinsky's jurisdiction.

The fat man is in charge.

He goes over to the sink. I figure he's going to wash off his hands after crawling around searching for evidence on the floor of a toilet stall. Instead, he ducks down so he can drink straight from the tap.

"How's this fucking thing work?"

"Motion detector," answers one his guys. This one has a major belly too and is working on a jumbo bag of Chex Mix, shaking it out over his face so he doesn't miss a single crumb. Guess everybody working the night shift is here for a reason.

"What fucking motion detector?"

"In the black circle. See it there?"

Slominsky waves his hand around the spigot.

"Fucking thing's broken."

"Stand up and lean in again," suggests his colleague. "You need to make motion that it can detect—"

"Sir?" It's Dixon. He's seen enough of the Saul Slobbinsky Show.

"What?" Slominsky stands up from the sink.

"The body? I'm here to identify it."

"Cool your jets, pal. He ain't going anywhere." He laughs. So does Mr. Chex Mix.

"Sir," Dixon demands, "what is your name?"

Slominsky snorts. "Me?"

Dixon nods. His eye slits are thinner than the space between tightly drawn blinds.

"You."

"Saul Slominsky."

"Your position here?"

"Senior investigator for the Burlington County prosecutor's office. This is my crime scene. You are here at my invitation."

"Then show me the goddamn body!"

Slobbinsky eyes the big man. They probably weigh the same. Two-hundred and fifty pounds. Only Dixon is six-three. Slominsky is more like five-two and the soldier's belly doesn't flop over his belt.

"Show it to me, now."

"Ease up, ace. Who'd you say you were again?"

"Sergeant Dale Dixon."

"And you know this Shareef Smith character how?"

"We served together. Operation Iraqi Freedom."

"You are, therefore, qualified to identify his body in lieu of familial representation?"

I think some insurance agent told Slominsky to say that so he doesn't get sued later by the family of the deceased.

"Yes. I have known him for several years."

"Did you know he was a junkie?"

"Come again?"

"Heroin. You know—scag. Schmeek. We found a dime bag on the floor of the stall next to his."

I check out the handicapped stall. Two guys move in on their hands and knees to pick stuff off the floor with tweezers and plop it into paper bags.

"We found his works over there too. Cute little leather wallet-type deal. Guess he came in here to take a dump and fly off to happy land. Decided to take the express route instead. Head all the way home to Jesus. Anyway, I figure Mr. Smith dropped his drug shit when he swallowed the bullet."

The guy crumpling up the Chex Mix bag nods. "That's what we figure," he says. "Death throes, you know? Flung it sideways. Kicked it over when he kicked the bucket."

"How do you know it was *his* drug paraphernalia?"

"We dusted it for prints."

"Do they match Corporal Smith's?"

"How the fuck should I know?" says Slominsky. "You think I got a microscope up my ass?"

"So your 'findings' at this point are pure supposition?"

"Hey, what's your problem, sarge? Your fucking boy has needle marks up and down his arms, okay? Probably started shooting up while you two were over there whacking Iraqis."

Slobbinsky heads toward the closed stall.

"Go on. Check it out. Look at his fucking arms. The fact that he's black makes the splotches easier to spot."

Slobbinsky swings the stall door open as wide as the hinges will allow.

Guess it's finally time for Dixon to see the dead man.

# 4

*Starky loses* her cookies.

I did the exact same thing when I saw my first corpse. Fortunately, Ceepak was there to prop me up so I didn't end up facedown in a puddle of my own puke.

Fortunately for Starky, we're in a humongous bathroom. I hustle her over to the other side, find a toilet, hold her up under both arms, turn my head and give her a moment.

"Sorry, sir," she groans after the second gusher.

"Take your time. Happens to all of us."

"Thank you, sir."

Another spasm. I think she's empty. We've moved into the dry heaves stage now. Means we're almost done. Don't ask me how I became an expert on the regurgitative process. Probably my misspent youth chugging warm cans of beer from my dad's stash of Busch out in the garage.

Truth be told, I too nearly barfed when I caught a quick glimpse of Shareef Smith. Didn't see much. Starky started making urp noises behind me. Duty called.

But what I did see was gruesome.

His head had exploded.

It's like it was a giant tennis ball somebody squeezed inside a vise until the trapped gas found a soft spot up top and burst free. Flanges of splayed bone gave him a crooked little red crown.

He was slumped backwards, propped up by the thick elbow pipe behind the commode. Blood had gushed out of his mouth and nose. His shirt—I think it used to be blue—was soaked with the stuff. So was this bib of tissues he was wearing around his neck. At least that's what it looked like: a thick circle of paper sitting on his shoulders, tucked under his chin and behind his head. It was like a Thanksgiving Pilgrim's collar, only bloodier. I don't know what it was, what it was made out of.

"Well, Sergeant?" I hear Slobbinsky say on the other side of the men's room. "That your boy? Sarge? Jesus, take your fucking time, why don't you? I got all night, here."

I guess Dixon is just standing there, mesmerized by the horror show behind door number three.

"You okay?" I ask Starky.

"Yes, sir."

"You want to wait outside in the car?"

"No, sir."

"How about some water?" I gesture toward the sinks lining the far wall. Someone has decorated them with vases of fresh-cut flowers. Not to honor the dead soldier, just to give this rank room a touch of class. Hey, I know they try their best to keep these restrooms clean. Got the clipboard on the wall indicating that somebody from HMM Host comes in every hour to swab the decks, fish the gum wads out of the urinals. But, come on: if thousands of strangers traipsed through your guest bathroom all day every day you could hose it down with a tanker truck full of Lysol and still end up with a room that reeked of urine mixed with industrial-strength ammonia.

"I'm good to go," Starky says, straightening up her uniform.

"Come on."

We hurry back to the other side of the restroom.

"Everything come out okay, miss?" Slobbinsky cracks when we

make our return. His colleague, Chex Mix man, snorts out a crumb-filled chuckle.

Dixon is still standing in the stall. Staring straight ahead.

"That's him," he finally says.

"You sure?" asks Slominsky.

"Affirmative."

"That mean 'yes'?"

"Yes."

Apparently, seeing his friend in such a grotesque pose has caused Dixon to lose some of his swagger. He turns and addresses the room. Looks solemn.

"That is the body of Corporal Shareef Smith. We served together in Echo Company. He was a good soldier. A good man."

Slobbinsky—the asshole—yawns. Checks his watch.

"Great. Thanks. The body is positively identified at One-fifty-six AM. Somebody write that down."

Dixon steps out of the stall. Reveals the mess behind him. I try to take it in. See it like Ceepak would.

The pistol is still gripped tightly in the young black man's right hand. Rigor mortis? I'm not sure. The gun hand rests on his right thigh. His head is twisted slightly to the left—probably from the force of the bullet's impact. Plus, it has that gaping explosion hole up top.

"Tell me what happened," says Dixon.

Slobbinsky shrugs. "He shot himself."

"I need more."

So do I. I check the walls of the stall. Gray gunk is splattered behind and above Smith's head. Blood streaks down the back wall. It starts where it should: in a straight line up from the exit wound. Ceepak has taught me to look for this kind of stuff. Trajectory paths. I just wish he were here to tell me where to look next.

Smith didn't pull down his pants when he entered the stall. Just sat on the toilet seat and did his business: a little heroin, a quick bullet to the brain.

The toilet paper roll near his right knee is clean. No blood splatter. Makes sense. Most of the blood exploded out of the back of his head when the bullet shot up through his skull. The rest of it ran in a thick river out of his nostrils and mouth. I think the heart keeps pumping even after your brain calls it quits. Need to check that one out with Ceepak.

All that blood ran down and soaked into that paper collar.

That paper collar.

I look above the roll of toilet paper. The seat-cover dispenser is empty. Just a cardboard box. None of those flushable sheets of tissue paper for you to drape over the toilet seat in an effort to avoid everybody else's butt germs.

That's what's around his neck.

He pulled out the whole stack, pushed his head through the hole cut in the center, and wore it like the cape the barber drapes over your head to catch hair clippings.

Why?

Why would a suicidal junkie bib himself with sanitary tissue paper before blowing out his brains?

He didn't want to make a mess?

Ceepak always asks me: What's wrong with this picture? What doesn't belong? Okay—how about a guy who tries this hard to be tidy on his way out the door?

And there's something else.

I'm not sure what it is. Not yet. But there's something else seriously wrong with this picture.

I reach to my belt. My cell phone has a camera in it. I should snap a shot when Slominsky isn't looking. I need a picture to figure out what else is wrong here.

"Tell me what the hell happened," Dixon says again.

"I can't say for certain," Slominsky answers. "Aren't any security cameras in here—this being a men's room and all."

"Give me your best guess. Based on the evidence and any witnesses you might have interviewed."

Slominsky sighs.

"Fine. Seeing how you two served together and all . . ."

Dixon nods to indicate he appreciates Slominsky doing him a solid.

"Okay. Here's what we figure. Your buddy comes in with his needle kit and some kind of Russian pistol with a six-inch silencer screwed on the muzzle. He closes the door, throws the latch, and locks himself in. Wants his privacy."

"Did anybody hear the pistol shot?" asks Dixon.

"Nope. Like I said—he screwed on a *silencer*. Must've worked. Nobody heard nothin'."

"Not even a pop?"

Another shrug from Slominsky. "Nothin'. Too much farting, I guess. Besides, that floor blower over there was going," he gestures toward this portable fan the maintenance crew must use to dry the tile after they mop. "Then you got your hand dryers whirling away, toilets flushing all over the place."

"Why would he do that?" asks Dixon. "Why would he use a silencer?"

"Hey—why would he wear a stack of sanitary tissues around his neck? Maybe your guy Smith doesn't want to cause anybody any trouble. Maybe he's just too damn courteous."

"You retrieved the round?"

"Yep," says Chex Mix man. "Dug a slug out of the wall. Back there where his brains are smeared."

Dixon nods. "Go on."

Another yawn from Slominsky. The man needs caffeine.

While he stifles the yawn, I pull the cell phone off my belt. Flip it open. Thumb the button to switch it into camera mode.

"Not much more to say. Janitor comes in for his scheduled eleven PM rounds. All of a sudden he sees these tennis shoes in stall number three. Doesn't say or do anything at first. Doesn't want to disturb some dude in there taking a dump or choking his chicken, you know what I'm saying?"

Nobody responds.

"Anyways," Slominsky continues, "the janitor swishes his mop around and some of the dirty water slops up on your guy's shoes. The janitor says he's sorry. Your guy, of course, says nothin'."

He lets that hang. Allows us to fill in the punch line: *Because he's dead.*

"Anyways, when he's all mopped up everywhere else, he knocks on the door to stall number three. Gets no answer. Asks if everything is all right and explains how he needs to mop up all the stalls. Still no answer. So, he goes outside, tries to find someone to tell him what to do. Some management type. It being after eleven, there aren't any of those hanging around the food court. This janitor, by the way, is Mexican. Doesn't *hablo* too much *Inglese*. He's legal, I think, but hey—you never know, you know what I'm saying?"

"Who opened the door?" asks Dixon.

"The janitor. He couldn't find nobody to help him figure out what to do so he comes back in and uses this little knife he keeps in his work clothes for peeling fruit and shit. Slips it through the crack, flips the latch up, grabs the door, swings it open—"

"And loses his lunch." Chex Mix man finishes for him.

"Where?" I ask.

Slominsky turns to me. Studies my face. Tries to figure out where he knows me from.

"Who the fuck are you?"

"Danny Boyle. Sea Haven PD."

"Sea Haven? Jesus, kid. You're what? Twenty miles outside your fucking jurisdiction."

"Where did the janitor vomit?"

"That's confidential."

"No it's not," I say back. "Where did the guy throw up?"

"Why the fuck do you want to know?" Slominsky is straining to remember who I am and why I piss him off so much.

"Because," Dixon jumps in for me, "if, as you suggest, he 'lost his lunch' when he opened the door, why is there no evidence of his vomit on the floor there?"

"Because he puked in that sink, okay?" He points to the one Chex Mix man is leaning against. "He held his gut, ran over, grabbed hold of the porcelain goddess, and let it fly! Jesus. You guys satisfied?"

"Yes," I say. "Thanks."

I see the lightbulb go off over Slominsky's greasy head. "Boyle," he says with a grin. "You worked that Tilt-A-Whirl job with me, am I right?"

That's one way to put it.

"Yeah," I say.

He turns to his buddy at the sink. "Frankie—I ever tell you about that one?"

"No."

"How about you guys?" He calls to the team working the floor around the handicapped toilet. "I tell you about Reggie Hart?"

"No." One of the CSI guys in the stall sits back on his heels to hear the story. "Who's he?"

"Reggie fucking Hart? You know—the billionaire."

"Trump?"

"No. This guy was even richer. When I showed up, that crime scene was fucked-up beyond all recognition. But we straightened things up, figured out whodunit, right, Boyle?"

"Yeah."

Actually, Slominsky didn't help us at all. I'm lying through my teeth here—something my partner John Ceepak would not let me get away with because he lives by this very strict moral code that doesn't allow him to lie, cheat, steal or tolerate those who do. Well, tonight I figure a little lie will get us out of this aroma-filled room a little faster.

"Yeah," says Slominsky like we're old pals from back in the day. "That was some case. Did some solid forensic shit on that one, didn't we, Boyle?"

"Mind if I snap a picture?" I ask, since, all of a sudden, we're old pals.

"Sure, Danny. Sure." He smiles. Strikes a pose. Thinks I want *his* picture.

So, I take it. Then I turn around and snap the shot I really want: Smith in his toilet stall, a ring of blood-tinged tissue wrapped around his neck.

"Thanks," I say.

"No problem, Danny." Slominsky is all smiles now. Guess it's a good thing I didn't contradict his version of the truth. "Let's see. What else can I tell you guys? Oh. Right. We searched his pockets. Found the Internet map in his shirt, which is how we found you guys. Had that phone number scribbled on it. We also found these."

Slominsky pulls a key ring out of his pocket.

"His car?" Dixon asks.

"Yeah. Poor bastard. Couldn't buy a break tonight. We found his vehicle in the lot. Seems that while he's in here doing the deed, somebody was out there breaking into his ride."

# 5

Someone ransacked Shareef Smith's Ford Focus.

"Bastards," mutters Dixon as we stare at the mess the burglars made.

"Happens all the time," says the state trooper who escorted us out into the parking lot.

Saul Slominsky stayed back in the men's room with Smith's body to, as he put it, "tag him and bag him." He wanted to wrap things up fast. Pack up the body and head home. Maybe grab a double Whopper with cheese on his way out the door.

Meanwhile, we're staring at the tumbled interior of a recently broken-into subcompact. No broken glass. Guess Smith forgot to lock his doors. Maybe he was in a hurry to grab a Whopper too. Either that or a hit of heroin. I see papers on the seats. Cigarette butts crowning a mound of gray dust in the cup holder. Someone yanked out the ashtray and dumped it there. There is no radio in the dashboard. Just a hole with loose, torn wires.

"Same old, same old," says the trooper. He's pretty young. Muscular. Balloons for biceps.

Dixon doesn't say anything. He looks shaken. Queasy. Like he just stepped out of the Hell Hole, this ride they used to have on the board-walk before they closed down Pier Four. You stand against a wall and the room begins to spin. It picks up speed and rotates faster—so fast centrifugal force pulls you away from the center and pins you against the wall. All of a sudden, you feel paralyzed, like a wet sock during the spin cycle. That's when they drop the floor out from under your feet and you don't even budge because you're glued to the wall.

It's when the room stops spinning, when you step out and try to walk through the real world that you feel wobbly. I think that's where Dixon is. Thrown for a loop. Wondering what the hell happened to one of his men who survived the horror show over in Iraq only to end up dead in a men's room on the Garden State Parkway.

"Small-time hoods," says the trooper, swinging his flashlight around inside the car. "They prowl these parking lots. Look for un-locked doors. Keys in the ignition. Folks on vacation typically pack a lot of pricey gear. Bikes. iPods. Satellite radios. Seatback DVD play-ers for the kids."

"So, what the hell happened there?" asks Dixon. Guess he found his land legs again because he sounds pissed. He's pointing at the steering wheel. "These hoods think Smith hid a DVD player in his steering wheel?"

"No, sir. They stole his air bag."

"What?"

"Happens six hundred times every week," explains the trooper.

I'm amazed. "On the Garden State Parkway?"

"No. That's a national figure."

Starky nods. I think my rookie partner spends her weekends memo-rizing the same crime statistics this trooper does.

Encouraged by Starky's interest, he continues. "The thieves sell these stolen air bags to disreputable repair shops who resell them to un-suspecting customers as replacements for bags that have deployed."

While he yammers on how easy it is to do—disconnect the car battery, unscrew four bolts—I check out the other side of the front seat. They rifled through the glove compartment too. It's emptied out. Stuff dumped all over the floor mats.

Dixon is looking where I'm looking.

"Probably searching for his drugs," he mutters.

"Yeah. Maybe. They probably hit the trunk too."

So Dixon and I move around to the rear of the vehicle while Starky and the trooper stay up front to swap crime-spree statistics.

Yep. The trunk lid has been jimmied open. You can see scratch marks and dings near the lock. Crowbar. Somebody in a hurry.

I instinctively reach into my hip pocket and slip on my lint-free gloves.

"What are those?" asks Dixon.

"Evidence handling gloves. Don't want to mess up any latent fingerprints on the trunk lid."

Dixon gives me the eye slits again. I must look like a pansy in my Mickey Mouse mittens.

I try to explain. "My partner always insists that I wear these things."

"This Ceepak guy?"

"Yeah. Otherwise, we might, you know, contaminate evidence."

"That crime-scene investigator. Slominsky. He wasn't wearing gloves."

*And that, my friends, is why we call him Slobbinsky.*

"Yeah," I say with a slight shrug. "His call. Anyway, it's not as important in there. Too many random fingerprints on a public restroom door to do us any good."

Dixon nods. "There'd be thousands of them."

"Exactly. But back here," I say, indicating the trunk, "we have a decent shot at lifting something usable. Wouldn't be too many other prints. Just your guy Shareef. The owner of the vehicle. And the bad guys."

"Shareef *was* the owner of the vehicle," says Dixon.

I shake my head. "I don't think so. Check out the rearview mirror. See those bracelets and feathery gewgaws hanging off it? Women do that. Not guys. Could be his girlfriend's ride."

Dixon nods. "Interesting."

I shrug. "You work the job, you pick up little things."

Especially if you work the job alongside John Ceepak.

Fully gloved, I raise the trunk lid.

"Fuckers," mutters Dixon.

Same story. The trunk is empty. Somebody gutted it. Ripped up the carpet, which has a big splotchy oil stain on the right. I lean over, sniff at it. Motor oil. Up near the spare tire, I see more ripped wires. An empty bracket that used to hold something, probably a CD changer.

"Do you think they knew Smith had the heroin?" asks Dixon.

"It's a possibility," I say because that's what Ceepak always says when we're just getting started, dumping the box of jigsaw puzzle pieces out on the card table, so to speak.

I lower the lid and call up to the trooper.

"Excuse me?"

He doesn't respond. He and Starky are still gabbing.

"In fact," I hear him say, "the NICB estimates that each year fifty thousand air bags valued at fifty million dollars—"

"Officer?" I say. Louder. "We need you back here."

He and Starky mosey around to join us.

"You guys should dust back here for prints," I say.

"Where?"

"Around the lock. Wherever, you know, you'd grab hold to open the trunk."

"Okay," he says. "I'll call headquarters. Requisition a team with the crime kit."

"Thanks."

"Officer Boyle?" says Dixon.

"Yes?"

"I'd like to return to my men."

"Sure. Of course."

"Nice meeting you, Wilson," Starky says to the trooper.

"Same here, Samantha."

They both smile. The way people do in those Find Your Soul Mate ads on the Internet.

"You ready to roll?" I say to Starky.

She snaps to. "Yes, sir."

"Good."

I check my watch. Nearly 2:30 AM. Too late to call Ceepak. Unless, of course, he's still driving around town in his wife's Toyota. I'll catch him tomorrow.

I need to talk to him about what's wrong with all these pictures.

## 6

*My regular* partner, John Ceepak, is now a coach in our local Babe Ruth League.

He got married a while back and officially adopted his wife's son. T. J. Lapczynski. Well, he used to be a Lapczynski. Guess he's T. J. Ceepak now. I would be—just to cut down on the consonants.

Anyway, T.J. is seventeen and, as it turns out, he's a pretty awesome ballplayer. Doesn't look like anybody you've ever seen on a baseball card, however. He has thick blond dreadlocks that he usually bundles up in a bandanna so they stick up like a feathered headdress. Not to mention this wild tattoo ringed around his forearm. He actually makes a Babe Ruth baseball uniform look cool.

Unlike Little League, the Babe Ruth League is for older kids. Sixteen- , seventeen- , eighteen-year-olds. Something for high schoolers to do over the summer besides the usual stuff: beach, beer, and babes. The stuff I used to do. I think Ceepak coaches T.J.'s team for two reasons: one, he likes the kid, wants to help him grow up. Two, the Babe Ruth League has a code, just like he does. Theirs is called the Sportsmanship Code. All about developing a strong, clean, healthy body, mind and soul. Ceepak's covers lying, cheating, and stealing. He got his from West Point. The Babe Ruth League? I guess a committee wrote it. I'm sure the Bambino didn't. He liked his beer, booze, and broads too much. I think *broads* is what Babe called babes.

Anyway, the older kids hit the field every Saturday at 2:00 PM when the mercury usually races up into the nineties and the humidity stays in sync with it. These guys can handle the potential heatstroke situation better than the younger kids who start playing around eight in the morning.

I drive my Jeep over to the ball field in the center of Sea Haven. It's right across from our police station, the courthouse, and the town hall in an island of municipal services situated off Cherry Street at Shore Drive. Behind the center field fence, just beyond the painted signs advertising Pudgy's Fudgery and Santa's Sea Shanty, you can see the parking lot for the Sea Haven sanitation department. You hit a homer into the open end of a garbage truck, you win a case of Pepsi. You sure don't want the ball back as a souvenir.

I see Ceepak down on the bench. His team, I think they're the Stingrays, are up to bat. Their uniforms are royal blue. Maybe they're the Blue Jays. Or the Royals.

Ceepak is clapping his hands, shouting, "Good eye, good eye" to the batter, who's just earned a free walk to first base.

"Hey, Danny!"

It's Rita. Mrs. Ceepak and T.J.'s mom. She's up in the bleachers, waving at me.

"Hey, Rita."

"You're just in time," she calls down. "T.J.'s up next!"

"Cool."

I climb up and take the empty seat beside her. There's a smattering of parents and siblings cheering both teams on.

"Who's winning?" I ask Rita.

"They are."

"What's the score?"

"Seven to six. Bottom of the ninth. Two out. Runner at first . . ."

I smile. "And T.J.'s at the bat?"

"Yeah." Rita's all kinds of excited. As she should be. This is it. The ultimate baseball cliché. Two down. Bottom of the ninth. Does T.J. save the day? Or is he the goat who loses the game with the final strikeout?

"Come on, honey!" Rita cheers.

I cringe. *Honey?* If my mom ever shouted that when I played ball, I would have opted for orphanhood.

T.J. turns around. Looks up into the stands. Gives his mom a devilish wink. Guess he's cool with whatever she chooses to call him.

"Knock it out of the park, honey!" she shouts.

T.J. takes a practice swing in the batter's box.

I think he's contemplating going for the back end of that garbage truck.

"Keep your eye on the ball," urges Ceepak from the dugout because baseball coaches have been saying that same thing since the first cave guys tossed round rocks at other cave guys swinging clubs.

Ceepak looks like he could've played pro ball. He stands six-two, works out every morning, and has Popeye-sized muscles like that disgraced slugger what's-his-name. Ceepak, of course, never uses steroids. That would be cheating.

The runner at first base is taking a pretty healthy lead off the bag. About ten feet. He's ready to dash to second the instant T.J. makes any kind of contact. With two out, you run on anything.

Rita reaches over. Grips my knee. Squeezes hard.

"I can't take this!" she says.

Me neither. Mrs. Ceepak has a good grip.

The pitcher hurls a fastball.

T.J. swings. Misses. Strike one.

"That's okay," says Ceepak. "You'll get the next one."

T.J. takes a few cuts of the bat to stay limber.

"Come on, T.J.!" shouts the guy leading off first. "Bring me home."

The pitcher goes into his windup.

T.J. waits at the plate.

This ball flies faster than the one before it. I hear it thwack into the catcher's mitt.

"Stee-rike two."

The umpire is good. Dramatic. Got the whole arm-pump thing going, big-time.

T.J. takes off his cap. Swipes away some sweat. Pushes back his soggy dreads. Finds room for them up under his hat. He knocks some dirt out of his cleats. Spits. Even does a quick sign of the cross.

Now he bends his knees. Cocks the bat. Takes his stance.

Rita squeezes my knee a little harder. This is it.

The pitcher squints. Reads the signal from the catcher squatting behind home plate. Nods. Raises his leg. Goes into his motion. Strains. Lets rip what's probably the fastest fastball he's ever thrown in his whole life.

T.J. swings.

Smacks it.

Hard!

Man, he got all of it!

The ball sails over the shortstop's head, flies into left field, and hits the dirt right in front of the home run fence.

I look back and the guy who had been on first is already rounding second. T.J.—who can totally fly—is not too far behind him.

The left fielder finally finds the ball underneath a billboard for Pizza My Heart. The first runner is past third, heading for home. The left fielder flings the ball. Now T.J. rounds third. The ball hits the pitcher's mound, kicks up some dust, and bounces toward home. T.J. slides. The catcher snags the ball. They both disappear behind a cloud of dust.

"Safe!" screams the umpire.

T.J. beats the tag! The Stingrays win! The Stingrays win!

The crowd—all twelve of us—goes wild. So do the guys on the Stingrays bench. They mob T.J. behind home plate. They slap high fives and whoop and holler.

"An inside-the-park home run!" Rita screams. "Whoo-hoo."

"Unbelievable!" I shout back. I'm sort of jumping up and down too. The bleacher boards tremble.

"Way to go, Tony!" screams this other dad in the bleachers. "Way to hustle." Guess Tony was the kid who scored in front of T.J.

Everybody is going cuckoo for Cocoa Puffs.

Everybody except Ceepak.

Down on the bench, the Stingrays coach is not celebrating. It's like that "no joy in Mudville" deal. You'd think the mighty Casey had just struck out.

Ceepak walks out to the field. Shakes his head. Even from a distance, I can see him heave a huge sigh.

"Ed?" he says to the umpire. "Ed?"

He motions for the umpire to meet him halfway up the third base line. Looks like they need to talk.

Ceepak turns, points toward the bag at third base.

The umpire takes off his mask. Gives Ceepak a puzzled look.

Ceepak nods.

Another look. Quizzical this time.

Ceepak gives him another grim nod.

The umpire shrugs. Then he turns back toward home and points at the runner who scored first. Tony.

*"You're out!"* He pumps his arm like a locomotive chugging up a hill and gives the kid the old heave-ho.

"What?" Tony shouts back. "Out? No way, man!"

"You're blind, ump!" The boy's father up in the bleachers agrees with his son.

"Tony?" Ceepak says, sounding calm but firm. "You didn't touch the bag at third base."

"Yes, I did, coach."

The way he says it? The kid knows he didn't. He took a short cut.

"Tony?" says Ceepak. "Don't make it worse. You broke the rules. Therefore, your run doesn't count. Neither does T.J.'s. You are out number three. The game is over. The Tigers win."

The crowd is, as they say, hushed. Nobody saw it, not even the third baseman who was waving like a lunatic at the left fielder to hurry up and throw in the ball.

Nobody saw it except Ceepak and that's really all that matters because, like I said, my partner will not tolerate cheating—even if the cheater is wearing the same color uniform he is.

# 7

"Deal With it, dude," is the sage advice T.J. offers to his teammate Tony.

Guess he's used to the Code, now that he's been officially adopted into the family Ceepak. Tony? Not so much. He clutches the backstop with both fists and makes like a gorilla.

"John was right," Rita says as we watch Tony rattle his steel cage. "If the boy doesn't play by the rules . . ."

But down near the bench, Tony's father has some less sympathetic words for my partner.

"Why don't you just forfeit every game in the first inning? What kind of coach turns in his own players?"

Ceepak ignores the rant and keeps slipping bats into the team's canvas equipment bag. Tony's dad won't let up—which maybe he should. I mean he's this totally out-of-shape guy who probably sits in an air-conditioned office all day except for when he's driving to it in his air-conditioned car. The only muscles he ever works are the ones in his mouth. Ceepak, on the other hand, is in good enough shape to jump out of airplanes again with the 101st Airborne. And once he hit the ground, he could probably run ten miles with a sixty-pound knapsack strapped to his back and still not be out of breath. Tony's dad is already winded—just from being a blowhard.

"How'd you get this job, anyway?"

Now Ceepak shrugs. "Same as the Army. I volunteered."

"Well, I'm going to have a word with Ron Venable. He runs the whole damn league. Works in my office, you know."

Ceepak stops stuffing the bag. Smiles.

"Please do discuss this with Ron, Mr. DePena. However, until he declares that the Babe Ruth League no longer follows the official rules of baseball as set forth by the commissioner of the Major Leagues, I suspect your son will still be considered out for not touching the bag when he reached third base."

"Aaaahh!" Mr. DePena throws up both his hands in disgust. Flips them dismissively. "Tony?" he yells to his son, who's still shaking the backstop.

"What?" Tony yells back.

"Grab your gear. This man is a moron! We're leaving!"

"Aaaahh!"

"Now!"

"See you 'round," T.J. says to Tony.

"Aaaahh!" Now Tony throws up both *his* hands and flicks them at T.J. Like father, like son.

Ceepak glances up into the stands to share a "can-you-believe-this?" look with Rita. Then he sees me.

"Hello, Danny."

"Hey."

He makes his way over to the bleachers as I climb down.

"Did you catch the game?"

"Just, you know, the last part of the last inning."

"Ah," says Ceepak with a sly grin. "So you arrived just in time to see us lose?"

"Yeah."

I help Ceepak load the baseball gear into the trunk of the family Toyota—the same car I saw on the road last night well after my partner's usual bedtime.

"Want to head over to the Pig with us?" Rita asks. "We're packing up the party stuff."

Rita used to be a waitress and bank teller. Now she's what they call a small business owner: she runs a gourmet catering company with Grace Porter out of Grace's restaurant over on Ocean Avenue—the Pig's Commitment, so-named because of that ancient joke about a plate of eggs and bacon. The chicken is involved. The pig is totally committed.

"We're making pigs in a blanket," says T.J., who helps his mom on party days. "Not the skanky cabbage kind. The kind with hot dogs and crescent rolls."

Tempting.

"I sort of need to talk to Ceepak," I say.

Ceepak cocks an eyebrow. "What's up?"

"It's this run we went on last night." I don't want to say too much else in front of Rita and T.J. "Starky and me. Around one-thirty AM, we escorted an individual to a crime scene down on the Garden State Parkway."

"A wreck?" asks Rita.

"No. It was—this guy had to go down there and identify a body. One of his Army buddies."

Rita closes her eyes. Shakes her head. Probably says a silent prayer.

"What happened?" asks Ceepak.

"The janitor found a body in the men's room at a rest area. The one near exit fifty-two. I know it's out of our jurisdiction and all. . . ."

"Indeed," says Ceepak.

"But some of what I saw doesn't fit with what the crime-scene investigator says happened."

Ceepak flicks his wrist. Checks his watch. "I'm scheduled to help Rita at the restaurant from sixteen hundred hours until the party commences at nineteen-thirty."

Military time. Man, I'd hate to see the Ceepak family calendar. Probably looks like a battle plan. Maybe he even has miniature tin soldiers, one for each member of his brood, that he slides around the kitchen table with a stick to show everybody their daily troop movements.

"It's okay, John," says Rita. "Stay here and talk to Danny. There's not much more to do for the party. Grace has all the food ready to go. We just need to pack it up and throw together the pigs in a blanket. Maybe you guys can help us load up the van and schlep everything over to Crazy Janey's?"

Crazy Janey is this New York City radio personality. Dirty Larry's sidekick. He makes the fart jokes, she laughs at them. Then she does the traffic report. Anyway, Crazy Janey has a summer place here in Sea Haven, down on the southern beaches where all the TV stars and music people and other assorted billionaires build their sand castles. Once a summer, she throws a huge party. Sets up a gigantic wedding tent out back. Hires a band. I think she had Puff Diddy last year. Invites everybody who's anybody, which, I guess, is why I've never received an invitation. Celebs show up from New York and Philly— even L.A., because they all need to pay homage if they want to plug whatever they need to plug on Dirty Larry's nationally syndicated talk show.

"Do you need help parking cars?" I ask. Sometimes Rita's catering company (which, by the way, they call the Flying Pig) hires off-duty cops to valet park at the big events. We earn a few extra bucks; nobody parks in front of fire hydrants. It's what you call a win-win situation. "I'm totally free tonight." And my plasma-screen TV fund needs all the help it can get.

"Yes," says Rita. "It's going to be huge. The guest list is nearly five hundred names long. A senator is coming. And that actress. You know, the one from that movie."

Sure. Her.

"We'll be there," says Ceepak.

"Great." Rita gives her husband a quick kiss.

Ceepak extends his hand to T.J. "Good game today, son. You really nailed that last pitch and Dominick Monetti has the fastest fastball in the league."

"Thanks," says T.J. "Too bad Tony had to go and blow it like that."

"Did you have fun?" asks Ceepak.

T.J. shrugs. "Yeah. I guess."

"Then you won."

Now T.J. cringes the way I would've if my mom ever screamed, *"Way to go, honey"* in front of all my buddies. I know T.J. basically digs Ceepak, likes having him in his life, but, every now and then, since he's human and seventeen, I know he can't believe how incredibly corny his newly acquired old man can be. Like an overgrown Boy Scout. Or Dudley Do-Right.

Me?

I'm sort of used to it.

We head over to the house, which is what we call the police station.

"What's up, gentlemen?" says the desk sergeant, Reggie Pender. "You on the clock?"

"Not today," says Ceepak.

"So what brings you into the office on this fine and glorious Saturday afternoon?"

"The coffee," I say. "Nobody knows how to make it like we make it here."

"You mean burned?" replies Pender.

"Roger that," says Ceepak. "We need to borrow the I.R."

Pender raises an eyebrow. "You interrogating a witness?"

"Negative," says Ceepak.

"A suspect?" Pender is a big guy. When he gets excited, he throws his whole body into it. "Is it those Feenyville Pirates? You two finally catch those rascals red-handed? They the ones running the dope?"

"I just need to talk to Ceepak. About that thing last night."

"The suicide?" asks Pender.

Now Ceepak looks really interested.

"Did you know him?" Pender asks Ceepak.

"Who?"

"The soldier. The one who, you know." He jabs a finger into his mouth. Cocks his thumb. Bang.

"Danny?" This from Ceepak.

"Yeah. Like I said. We need to talk."


We're sitting at the long table. We grabbed a couple cold drinks out of the vending machine and the cola buzz helps. I'm downloading everything as fast as I can.

The noise complaint. The soldiers partying in the house on Kipper Street. The phone call from the state police. The drive down the Parkway with Sergeant Dixon. The rest stop. Corporal Shareef Smith in the toilet stall.

I leave out the part where I saw Ceepak's car headed home after 1:00 AM.

"I took a picture," I say. "With my cell phone."

I pass the phone to Ceepak. He studies the tiny display window.

It's a head-on shot. Shareef sitting on top of the toilet lid, the top of his skull blown open, the ring of pink-tinged tissue paper around his neck, the gore streaking down the tile above and behind his head.

"He put the sanitary toilet seat things around his neck," I explain.

Ceepak nods. Doesn't say anything. He's squinting at the screen. Putting himself into the crime scene. Probably seeing things in the pixels I didn't see in person.

"So he wouldn't make a mess, I guess."

"Unusual behavior for a suicide," says Ceepak.

"Yeah. That was the first thing that bugged me."

"Who did the crime-scene investigation?"

Oh, yeah. I almost forgot. "Saul Slominsky."

Ceepak nods. He remembers Slobbinsky, although he'd never call him that. Not out loud.

"He's with the Burlington County prosecutor's office now," I add.

Another nod. "They would be the lead investigative agency in this instance."

"They say they found drugs," I add.

"On the soldier's body?"

"No. I mean, he had needle marks on his arms, but his drug kit was on the floor of the stall next to his. They figure he dropped his works or kicked them over."

"They do?"

"Yeah."

"Busy man in the final moments of his life."

"I guess."

"Go on."

"Some small-time hoods broke into his car."

"They apprehended suspects?"

"No."

"Then how can you say the crime was perpetrated by 'small-time hoodlums'?"

"It's just what, you know, what everybody was saying last night. . . ."

"You mean what they were speculating."

"Yeah."

Ceepak. The guy's a stickler for stuff like that. Doesn't want to deal with speculation and wild guesses. He's Dan Aykroyd in *Dragnet*. Just the facts, ma'am.

"Anyway," I say, "some . . . unknown individual . . ."

"Or individuals."

"Right. They really tore through this guy's car. Ripped out everything. From the air bags up front to the CD changer in the trunk."

"Interesting."

"Yeah."

"What else?"

"I don't know. There's just something wrong with the picture. I can't put my finger on it but it's been bugging me. All last night. This morning."

"As it should."

"What? You see something?"

"Of course. The same thing you saw, Danny."

"That's just it, I don't *know* what I saw."

"That something wasn't as it should be."

"Yeah. I guess."

"It's the floor."

"What about it?"

Ceepak hands me back my cell phone.

"You tell me."

Great. I'm hungry for answers; he wants to play *Let's Learn Forensics.*

"I dunno."

"What doesn't fit?"

"On the floor?"

"Yes."

I hate when we play this. "There's nothing on the floor except the dead guy's sneakers."

"Exactly."

No blood.

Not just under the front of the toilet, under his bent knees, because, maybe, the sanitary tissues sponged up all the blood gushing out of his nose and mouth.

There's also none on the floor back near the rear wall.

Yeah. Ceepak's right. That's what's been bugging me.

If there are thick streaks running down the back wall, how come nothing dripped all the way down to the floor?

*8*

*Ceepak heads* to his locker because he needs his cargo pants.

Every day, my partner loads up his pockets—front, side, rear—with enough tools to open a CSI hardware store. And, of course, he tosses in a handful of Snausages in case we run into a snarling dog. Any Snausages left over at the end of the day go to his pooch: Barkley. Barkley's old. Snausages are soft. It works out.

We've decided to head down to the rest stop at exit 52 to "see what we can see," as Ceepak likes to say. Nothing official, mind you—we're not strapping on our weapons or anything. We're just two civilians on the road looking for a restroom and willing to drive ten or twenty miles to find it.

"Traffic's not too bad," I say.

Ceepak looks up from the passenger seat.

"No. It's all good."

"How about last night?"

"Come again?"

"When Starky and I drove the guy down here last night, I saw you in Rita's Toyota."

I glance over at Ceepak.

"Traffic conditions were extremely light last evening," he says.

"Yeah. They usually are. So why were you out so late?"

"I'd rather not say."

He's smiling but his eyes aren't. Time to change the subject.

"I think it's always best to examine the crime scene in person," I say because Ceepak said it to me once.

"Correct. Photographs can only tell us so much. Especially low-resolution images captured on cell phones."

"Slominsky had a guy taking pictures last night. We should look at his."

"That would work. However, the Burlington County prosecutor's office may not grant us access to their evidence seeing how we have no official standing in this matter. Not yet, anyway."

Excellent. I believe my man is trying to figure out an angle, some way to get us into the game. Ceepak, of course, always plays by the rules but that means he knows all of 'em—even the obscure ones listed in tiny print way back at the end of the rule book where nobody else bothers reading because they're bored or they just scored this hot new game for their Xbox 360 and want to play it already. Or maybe that's just me.

Before we left the house, we uploaded my cell phone photos to my Verizon Pix Place account on the Internet and printed out the money shot—Smith sitting atop the toilet. Ceepak keeps studying it, trying to glean one more clue from the horrible scene.

"The commode is a built-in," he says. "No tank as one would typically see behind a toilet at home. In his seated position, Smith is barely six inches from the rear wall. His head, canted at an acute angle after impact, is touching that wall. The expelled organic material from the exit wound created a dramatic splatter pattern in line with the established trajectory path."

"And then all the gunk trickles down," I add, realizing there's probably a more forensically correct term for *gunk*. Maybe *goop*.

"Right. The droplets elongated and slid down, developing tails pointing away from the initial point of impact. But, they end in a blur on the wall about a foot above the ground."

Just like tossing a can of paint against a wall. Eventually, some of it should dribble down to the floor. You splash it against a tilted canvas, you could end up in an art museum.

"Did Smith leave a suicide note?" Ceepak asks, folding up his printout.

"Not that I know of."

"Perhaps it was on his person?"

I shake my head. "Slominsky only found the MapQuest map to the party house. Smith had it tucked into his shirt. Chest pocket."

"Interesting," says Ceepak. " 'Your Chelsea suicide with no apparent motive.' " He's quoting Springsteen lyrics, one of his favorite autofocusing techniques. "Why would a young man like Smith take his own life?"

"Because of his drug problem?"

"Perhaps."

"Or, you know, he might've been bummed out. Depressed. About the war and all."

Oops. Didn't mean to say that. Ceepak could've figured that one out all by himself. He was there, served his time in hell. Saw and did some pretty horrible stuff. He has his dark days, trust me. I've been there for some. So, he doesn't need me to remind him about post-traumatic stress disorder or whatever they call it when you feel like shit for doing what you were told to do to defend your country.

"I mean, maybe—"

"It's okay, Danny. You make a cogent point. PTSD is a definite possibility. I just wish we knew more about this man."

"Do you have any friends in the Eighty-second Airborne?"

"A few."

"You should, you know, give them a call."

Well, duh. Man, I'm really saying all the wrong things today.

"Will do, Danny. Excellent suggestion." Ceepak, on the other hand, always says all the right things. Never busts my hump, even when I deserve it. The man has a high tolerance for my latent Danny-ness.

———

We pull into the parking lot at the exit 52 rest area.

The place is packed. I'm guessing a thousand cars are angled into slots on both sides of the main building. Some folks are over near the trees, walking their dogs, establishing canine rest areas in the grass already burnt brown by all the dogs who peed before them.

Two canopied pushcarts near the south-side entrance are open for a brisk business selling sunglasses. It's bright today. The sky's as blue as the freshly painted lines in the handicapped parking zones, one of which is occupied by an obese guy wolfing down a Whopper, his belly pressed tight against the steering wheel, even though his seat is slid back as far as it can go without becoming the backseat. Guess being a blimp is his handicap.

We enter the main building. If there's a thousand cars, there must be two thousand people. Most of them sipping something. Snapple. Grande mocha whip-a-chinos or whatever words Starbucks invented this month. Jumbo tubs of Pepsi.

"Where's the men's room?" asks Ceepak.

I point. He nods.

Then he turns around. Studies the walls.

I do the same thing.

I see this huge ad for the Trump Marina casino in Atlantic City. A sexy lady in a tight red dress and stiletto heels with a come-up-to-my-suite twinkle in her eye is holding a pair of dice. The headline reads: *First. Best. Wildest.*

I can't tell if Mr. Trump means his casino or this girl.

"Only one security camera," says Ceepak.

Apparently, he wasn't looking at the poster with me.

"See it, Danny?"

He points.

"Wouldn't tell us much. Doesn't seem to cover the entrance to the men's room. It's aimed toward the gift shop." Ceepak does a three-finger hand chop at the store with all the pegboards dangling brightly colored bags of candy, chips, crackers, and antacids. "Low potential for shoplifting in the opposite direction."

Yeah. There ain't much worth stealing in the restrooms.

"Security camera footage won't help us very much," says Ceepak. "Let's hit the head."

You ever walk around a men's room staring at stuff?

Guys inside doing their business give you the evil eye, wonder what the hell you're gawking at. This doesn't stop Ceepak. He pulls a small digital camera out of his left thigh pocket.

Guys shuffle closer to the urinals.

The layout is just like I remember it. On each side, there are a half-a-dozen urinals on a tiled wall leading down to three sinks. Fresh-cut carnations stand guard in slender vases atop the porcelain washbasins. There's a paper towel dispenser, big-mouthed garbage barrel, and electric hand blower attached to the wall perpendicular to the sinks. Everything has electric eyes. The urinals. The sinks. Maybe even the towel dispenser. You never have to touch anything to make it work.

Except, of course, the doors to the toilet stalls.

"Stainless steel," Ceepak comments as he studies the four doors on our side of the men's room. Three regular, one wider for the handicapped toilet. All currently closed and occupado.

Stainless steel is an excellent surface for grabbing fingerprints. All five billion of them. The men's room is currently crowded. If a toilet opens up before a urinal, you can bet the next guy in line is going for the stall and everybody behind him will just have to pray he raises the seat.

Ceepak faces the closed door on the walled-in box where they found Lance Corporal Shareef Smith.

"You say it was locked? From the inside?"

"Yeah. The janitor had to flick the latch open from out here."

Ceepak snaps a flash photo.

"Hey!" says whoever's inside. Some guy in those new Nikes and Calvin Klein underwear.

"Don't worry, sir," says Ceepak. "You're not in the picture."

"Jesus H. Christ," mutters the man behind door number three as he rises off his throne. The toilet does its thing and automatically flushes itself. The door swings open and Calvin K. comes out hitching his belt.

"What's your problem, pal?" he asks Ceepak, who's already busy lining up his next shot: a close-up of the toilet itself.

"Sorry. I didn't mean to intrude on your privacy."

The flash strobes.

The guy who just finished up stomps away.

Doesn't hit the sink.

Men.

Why do they even give us sinks with fancy automatic faucets? They should just hang up a few more urinals on the wall and let us wipe our hands on our pants in peace.

"You usin' it?" asks a man who's doing a nervous Texas two-step to keep his mind off what he really needs to be doing.

"Sorry," says Ceepak. "We'll only be another minute."

We?

Ceepak steps into the stall. I don't follow. I could easily fit in there with him but two guys squeezing into the same toilet booth at the same time might earn us more stares than Ceepak's Kodak moment with the commode. People might think we'd just been playing footsie between stalls and have decided to run for Congress.

Fortunately a urinal opens up and dancing man doesn't explode.

"They've cleaned it up," says Ceepak, examining the rear wall.

"Yeah."

"Completely scrubbed it down. There's not a trace of evidence. Nothing. Not even any stained grout."

"Well, they clean in here every hour."

"Come again?"

"They clean in here every hour."

"You're certain?"

"Yeah. There's a chart on the wall in the hall. It's a grid. Days across the top. Time down the side. The janitors have to initial the box when they come in and clean up. Note the time."

"Show it to me."

I lead the way to the mounted clipboard. It's attached to the frame of an HMM Host poster proclaiming *The HMM Five Star Advantage. Cleanliness, Quality & Service.* I look at the boxes. Somebody came in at 4:03 PM. And 3:05. And 2:06. Every hour, pretty much on the hour, since midnight.

"Fascinating," says Ceepak. He taps the last line on the poster: *For immediate attention please see manager.*

I don't get it. "What?"

"Let's suppose, for the sake of argument, that this was not a suicide."

"Okay."

"Let's say someone lured Corporal Smith into the men's room."

"To murder him?"

Ceepak nods. "They knew they had almost an hour to get away— more if they could make certain that there was no need for 'immediate attention' and, therefore, no reason for the janitor to disturb the occupant seated in stall number three."

Now I get it.

No immediate attention required.

No blood on the floor.

## 9

If somebody shot Shareef Smith, made it look like a suicide, and then wiped up any blood that dripped down to the tiled floor, they might've had an hour or more to get away.

"Perhaps even longer," says Ceepak. "Let's suppose the murder took place prior to a shift change. The new janitor coming on duty would not realize that the shoes indicating the presence of a patron in stall number three had been there for over an hour."

We're in my Jeep. Driving back to Sea Haven.

"Wait a second," I say. "Somebody in that bathroom should've heard something. Seen something."

Ceepak nods. "Perhaps."

"Hey, if I was in one of the stalls next to Smith's, I would've known if two guys next door started doing something weird. Even if I didn't hear the shot because the pistol had that silencer, there had to be some sort of scuffle. And when the bad guy bent down to wipe up the floor, I would've seen that."

"You raise valid points, Danny."

Yeah. I do that every once in a while.

"But," Ceepak says, "we know the handicapped stall to his right, let's call it stall number four, was unoccupied."

"We do?"

"Yes, Danny. That's where Slominsky's people found Smith's drug kit."

"They said he kicked it over there. Or dropped it."

"From his left hand."

"Yeah. Because the pistol was in his right."

"That would be some bounce," says Ceepak.

He's right. Out of the left hand, down to the floor, and over to the stall on his right? The little leather pouch had to have legs or a skateboard.

"If someone had been there," Ceepak continues, "they would have reacted when the drug kit came sliding across the floor and hit their foot."

And, if a wrapped-up satchel of hypodermics and heroin bags smacks into your shoes, you usually tell somebody about it. You might even summon a janitor for some of that immediate attention.

"'It's a death trap, it's a suicide rap,'" mumbles Ceepak. More Springsteen. "Born To Run." I think the Boss was singing about escaping his boring hometown. Ceepak, on the other hand, is thinking about a toilet on the Garden State Parkway. A death trap someone wants to turn into a suicide rap.

"Should we call the Burlington County prosecutor's office?" I ask.

"Not yet. It's all speculation at this point. We have no hard evidence."

"So what do we do?"

"Tell me again about the burglarized car."

"They ripped out everything. Radio. Air bags. Stuff in the trunk."

"How was the trunk opened?"

"Can't say for sure but it was dinged and scratched up pretty bad. Like somebody in a hurry went at it with a crowbar."

Ceepak glances at his watch.

"Rita doesn't need us at the party site for another two hours. Let's head out to Feenyville."

Oh-kay. That's kind of random.

Feenyville is this scuzzy trailer park up on the north end of the island. It's run by a nice old guy who doesn't have a clue what the riffraff
he rents to are doing instead of going to work or leading respectable
lives. Fred Feeny opened the "RV Park and Boat Basin" forty years ago
and calls himself the mayor of Feenyville, which, nowadays, is basically sixteen mobile homes sitting on cinder blocks in a scraggly patch
of crushed seashells.

In the old days, Feenyville was like a KOA. A place for families to
park their campers, dock their boats, and enjoy the ocean. Nowadays,
it's . . . well . . . it's a trailer park. Guests from the Jerry Springer show
stay there, if you catch my drift.

We cross the bridge into Sea Haven.

"It might be prudent to discuss this matter with the Feenyville Pirates," says Ceepak. "As you recall, the crude use of a crowbar to gain
illegal access is one of their favorite m.o.'s."

The Feenyville Pirates is what we all call this bunch of scallywags
who currently rent parking spots from the tolerant Mayor Feeny. Six or
seven scruffy guys and their equally scruffy significant others who are
responsible for a lot of the petty burglaries that take place on the
island—particularly in the off-season. Last winter, we caught a couple
of them breaking into an empty McMansion just off the beach. They
had dented and scraped the bejeezus out of a storm window trying to
pry it open. We busted them, confiscated their crowbar. Guess they
swung by Sears and shoplifted a new one.

"As it happens," says Ceepak, "last Tuesday I tailed one of the pirates to that same rest area."

"Was he carrying a crowbar?"

"Roger that."

"Which one was it?"

"Mr. Nicky Nichols."

"He's the big dude, right?"

Ceepak nods.

It's hard to forget Nicky Nichols. He's nearly seven feet tall and
looks perpetually stupid due to his cartoon-dog eyes and open-mouth
breathing habit.

"Nichols parked his vehicle next to an empty station wagon," says Ceepak. "A Volvo with a DVD entertainment system mounted into the ceiling above the backseat."

Kids today. They never have to stop watching their Disney movies.

"He walked over to the Volvo, raised its hood, and bent over to fiddle with the engine. When I approached and asked him what he was doing, he told me that the station wagon, which had Missouri license plates, belonged to a neighbor at the trailer park and he had come down to jump-start its dead battery. I asked if he'd like to borrow my jumper cables, since the only tool he was carrying was that crowbar."

"You think he was going to steal the battery?"

"No, Danny. The air bags."


We crunch into Feenyville.

It's set off from the road by a sun-bleached stockade fence. A teenager in a terry cloth halter top pedals past on her bike, the tires slipping sideways in the powdery mix of sand and shells. We crawl past the first trailers. Their undercarriages and PVC plumbing are hidden behind skirts of pressure-treated latticework. Some trailers fly the American flag off their TV antennas, one has a Jolly Roger flapping on a rusty pipe. Pirates are brazen that way. Most of the aluminum homes have dented chairs set up in circles around corroded grills. These are Feenyville's backyards.

Up ahead, I see two guys hunkered under the hood of a 1980-something pickup truck. One guy is standing on an upturned cinder block to make him tall enough to tinker with the engine. The other guy doesn't need any kind of booster block. It's Nicky Nichols, all seven feet of him. Bent over like that, he can probably scrape his knuckles on the ground underneath the driveshaft. Now I hear music. Rap. Thumping bass. Angry chants.

Ceepak and I climb out of our car.

The pirate mechanics remain oblivious to our arrival. The rap song is loud, like syncopated thunder.

"You got a wrench?" Nichols shouts to his friend.

"What?" the other one pops up. Bangs his head on the hood. "Fuck!"

I recognize him too. Mr. Shrimp. Guess it's a pirate name—like Mr. Smee from Captain Hook's crew. However, if "Mr. Shrimp" was my handle, I think I'd sign up with some other bunch of buccaneers with tougher-sounding nicknames. Mr. Shrimp is, or course, short. Not exactly a dwarf, but Napoleon short—like five-two. He has this bushy white beard and a red bandanna that makes him look like one of those coconut-head pirates they sell at the Treasure Chest. He also wears glasses, which, if you ask me, sort of ruins the whole pirate look. An eye patch, maybe. Corrective lenses? Not so much.

Nichols sees us. I can tell because he's standing there frozen. Dumbfounded. Straining to remember who we are. When he tries to think like that, the circular *O* of his mouth shrinks down into a wrinkled pucker.

Now Nichols crosses both arms over his chest genie-style and attempts to say something threatening.

"What do you want?" is the best he can manage.

"Yeah," adds Mr. Shrimp. "Whattayawant?"

"We'd like to ask you two gentlemen a few questions," says Ceepak.

"You're cops!" The fifteen-watt refrigerator bulb in Nichols's brain clicks on. "Last winter. You arrested me."

"That's right. I'm Officer John Ceepak. This is my partner, Officer Danny Boyle."

"Where's your badges?" inquires Mr. Shrimp. He puts a lot of head bobs and shoulder twitches behind every word.

"We're off-duty today."

"So what're you doin' here?"

"We'd like to talk to you about air bags."

"You in the market to buy some?" asks Nichols.

You look up *dumb* in the dictionary, you'll see this man's mug shot.

"Nicky?" snaps Mr. Shrimp.

"What?"

"We're not here to make a purchase," says Ceepak. "We're looking for an air bag that someone illegally removed from a Ford Focus parked at the exit fifty-two service plaza on the Garden State Parkway last night."

"Is that so?" Mr. Shrimp jiggles his shoulders. "Well, we was right here, all night."

"Yeah," adds Nichols. "Except when we went out."

"Nicky?"

"What?"

Mr. Shrimp doesn't say it; just mouths the words: *Shut. Up!* He could've added, *You. Idiot.*

"We know you two gentlemen are actively engaged in the business of selling replacement air bags to unscrupulous auto-body repair shops on the mainland," says Ceepak.

Now Nichols looks offended. Well, as offended as he can given his limited range of facial expressions.

Suddenly, the rap song ends and a new song starts. Heavy metal. The CD player in the old truck must have a shuffle mode—one of those six-CD changers people bolt inside their trunks.

*Like Shareef Smith had bolted inside his Ford until somebody ripped it out!*

I recognize the tune: "Cum on Feel the Noize." Quiet Riot. The same heavy metal anthem Dixon and his troops were blasting out the windows of their party house last night.

# 10

"That's Echo Company's theme song!" I say to Ceepak. "They were playing it at that party we broke up! The ten-forty-three!"

Ceepak nods.

"I'll bet that's Smith's CD changer!" I'm pretty jazzed. "They stole it out of the trunk and it was loaded with Smith's CDs!"

"No way. That's my music, man!" says Mr. Shrimp. "I didn't steal that shit from anybody."

"Shit" seems like an extremely appropriate descriptor for the fuzz-box power chords currently ringing out of the truck's gigantic speakers.

"You like Quiet Riot?" I ask.

The Riot singers strain to be heard over the chugging drums. Fortunately, the words are all pretty much the same: *Come on feel the noise.* Over and over. And then a guitar solo. The kind Wayne and Garth used to diddle in the air.

"You actually like an eighties hair band?"

Mr. Shrimp puffs out his chest. "You got some kind of problem, Officer?"

Well, yeah. The song sucks.

"It's a free country!" says Nichols.

I guess so. Especially if you steal everything. Then, yeah, it's all pretty much free.

"This is America," adds the short guy, who's hurling all of his tough-guy machismo in my general direction because it's obvious that Ceepak, the six-two tower of power standing to my left, could peel and eat Mr. Shrimp for breakfast. "We can listen to whatever we want!"

"You stole that CD changer from Corporal Shareef Smith," I reiterate my point. Loudly. It's the only way to be heard over the cascading guitar riff. "That's his song. His CD! His CD changer!"

"You got any proof?"

"Yes," I say and try to think of something I could offer as evidence besides my hunch. But then I see Ceepak shake his head.

"He's right, Danny. We have no proof."

This is when I wish Ceepak's code allowed us to tell a lie every now and then. I wouldn't do it all the time, mind you. Only when it was important or, you know, convenient.

"See?" says Shrimp. "You two ain't got nothin'!"

Nichols tries to chuckle. "Heh. Heh. Heh." It comes out slow—a dying lawn mower huffing out fumes as it runs out of gas. Mr. Shrimp leans into the cab of the truck. Yanks up on a wire. The music dies.

"However," says Ceepak, "this does not mean we intend to let this matter drop."

Nichols's face shifts slowly from amused to puzzled.

"I suspect Officer Boyle's instincts are correct. I suspect you stole the CD changer from the trunk of Corporal Smith's vehicle. I further suspect that you two forgot to exchange his CD collection for music of your own. However, my suspicions and suppositions aren't enough. We will need to gather more evidence if we hope to convince the Burlington County prosecutor to proceed with a criminal case against you two."

"Good luck," taunts Shrimp.

"We won't need luck," says Ceepak. "We'll simply need access to all the evidence surrounding Corporal Smith's trip to the rest stop last night and his supposed suicide."

Ah-hah.

Long live the code.

Ceepak just found our angle. Possession of stolen property here in Feenyville is definitely within our jurisdiction, so Saul Slominsky may be forced to share his forensic evidence with us. Who knows? Maybe these two knuckleheads *are* the ones who did it. Maybe they killed Smith then staged it to look like a suicide. Motive? I don't know. Heavy metal envy.

Okay. It's a flimsy case. But, we officially have our foot in the door, or, more correctly, the toilet stall.

"Thank you for your time, gentlemen," says Ceepak.

"Somebody's dead?" asks Nichols, his brain still locked in that time lag mode.

"Yes," says Ceepak. "The man whose CD player we suspect you stole."

"Suicide?" says Shrimp.

"So someone would have us believe."

The way Ceepak says it? It sounds like Mr. Shrimp might be the *someone* he's talking about.


"Do you think they did it?" I ask when we're back on the road, heading down Ocean Avenue toward the center of Sea Haven.

"I suspect everybody until the last minute," says Ceepak. I guess he's been reading mystery books again. He does that in his spare time when he's not watching forensic shows on the Discovery Channel or helping Rita run the catering business or coaching his stepson's base-ball team.

Or sneaking around town in his wife's car after 1:00 AM.

We're heading over to Kipper Street and Beach Lane. The party house. Ceepak made a few calls and found out from his state trooper pals that Smith's vehicle was towed over to the rental house around noon. Since Slominsky figures it was a suicide and that Smith killed himself in the men's room, not the front seat of a Ford Focus, the car is no longer of any interest to anybody connected to the case.

Nobody, of course, except us. We need to investigate that trunk some more. See if Nicky Nichols and Mr. Shrimp left any evidence behind when they tore out the dead man's CD changer. Maybe a curly hair from the little one's beard. Maybe DNA-rich drool from Nichols's droopy lips.

"We'll need to look at video footage from the parking-lot security cameras," Ceepak says as we turn off the boulevard and cruise down the residential side street. "Try to locate witnesses."

"When do you think Nichols and Shrimp broke into the car?"

"When Smith went inside to use the restroom."

"So *our* witnesses might also be witnesses to whatever really happened in that men's room?"

"Roger that."

Awesome. We're on a parallel path. Our investigative duties will just happen to coincide with whatever went down when Smith stepped into that toilet stall. Maybe some of the people we talk to will just happen to mention whatever they saw in the bathroom. Especially if we just happen to ask them about it.

Couldn't handle the dark mental shit that comes with doing the job."

"Many soldiers experience emotional stress when confronted with the realities of war."

"Jesus. Did you do your tour as a fucking shrink?"

"No. Military police."

"MP? Then you've seen Smith's type. Hell, maybe you even arrested him. Fucking hophead. Got into that serious Afghan shit flowing across the border from Iran, big-time."

"Heroin?"

"And hash. Used to fuck himself up royally before we'd saddle up. Every mission, Smith was high as a fucking kite. Couldn't trust that weak sister to cover your ass worth a damn."

"I'm told they found drug paraphernalia near his body last night."

"Roger that. Guess he smuggled some of that happy horseshit and a Russian PB/6P9 pistol home with him. I wanted to wash him out of our unit but the boys with the brass brains wouldn't let me. Seems we were short on manpower. Too many guys checking out after a single tour."

Now the other guys stare at Ceepak, like it's his fault one of their buddies became a junkie who hated being a soldier so much he put a pistol in his mouth and pulled the trigger.

Dixon jabs a stubby thumb in my general direction. "Your partner here tells me you won some medals."

"One or two."

"You pick up a Purple Heart?" Dixon asks Ceepak.

"No."

"Guess you weren't there long enough. Rolled into Baghdad just in time to watch them pull down that Saddam statue and said, 'hasta la vista, baby'—hightailed it home before the Hajis started blowing up every fucking American convoy they could with their roadside IEDs."

Now it's Ceepak's eyes doing the narrowing. I know he saw his share of improvised explosive devices during his stint in Iraq. I also know he came under some pretty serious enemy fire. He got one medal, the Bronze Star for heroic service in combat, when he risked his life to run up an alley in Sadr City and drag a guy to safety—some gunner he didn't even know—while Sunni snipers up on the rooftops tried to nail him. My man may have only served one tour of duty but he's definitely done his time in hell.

"I was never wounded," Ceepak answers without any emotion. "Not in Iraq."

"Me neither. Too fast." Dixon does a quick juke step and head fake, like he's a point guard for the Nets. "Kept dodging the bullets and the bombs. Now, my man over there, Lieutenant Worthless . . ." He points to the tall guy doing tong duty at the grill. "Old Worthless took a Haji bullet in the leg."

I remember now: he had a limp when he came out with the cell phone to tell us about Smith last night.

"They gave him all sorts of medals for that one. Right, Worthless?"

"Yeah."

"You pack your Purple Heart?"

"It's inside."

"Well, shit, Lieutenant—pin it to your swimsuit. That and a beach badge will get your pecker wet." He turns away. Walks back to the beer cooler. Fishes out a green bottle. Heineken. Twists it open. Takes a swig. Takes his time. "You gentlemen need something?" he finally asks. "Or is this just a condolence call?"

"We need to examine Corporal Smith's vehicle," says Ceepak. "More specifically—the trunk."

"Why?"

"We have reason to believe that he was the victim of a burglary last night. We think some local thieves stole his CD changer."

"Really?" Dixon shakes his head. Starts to laugh. "Jesus, Ceepak. The pussy freak blew his brains out in a fucking crapper. You think he or I or any of these men give two shits about a goddamn CD changer?"

"No, I do not. However, I think investigating this criminal incident might lead us to the truth behind what happened to Corporal Smith last night."

"Come again?"

"He didn't commit suicide. I'm sure of it."

"What?"

"Shareef Smith was murdered."

# 12

*It's rare* that Ceepak makes a pronouncement like that.

Usually, you ask him, "Was this guy murdered?" he says, "It's a possibility." I think there's something about a fellow soldier's unseemly death that's hit him hard.

"You're telling me somebody murdered one of my men?" snaps Dixon. All of a sudden, Shareef Smith isn't a "pussy freak" who couldn't handle the stress of battle. He's back to being one of the guys.

"I believe so."

"Jesus."

"I have no proof at this juncture."

"Fuck."

"As you know, I wasn't on scene last night, but Officer Boyle was able to describe what he saw in sufficient enough detail for me to note inconsistencies that make me uneasy."

"I was there," snaps Dixon. "He had the Russian pistol in his hand. Took a mouth shot. Blew his brains out. Splattered them against the back wall."

"But there was no blood on the floor."

"Come again?"

"Somebody cleaned it up."

"No. He had those tissue rings around his neck."

"The sanitary seat covers."

"Right. That caught all the blood."

Ceepak shakes his head. "As you stated, there was blood and organic matter splattered against the rear wall, which the tissue paper would not, in fact, *could not* catch. In a crime-scene photograph taken with Officer Boyle's cell phone you can see the droplets streaking down toward the floor. The floor itself remains clean."

Dixon squints. Tries to remember what he saw. Tries to find a logical explanation. "Maybe it didn't drip down that far."

"Negative. I suspect somebody mopped the floor, which would also explain how the drug paraphernalia ended up in the adjoining stall."

Of course. The mop head slapped the drug stuff over into the next booth like a hockey stick smacking a puck.

Dixon looks unconvinced. "Somebody mopped up while Smith was still sitting on top of the toilet?"

"Roger that."

"Who? The janitor?"

"Doubtful."

"Who?"

"Too soon to say."

"Jesus!"

"Rest assured, Sergeant, we are going to investigate our suspicions further. That's why we need to examine Smith's vehicle. Specifically, the trunk."

"You think the killer hid in the trunk?"

"No. As it stands, we have no official interest or jurisdictional standing in what happened inside the rest area washroom. However, the burglarization of Smith's vehicle by certain local recidivists might grant us limited access to all evidence associated with his death."

"We're looking at two of the Feenyville Pirates," I say, since Dixon seems stuck on Ceepak's choice of the word *recidivist*. I can see he's struggling to come up with a definition. "Repeat offenders named Nicky Nichols and Mr. Shrimp."

Ceepak turns. Nobody else can see what I see in his face: a wee wince—a small crinkling of the lines around the eyes. Oops. I don't think I should have said that.

"What?" says Dixon. "Fucking pirates?"

"We have two small-time criminals on our radar for the burglary and, as I said, pursuing that investigation may open up access to evidence related to the corporal's death."

Dixon yanks open the gate. Steps off the patio. Goes nose to nose with Ceepak in the patch of gravel near the garbage cans.

"What do you mean 'may'?"

"I cannot guarantee that the Burlington County prosecutor's office will welcome our interest in what they consider a closed case."

Dixon leans forward.

"Let me see if I have this correct, Officer Ceepak. You're telling me that two local yokels murdered one of my men in a lousy latrine on the goddamn Garden State Parkway but you can't do anything about it?"

"Actually, we have no reason to suspect the locals were the ones who—"

Dixon turns his back on Ceepak, addresses his troops. "Gentlemen? Listen up. We will not be breaking camp tomorrow as previously planned."

"How long are we staying?" asks Lieutenant Worthless.

"As long as necessary."

"Just a moment," Ceepak tries. Dixon isn't listening.

"We may need to bring this shitty little town some goddamn noise!"

"Sergeant Dixon, please!" says Ceepak. "There is no need for you and your men to pursue vigilante justice."

"That's your opinion."

"I realize you are upset. But we can not and will not condone citizens taking the law into their own hands."

"Somebody has to."

"Justice will be served. The truth will be uncovered."

"Oh, really? Swell. Put it on a greeting card. Sell it to Hallmark."

"Give me twenty-four hours."

"To do what?"

"To see if I can determine who did this."

"And if you can't?"

"We'll have that beer and talk about next steps."

Over at the grill, I hear the whomp of flames. Everybody's been riveted on Ceepak and Dixon. Lieutenant Worthless hasn't been minding the meat. It's flaring like waxy fireplace logs.

"You have my word," says Ceepak.

"Your word?"

"Yes, sir. And I will not lie nor tolerate those who do."

"You West Point?"

"No. I simply choose to live my life according to their code of honor."

Dixon gives Ceepak a look. "Really? Well, my men and I have a code too: We look out for our own and will not tolerate any individual who seeks to do any one of us harm."

"All I'm asking is one day."

Dixon is thinking about it, I can tell. His breathing is almost regular. Finally, he turns around and calls out to the biggest ox on the patio. "Butt Lips?"

"Sir?"

"Do we have twenty-four hours' worth of liquid refreshment inside the wire?"

"Yes, sir."

"Handy Andy?"

"Sir?" It's the kid with the kielbasa nose.

"How are we doing on acquiring cable TV?"

"We're wired up and good to go, sir."

Dixon nods. Returns his attention to Ceepak.

"Very well. You have twenty-four hours, Officer Ceepak. This time tomorrow. Sunday. Seventeen-hundred hours. But that's it. There will be no deadline extensions."

"Thank you. Now, may we inspect the trunk?"

I hear car tires crunching across gravel.

"You'll need to ask the ladies," says Dixon, indicating the car that just pulled into the parking pad. "Smith's sisters. Apparently, the vehicle in question belongs to one of them."

*13*

*A dark* red Dodge that rolled off the assembly line sometime back
when Reagan was president parks next to my Jeep. I can see two sil-
houettes in the front seat but nobody gets out.

"The troopers contacted Smith's family," says Dixon. "Alerted his
sisters as to what happened. Told us the ladies would be coming up today to claim the vehicle and make arrangements for the body."

Ceepak nods.

We're all standing along the fence. Seven men staring at the two black
women in the car. We must look like the receiving line at an Irish wake.

Finally, I hear the clunk-thud-screech of heavy car doors opening.
Two at once. Both of Smith's sisters step out of the beat-up old Dodge.

"We come for the car," says the one standing behind the door on the
driver side. "Tonya needs it for work Monday."

Tonya seems to be the shy sister. About my age and very pretty, she
stands behind the door on the passenger side. She's thin and, right now,
looks like she wishes she were even skinnier so she could become in-
visible. She won't lift her head to meet any of the fourteen eyes staring
at her.

"Which one of you has the keys?" The driver-side sister, on the other hand, is no shrinking violet. I figure she's older, maybe thirty. She talks with a sassy swagger and looks tough enough to take out half of Dixon's unit, especially if she packs all 290 of her pounds into the first punch. "Maybe you gentlemen didn't hear me. I said, 'Who has the damn keys to Tonya's ride?'"

"Butt Lips?" Dixon calls out.

"On it, sir." Rutledge, aka Butt Lips, heads into the house to retrieve the car keys. Ceepak takes a step toward the women. When he does, Tonya, the shy one, retreats half a step. The other one? She doesn't budge.

"Ma'am, we are all very sorry for your loss."

The driver doesn't answer. She gives Ceepak a bull snort out both nostrils and stands her ground.

"Will you be taking the vehicle home to Maryland?" Ceepak asks. He's not that good at guessing where people are from by the way they snort at him. He just knows how to read the license plates on the Ford and the Dodge: *Maryland.*

Now the big sister glowers at him. "You a soldier?"

"No," says Ceepak. "I'm with the local police."

"But he used to be a soldier," I chime in. "Over in Iraq."

I figure she might relax if she knows everybody here except me played on the same team as her brother. But she doesn't. In fact, she looks angrier.

"Local police have a problem with Tonya picking up her own damn car?"

"Of course not."

"Then it's none of your damn business where we're headed, am I right?"

Ceepak gestures toward the smaller of the two cars. "Would you mind if we inspected the trunk before you drive home?"

"Why?"

"Part of an ongoing police investigation."

"What kind of investigation?"

"We think we know who stole the air bags and CD changer."

"They took the air bags?"

"Yes, ma'am."

She shakes her head, disgusted. "Who has the damn keys?"

Rutledge comes back out to the patio. Tosses a key ring to Dixon, who snatches it in midair. He steps forward and dangles the key ring off the tip of his index finger in front of the big sister's face. Swirls it around some.

"Miss Smith," he says, "these keys are hereby presented to you on behalf of a grateful nation and the United States Army as a token of appreciation for your loved one's honorable and faithful service."

Geeze-o, man.

I think Dixon is mocking a dead soldier's sister.

The big sister rips the key ring off his wiggling finger. Mutters something nasty. I hope it was "fuck you."

"Excuse me?" says Dixon.

Apparently, it was.

The back of his neck flushes red with rage. If he had any hair back there, it'd be standing up like dog hackles.

"What'd you say?"

Ceepak steps forward. "Let it go, Sergeant Dixon."

Dixon pivots. Glares.

"Let it go," Ceepak says again.

"This woman disrespected me."

"And I'll do it again," she says. "In fact, I'll tell you to go straight to hell you ever talk that kind of trash about my baby brother again."

Dixon grins. "Perhaps you misunderstood me, Miss Smith. I said nothing derogatory against your brother."

"Uhm-hmm. I heard the words behind your words."

"Sarge?" It's the lanky guy they keep calling Worthless. The lieutenant. The guy who should be in charge but, apparently, isn't. "Let it go."

Dixon's skin tone steps down to code orange from its previous status at red.

"Tomorrow," he whispers to Ceepak. "Seventeen-hundred hours." He turns. "Gentlemen? Inside."

The short dude in the do-rag, Hernandez, hops to and shoves open the sliding glass door. The soldiers head into the rental house. Hernandez is the last man in and slams the patio door sideways and shut.

I hear sizzling over on the grill. Those sirloins are officially shoe leather.

"You drive that one, Tonya," says the big sister when the soldiers are all gone. "I'll follow along behind you."

"Jacquie?" The shy girl speaks.

"What?"

"The police officer said he needs to inspect the trunk."

"What for? It won't do Shareef any good."

"Jacquie? Please."

The big woman, Jacquie, lets out a hurricane gush of exasperation. "Fine." She flings the key ring at my partner. "Five minutes."

Seems everybody's giving us deadlines today.

"Thank you." Ceepak moves around to the rear of the Ford. I follow. So does Tonya.

Jacquie grumbles as she climbs back into her Dodge. "Gonna take us all night to drive home to Baltimore. Gonna be all kinds of bad traffic. . . ."

She keeps jabbering but it's mostly a mumble—a TV set in the living room nobody's really listening to.

We lift the trunk lid and see less than nothing. Literally. If you ask me, Nicky Nichols and Mr. Shrimp travel around town with one of those portable Dustbusters you can plug into your cigarette lighter and tidy up after they break in. The carpet still has that greasy splotch on the left, but no way are there any hairs or fibers we could put under the microscope to help us nail Nichols and Shrimp.

I, once again, see the metal bracket and torn audio wires.

"They stole my CD changer," says Tonya.

"Hopefully," says Ceepak, "we will be able to recover it for you soon."

"Tonya?"

Jacquie's back. If our five minutes are already up, her watch must be from a different time zone.

"We need to leave here. Now." She turns on Ceepak. "Listen up, po-po. Tonya and I are leaving. And don't you fools be comin' down to Baltimore, knocking on our door, getting all up in our business. We are through with you, them, and the entire United States Army. Is that clear?"

"Of course," says Ceepak.

"It was new," says Tonya. "The CD changer. Brand new. I bought it last month."

"Little sister, you do not need to be talking to this man!"

"I may have the receipt. Would that help?"

"Yes, ma'am. It would help us identify the unit's serial number." Ceepak hands her a business card. She stares at it. "If you find the paperwork, please call me."

"Tonya?" says Jacquie. "We still need to go talk to that damn funeral home man."

Ceepak lowers the trunk lid.

"Thank you for your time. Again, we're sorry for your loss."

Jacquie turns on her heel and heads back to her car. "We are out of here."

Tonya doesn't move.

"You were Shareef's friend, right?" she asks.

"No. We never met."

Now she looks puzzled.

"Tonya?" Jacquie is hollering out the passenger-side window of her car. "How many damn times have I got to tell you? We need to leave here. *Now!*"

Ceepak looks at Tonya. Musters up his considerable stockpile of honesty and integrity and puts it right there in his eyes so she can see it. "Is there something you want to tell me, Ms. Smith?"

She nods. "Shareef called me."

"Last night?"

Another nod. "We talked some."

"Tonya?" Jacquie is furious and yanks open her door again. When she slams it shut behind her, the whole chassis rocks. "Get in the damn car, girl!"

Tonya keeps talking. "He said he was in a parking lot. At a rest stop. He told me he was fine, feeling strong."

"Tonya?"

"Then he had to run because his friend showed up."

"His friend?" says Ceepak.

"That's enough," snaps Jacquie.

"I thought it might've been you," says Tonya.

Jacquie grabs Tonya's elbow. Rough. "But you were wrong weren't you, baby sister? Shareef was wrong too! Dead wrong! He never had no damn friends. Not this man, not those others, not any of 'em!"

## 14

"Danny? Did you get more ice?"

"Yeah."

"Great. Sam? Can you give him a hand? We need it at the poolside bar. Thanks, guys."

Rita hustles up the driveway through the wrought iron gates to Crazy Janey's French chateau beach house. The place is a mansion. Samantha Starky and I have been valet parking cars for a couple hours, ever since the gates swung open at 7:30 PM. We're both wearing black pants and little red jackets. Kind of look like organ grinder monkeys. Of course, Starky makes a much cuter monkey than I do.

The red tunic hugs her in a way that shows off a shapely figure. This might be the first time I've ever seen her out of uniform. I mean she's in a valet parking uniform but not the drab dress-blue polo shirt that sort of makes everybody wearing it look like a lumpy airplane pillow. And without the cop cap, her hair is kind of bouncy, not strangled into a ponytail poking out the back of her hat.

She cleans up good, as they say.

"I can carry two bags," she says.

"Great. I'll grab the rest." I go ahead and hoist four bags so I can prove to Starky and the world just how manly I am. Mistake. Each bag weighs thirty pounds and the bottoms are filled with the sloshing water of melted ice, some of which is dribbling out of vent holes and soaking my shoes.

"We can make another trip," suggests Starky.

"That's okay," I grunt. "I'm good to go."

Of course, it's all uphill from here. Up the driveway. Through the gates. Up around the fountain. The bags seem heavier with every step.

"Did you see Paris Hilton?" asks Starky as we hike up the hill. I'm leaking a trail of droplets, my bags barely an inch off the pavement.

"Nah." I'm keeping my words to a minimum. Hoarding my oxygen. It's another hundred yards around the triple garages to the backyard, two hundred feet from there to the kidney-shaped pool. My arms are about six inches longer than they used to be. Carrying 120 pounds of ice will do that to you.

Starky and I are working our butts off tonight, because Ceepak isn't here to do all the jobs he was supposed to do. He talked to Rita earlier and, I guess, they both decided it was more important for him to head down to the state police barracks and talk with some of his trooper pals, see if we could gain access to any of the Smith suicide evidence, now that we officially suspect a pair of Sea Haven pirates were the ones who broke into the dead man's vehicle. Ceepak probably advised his wife that we only have about nineteen hours left to figure out who really killed Shareef Smith or, without a doubt, Sergeant Dale "Stone Cold" Dixon will send out his troops to do the job for us. They'll probably do the judge and jury's jobs too. You know—the sentencing and execution parts. I think they're all firmly in favor of the death penalty.

I guess when you marry a guy who comes with a rigid moral code, this sort of thing happens now and then. He gives his word to someone, you suffer the consequences.

But wait—it's almost 9:30. Ceepak's been gone for three hours. The state barracks are only like a thirty-minute drive down the Parkway. He should definitely be back by now.

Maybe he's allergic to ice.

We round this bend in the garden path and weave our way through a few hundred of Dirty Larry and Crazy Janey's close, personal celebrity friends. The girls in the crowd—mostly supermodels and adult movie actresses or both—are all wearing bathing suits. Skimpy bikinis, mostly. But none of them are actually in the pool playing Marco Polo. We pass this one blonde and I swear it looks like she's wearing three folded napkins. Cocktail napkins. Folded in half. Tiny triangles.

I hear a wolf whistle. T.J. He's over in the poolside tent, setting up beverages for the beautiful people. He waves us over.

"We need to ice down this champagne, pronto," he says. "The senator's all set to make a big toast."

T.J.'s already lined up three-dozen magnums of Moët & Chandon in foil-lined bins.

I plop my ice bags on the ground and try to reestablish some semblance of circulation to my limbs. Starky repeatedly smacks and smashes her two bags on the concrete to break up the clumped-together cubes. Gives one bag a good karate kick. Then, she tears open the top with her teeth, gives the whole thing a good shake, and dumps ice into the channels between champagne bottles. She's not even breathing heavy. Maybe I should sign up for Tae Kwon Do.

"We have a senator here?" I ask to kill some time so I don't have to lift anything heavy for another ten seconds or so.

"Senator Worthington," says Starky. "The senior senator from Pennsylvania. I parked his Lexus while you ran to the store for ice. It's a very nice car but he's a terrible tipper. Gave me seventy-five cents."

"Man, you should've kept driving," says T.J. "You could've held his Lexus hostage. Hey, Danny?"

"Yeah?"

"Did you meet Springsteen?"

"No way. He's here? Springsteen?"

"Yeah. He played a couple songs. You know—'Crazy Janey and her mission man were back in the alley trading hands.' "

"Oh, man! He sang 'Spirit in the Night'?"

T.J. chuffs a laugh.

"Gotcha!"

Kids. You gotta love 'em. Can't shoot 'em.

"I'm yanking your crank," T.J. says as I dump my first load. I make sure a couple cubes tumble out. I also let the water slosh onto his sneaker.

There's some commotion across the pool.

Eight brawny guys in dark suits and sunglasses who look like linebackers with curly wires trailing out of their ears. One of the guys talks into his sleeve, just like in the movies. I don't think he's talking to his buddy Mr. Cuff Link. I think they're Secret Service agents or some kind of private security guards—either for Dirty Larry, the king of all airwaves, or the senior senator from Pennsylvania. Right now, I'm guessing they work for the senator because they have crew cuts and shaved heads. I'm certain Dirty Larry's security posse dresses in the latest gangsta rap fashions and none of these guys are wearing necklaces that resemble hubcaps on chains.

The security team scans the crowd, sweeps it with their hidden eyes. A couple talk to their sleeves some more.

Rita swings by the booze tent carrying a tray of pigs in a blanket—golden brown pastry shells wrapped around sizzling little wieners. Starving, I reach for a toothpick.

"Danny? These are for the guests. Hey—have you guys seen John?"

"Nope!" says Starky, the one off-duty cop not currently drooling like Homer Simpson in a doughnut factory.

"Darn," says Rita. "I wanted him to hear Senator Worthington."

"Is he the guy in the suit and the Army boots?"

"Yes, T.J.," says Rita.

Okay. I've read about Senator Worthington. Only because his fashion statement made the cover of this weekly newspaper I read whenever I'm in the express line at the grocery store with the mathematically challenged. You know—people who can't count to fifteen. The *Star Gazer* loves Senator Winslow "the Winner" Worthington because he always wears a pair of his son's dusty ol' Army boots. He says he wears the boots "so I never forget the daily sacrifices being made by my son and all our brave troops with boots on the ground over in Iraq."

Geeze-o, man.

Hey, call me cynical, but the wearing-my-son's-old-Army-boots bit sounds like a slick political PR stunt to me. Something for the TV cameras. This is why, when he speaks, he never stands behind a podium, unless it's made out of Plexiglas. It's all about the boots.

And it's working. Everybody says Worthington is a shoe-in to be the next Republican candidate for the presidency.

"Testing, one, two, three . . ."

On the other side of the pool, they've set up a small raised platform. Dirty Larry, the nationally syndicated potty mouth, is on stage, shaking his shaggy hair and tapping on the microphone.

"Can you hear me, Janey?"

"When can I *not* hear you?" Crazy Janey, our hostess and Larry's loyal sidekick, screams from over near the diving board.

"Okay, everybody," says Larry, "before we fill the pool with Jell-O and really get this party started . . ."

The crowd laughs. I might've joined them except I'm busy heaving another bag of ice.

"I want to introduce a truly great American. Not as great as me, of course. He's not syndicated in one hundred and twenty-seven markets. . . ."

The crowd claps. I dump ice.

"Ladies and gentlemen, it's my pleasure to introduce an American who isn't afraid to speak up for our brave men and women in uniform, maybe because he walks a mile in his son's shoes every day. A son, by the way, who was wounded in combat and awarded the Purple Heart. Ladies and gentlemen, if you want my opinion, which, of course everybody does, this man should be and will be the next president of these United States. Why? Because I'm too busy to run myself!"

A few more chuckles. Enough noise for us to start popping champagne corks into towels.

"Friends, I give you the senior senator from the great state of Pennsylvania—Winslow W. Worthington!"

Dirty Larry signals for the senator to clomp up on stage in those Army boots.

Everybody claps so I flap flippers like an obedient seal.

"Danny?" says Starky. "Start pouring. It's almost time for the toast!"

So, while the esteemed senator rambles on about how happy he is to be here and jabs the air with his thumb like Clinton used to do, we pour bubbly into plastic champagne glasses. Well, I guess they're not really glasses but you can't call them champagne "plastics." Not very classy and, trust me, Crazy Janey is definitely paying the classy rates for this shindig.

The senator talks some more.

We pass out the champagne.

The senator talks even more because that's what senators do.

Rita makes her way through the crowd and reaches the stage so she can hand a cup of bubbly up to the senator.

The eight guys with the sunglasses and earpieces flanking the senator on all sides of the stage won't be drinking this evening. It's hard to whip out your Uzi if you're sipping champagne.

Finally, the senator stops speechifying long enough to raise his plastic goblet.

"And so, my friends, I propose a toast!"

Everybody raises their glasses when the senator raises his.

"Goodness gracious," he says. "Words fail me."

"Impossible," cracks Dirty Larry, who, unlike the senator, never runs out of words, especially if there's any kind of microphone close by.

"What makes this the grandest summer evening of all?" the senator continues, sounding all choked up. "The answer is quite simple: my only son is here tonight. Oh, yes—he could have come home to his family months ago when he won that Purple Heart Larry mentioned. However, when his wounds healed, my son told me he didn't want to abandon his other family: the brave men of Echo Company."

The crowd applauds. They know a hero when they hear about one.

"Ladies and gentlemen, my son is here on a brief furlough to savor some of the freedoms he has fought so valiantly to defend. And, to make this night even more special, he's brought along a few friends!"

A murmur rumbles through the crowd. I notice that Starky is up on the tips of her toes. The senator swings his arm grandly to the right.

"Son? Come on up here with your buddies and take a bow!"

Five men in uniform rumble up the steps and line up behind the senator.

"Ladies and gentlemen, I give you Second Lieutenant Winslow G. Worthington and his courageous comrades from the fighting Eighty-second Airborne!"

The crowd goes wild.

Well, everybody except me.

Winslow G. Worthington? He's the soldier with the limp.

The one Dixon calls "Lieutenant Worthless."

# 15

"You from New Jersey, Officer Starky?"

"Yes, sir."

"You what they call a Jersey girl?"

" 'spose so, sir."

"How come you don't have the big hair?"

Just our luck. After the toast, Sergeant Dixon is still thirsty. So he and three of his buddies, the ones he calls Handy Andy, Mickey Mex, and Butt Lips, are in the booze tent, helping themselves to champagne. A magnum each. That's one and a half liters—twice as much as a normal bottle.

When it comes to alcohol consumption, these guys don't know from normal. Especially Butt Lips. He's huge. A real two-fisted drinker. One magnum in each paw.

Dixon leans in with a leer. "So, what do you do for fun down here, Jersey girl?"

"Sarge?" It's Lieutenant Worthington. Two of the senator's bodyguards flank him. "Dad says we should roll."

"So soon?" says Dixon. "What a shame. Officer Starky was about to give me her phone number."

"It's the same as mine," I say. "Nine-one-one."

"Cute, Boyle. Cute."

"I try."

"Yeah. Well, why don't you and Ceepak try spending some time figuring out who the fuck killed one of my men instead of valet parking cars at fancy-ass parties?"

"Sarge?" Worthington shakes his head. "Not here."

"You giving the orders now, gimp?"

Worthington blinks.

"So, you guys want to hit the boardwalk tomorrow?" Dixon asks nobody in particular.

"Sure, sarge," says Butt Lips. I think I know how Rutledge got his nickname: he kisses a lot of heinie.

"Might give us something to do before we do the job the local constabulary seem unable to do." He holds up a hand. "But, I gave my word. Gave Officer Ceepak twenty-four hours, of which he only has what? Twenty left?"

"Nineteen, sir," says Handy Andy. He is, indeed, handy. Knows his math.

"So, we'll head over to the boardwalk and kill some time riding the rides before we head out to kill whoever—"

He stops.

Here come two more musclemen in sunglasses and suits. They look like the downfield blockers for a tailback if, you know, offensive linemen were allowed to carry concealed weapons under their uniforms. They halt. Separate.

Here comes the all-American from Pennsylvania: Senator Winslow W. Worthington. The four other bodyguards from the eight-man crew are tailing him, still scanning the crowd for trouble other than someone popping out of their bikini top.

"Win?"

"Yes, Dad?"

"It might be prudent for you and your friends to call it a night."

"Yes, sir."

"Good seeing you again, Sergeant Dixon," says the senator. He looks like his face should be chiseled into marble. White swept-back hair— like George Washington with better teeth. If this senator-president thing doesn't work out, the elder Mr. Worthington could become a male model and pose as the wise-and-loving father of the bride in tuxedo ads.

The senator extends his hand. Dixon puts down his champagne jug so he can shake it.

"Thank you for watching out for my son, Sergeant."

"Yes, sir."

I note that Dixon is standing more stiffly now, like someone just shoved a ramrod up his butt.

The senator snaps Dixon a crisp salute, which Dixon returns just as sharply. The man sobers up quicker than anybody I've ever met.

The noble statesman and his bodyguards breeze up the garden pathway to shake a few more hands on their way out of the party.

Dixon picks up his super-sized bottle and drains the last drops. "I'll drive."

"We have the Denali, sir." This from one of the security guys guarding the senator's son. "We'll transport you and your men back to Kipper Street."

Dixon gives the guy a wobbly salute off the brim of his khaki hat. "Sir, yes, sir."

Guess he was faking that sobriety for the senator.

And so the war heroes depart. They shuffle into this huge SUV that somebody parked on the patio next to the pool. I guess when you have Pennsylvania plates reading *US SEN 1* you can park anywhere you want. The two bodyguards climb in up front. The one riding shotgun probably actually has a shotgun.

"Thanks, Danny," says Starky when the soldiers are safe and secure behind locked doors and tinted glass.

"No problem," I say.

She seems sort of embarrassed. "I know they're war heroes . . ."

"Doesn't mean they get to be assholes too."

"Yeah. Anyway, thanks."

"You're welcome. But you know—you could've taken them out with some kind of karate kick or one of those Tae Kwon Do moves . . . ."

"Not all five. Only two or three."

"Hey, I'd help. And don't forget—we have Ceepak on our team."

"Not really. He's not here."

Oh, yeah. In any altercation, no matter the martial art, your kicks and karate chops are much more effective against your adversaries when you're actually there.

Ceepak finally shows up around 11:30.

"Sorry I wasn't available to help this evening," he says to Starky and me when he finds us out front. The toasts are all over, so we're back on active valet parking duty. We can hear the music and laughter drifting up over the wrought iron fence. Occasionally, we pick up the splash of a cannonball as somebody either jumps or gets pushed into the pool. Probably the latter. The splashes are always followed by hysterical laughter and "boo-yeahs" and "whoo-hoos" and whatever else drunks can come up with after they toss somebody into chlorinated water. I don't think any of our revelers will be claiming their cars any time soon. The night, as they say, is young.

"John?" Rita comes down the driveway. "Is everything okay?"

"Fine."

"You took care of it?"

"It's all squared away."

Starky and I shoot each other a glance. We have absolutely no idea what Ceepak and his wife are talking about.

So I ask.

"What's up?"

"Personal matter," says Ceepak.

Wow. How un-Ceepakian. Taking care of personal business when we only have like seventeen hours left to figure out who killed Shareef Smith before Dixon and his crew do it for us? Totally off task.

"Anything we can help with?" I ask and gesture to include Starky. Might as well drag her into this since we're both kind of counting on

Ceepak to help us out the next time Sergeant Dixon leches after Starky.

"I'd rather not discuss it," says Ceepak.

"Same here," says Rita.

Guess if they don't say anything, they can't lie about whatever it is they're trying to hide from us.

"Glad you're back," Rita says to Ceepak and gives him a quick peck on the cheek. "I need to be up at the pool. Time to serve ice cream. Want me to fix you a cone or a sundae or something?"

"No, thanks."

"We have water ices too."

"I'm good."

"Okay. If you change your mind . . . ."

"Actually, Rita—if it won't create too much of an imposition, Danny and I need to take off. The same janitor who was on duty at the rest area last night is there tonight. We should talk to him ASAP."

"Your friends at the state police set up an interview?"

He nods. "They're also working on access to the physical evidence. They understand our sense of urgency."

"Great. Okay. You guys go on. I'll ask some of the waiters to help Samantha with the cars when the party breaks up."

"Appreciate it," says Ceepak.

We hear another splash and a wild squeal of whoo-hoo delight. Now, they're applauding. Cheering. Why do I think Dirty Larry just got dunked?

"I gotta go . . ."

Rita dashes up the driveway.

"Danny? Where's your Jeep?" Ceepak asks.

"Way down the road. I had to save the good spots for the guests."

"As you should. The walk will do us good. Help us clear our minds. Formulate questions for our interrogation of the janitor."

Yeah.

Maybe I'll ask him what's better: Lysol toilet bowl cleanser or Scrubbing Bubbles.

Then maybe I'll ask him if he knows what the hell Ceepak and his wife are trying to hide from me and Starky.

# 16

"Who do you think his friend was?" I ask.

"Come again?"

"Smith's sister. She said that when she talked to Shareef last night, he had to hang up when his 'friend' pulled into the parking lot."

I see the sign indicating that the exit 52 rest area is two miles down the Parkway. The sign also advises passing traffic that the next rest area is thirty-six miles away. It's giving fair warning: if you gotta go, you better go now or forever hold your peace.

"So why'd she think that friend was you?"

"Not knowing, can't say."

"Did you know Shareef? Over in Iraq?"

"No."

"Maybe you busted him or something when you were an MP."

"I suppose that's a possibility. However, few of the soldiers we wrote up considered us 'friends.'"

"So who could this 'friend' be?"

"The possibilities are endless. Maybe Shareef had friends from Baltimore who moved to New Jersey. Maybe another soldier from his regiment lives in the area. Or, perhaps, it was simply his way of politely getting rid of his sister in order to make contact with a drug dealer."

"So how do we narrow down the field?"

"I've asked the state police for access to any and all security camera footage from the parking lot. We may soon have visual evidence regarding who broke into Smith's vehicle as well as who visited him right before he went into the building to use the bathroom."

Yeah. Smith used it to shoot up drugs. Somebody else used it to shoot Smith.


We pull into the parking lot of the rest stop.

The sea of asphalt is nearly empty. Pools of soft light are lined up in tidy rows underneath towering lampposts. High-flying bugs, some the size of winged bricks, flutter up where the mercury vapor glows. Not too many cars in the slanted spaces at this hour but more than I'd expect to see at midnight on a Saturday.

I see a bunch of buses too. The kind with cushy seats, carpeted walls, aluminum toilets, and chair-back TVs. The kind loaded up with senior citizens heading home after transferring their bank balances to the casinos down in A-C.

"Mr. Delgado will meet us in the food court," says Ceepak. According to what the state police told him, Filberto Delgado was the janitor who flipped up the latch on the locked stall and found Shareef Smith's body. The one who threw up in the sink.

"I'm surprised he's working tonight," I say. "I mean, after what he saw last night. What he found."

"He may not have a choice, Danny."

True. The guys with the crappy jobs, the ones who clean up other people's messes all day every day, seldom get what they call a benefits package beyond a steady paycheck. Forty hours at minimum wage.


"I always work the eleven-to-seven shift," Mr. Delgado says. "I like nights. Not as messy."

We're sitting at one of the small tables near the atrium on the east side of the food court. The atrium was designed for folks who like to wolf down their pizza in sunshine magnified to hothouse levels by an arching ceiling of glass. At midnight, however, the sun's not so intense, but the daytime heat is still trapped under the curved dome. The chairs sort of look like hard plastic versions of the wooden ones you might have around your kitchen table, except these are welded to the table's crossbeams, something most people don't do at home, even though I know my mom thought about it whenever my brother and I leaned back in our chairs and made the spindles pop out of their sockets.

"I clean the men's room every hour on the hour."

Delgado is probably forty. He's bald up top, keeps both side panels so neatly trimmed they could be putting greens. It looks like he irons his uniform polo shirt and black pants. His HMM Host baseball cap too. He's obviously Hispanic, but his English isn't nearly as deficient as CSI linguist Slominsky suggested it was.

"So you went into the men's room for the first time when?" asks Ceepak.

"Usually, it's the first thing I do—right after I clock in. Say, eleven-oh-five. Eleven-oh-six. I always clean the men's room first. It's a high traffic area. Men are messier than women. They stand. They miss. They do not flush."

True. Hence the dreaded "floaters."

Delgado rests his arms on the small square table. Feels something sticky. Looks annoyed.

He reaches for a spray bottle on his rolling Rubbermaid cart. It's parked next to our table and loaded up with all sorts of jugs and brushes and enough toilet paper rolls to last most guys an entire year, unless, of course, his girlfriend is staying over.

Delgado spritzes the laminated particleboard and wipes it clean with a paper towel he rips off the roll he has cleverly rigged to the front of his janitorial trolley. Gives the aluminum edging near his elbows a quick swipe with the towel too.

Ceepak smiles approvingly. He likes a man who takes pride in his work.

Delgado shakes his head while he balls up the soiled towel. "As you can see, Osvaldo worked the second shift again tonight. Osvaldo is twenty-five and lazy."

Sure. I can relate.

"He only does enough work to keep the boss from firing him."

The tabletop sufficiently de-sticky-fied, Delgado now expertly centers the plastic salt and pepper shakers.

"Sometimes, Osvaldo even cheats."

Uh-oh. That's a Ceepak code violation if ever I heard one.

"How so?"

"Last night, he made me late on my rounds."

Ceepak looks confused. "You initialed the clipboard at eleven-oh-five PM . . . "

"Yes. But this was before I saw that the tape had been pulled across the right side, closing it down for maintenance."

Interesting. This is the first time we're hearing this: the side of the men's room where Smith's body was found was roped off to the public.

"Sometimes, instead of cleaning, Osvaldo just pulls the tape across."

"The Retracta-Belt?"

Delgado nods. "The clipboard is in the entranceway, so I signed in at eleven-oh-five. But, when I walked down the hallway and saw that the right side was closed for maintenance, I went looking for my boss."

"And did you find him?"

"No. I think he took the night off. I could not find him after . . . you know . . . after I . . ."

Now it's Ceepak's turn to nod. "So," he says, "you came back into the restroom at what time?"

"Eleven-twenty. Maybe eleven-thirty."

"And, according to the clipboard, the last time the men's room had been cleaned was ten-oh-five PM?"

"Yes."

Okay, figuring this Osvaldo slacker finished mopping up sometime around 10:10 because he probably spent like two minutes cleaning up the "open" side, our killer had over an hour to get in, do the job, then head down—or up—the Parkway.

"Did you take down the tape?" Ceepak asks.

"Yes. So I could roll in my cart."

"Tell us what you saw when you first entered the right side of the restroom."

"Okay. First I see the portable floor blower. The big fan was still running, wasting electricity, because the floor was completely dry. They call this machine the tornado. It is very powerful. Very loud."

"Anything else strike you as unusual?"

"Yes. To my left, I see a mop bucket tucked into a corner where I could not see it from out in the hallway. The bucket was empty."

Now I nod. "Osvaldo," I say. "The lazy bum just left it there."

Ceepak shakes his head. "Danny—somebody else may have left it there."

Duh. Right. The guy who swabbed the floor underneath Smith's toilet to clean up all the evidence. The guy who knocked the drug gear into the neighboring stall.

"Was there a mop in that bucket?" Ceepak asks.

"No. It was empty."

"Where is that bucket typically kept between cleanups?" asks Ceepak.

"In the supplies closet. Over by the food court."

"Is there only one bucket?"

"No. We have several."

"I see."

"They roll on casters."

"Was one missing from the closet?"

"Yes."

Ceepak jots a note in his pad. "This is very helpful," he says. "Tell us what you did next."

"I saw the shoes in the stall. I thought it was unusual—somebody using the facilities even though that half of the restroom had been closed off. Also, his pants weren't, you know, pulled down."

Yeah. It always works out better if you drop your drawers before you sit on the throne.

"But, I said nothing. I cleaned the sinks. The urinals. Put fresh water in the flower vases. Restocked the paper goods. Finally, I started mopping the floor. I even hummed and whistled some, thinking the man in the stall would hear me and maybe, you know, hurry up."

But, as we all know, that didn't happen. Smith was already dead.

"I accidentally splashed some mop water on the man's shoes so I said, 'I am sorry.' He said nothing. So, I said, 'Sir?' Again, he said nothing. 'Are you all right, sir?' I asked. Still nothing. So, I go right up to the stall. Tap on the door. Nothing."

"That's when you went out again to look for the manager?"

"Yes. And again, I can't find him."

"The state police have informed us that Anthony Bosco, your manager, phoned in sick last night."

"I see," says the maintenance man. I'm guessing Mr. Delgado has never taken a sick day in his life.

"So you came back into the men's room . . ."

"Yes. I have a small knife, which I carry in my pocket. I opened it up. Used the long blade to slide through the crack and raised the latch. I pushed open the door. I . . ."

Delgado swallows hard. Remembers what he did next. Hopes he doesn't have to do it again.

Me too. We're a long way from the nearest sink.

Ceepak closes up his notebook.

"Thank you, Mr. Delgado. You've been very helpful. We may want to speak to Osvaldo. Do you know his last name?"

"Vargas. Osvaldo Vargas. He has family in Tulcingo. He should work harder, send them money. Instead, he likes to party with his wild friends."

Hey, come on—the guy's twenty-five. It's what we do.

"I'm sorry to have made you go through all this again," says Ceepak.

"Again?"

"I'm assuming you told this same story to the investigators last night?"

Delgado shakes his head. "No."

"No?" says Ceepak.

"The man with the mustache? The man in charge? He didn't seem in-terested. He only asked if I had a key to the snack shop. He was hungry."

We let Mr. Delgado go back to work. Those folks headed home from Atlantic City? While we were chatting, they were dropping limp French fries on the floor. Ketchup packs and napkins too. That's why there's white paper stuck to the heel of my shoe when Ceepak and I head out the front doors.

"Let's meet for breakfast first thing tomorrow at Grace's place. She's from Baltimore . . ."

Yep. That's why the Chesapeake crabmeat omelet is the only thing on the menu at the Pig's Commitment that doesn't include some kind of pork.

"She might be able to help us reach out to Smith's sisters."

Grace Porter is also black.

"Then, at ten AM," says Ceepak, "we need to be on the ninth hole at King Putt Golf. I believe they call it 'Victoria Falls.'"

Tomorrow is Sunday, a national day of golfing for many, I'm sure, but I figured we might be busy tracking down leads, not hitting the loop-dee-loop on Ocean Avenue.

Ceepak reads my puzzled expression.

"The choice of location was made by Saul Slominsky. I suspect he feels confident no one will recognize him there. Apparently there is a cave underneath the waterfall."

What do you know?

Slobbinsky wants to talk to us.

# 17

There's nothing like the smell of bacon grease in the morning.

It smells like somebody else fixed breakfast.

It used to mean my mom woke up early to plunk flabby strips into her skillet so they could shrink into crisp ribbons of deliciousness. Now it means Ceepak and I are already back on the job. Eight AM Sunday, we're at the Pig's Commitment, Grace Porter's place on Ocean Avenue. The whole building smells like a can of congealed bacon drippings with the consistency of Crisco.

Ms. Porter, the proprietress, is elderly and elegant and swears she improvises her secret rib sauce recipe every time she whips up a batch. Her restaurant doubles as a mini-museum for porker paraphernalia. The walls are covered, the shelves crammed. Ceramic pigs, plastic pigs, piggy banks of all kinds, pig-shaped cutting boards. Each table is set with a pair of mismatched shakers where the salt and pepper come tumbling out of pig snouts. The decor is enough to make a vegetarian weep.

Grace comes over to our table carrying my salvation: a freshly brewed pot of coffee. She's tall and slender, even though the lady spends most of her day surrounded by fatty foods. She's about as thick around the middle as one of the wooden chopsticks they give you when you order the pork pot stickers. She's sixty-something and wears a cool Kofi hat with African tribal squiggles all over the sides so she looks like a jazz musician or, as she likes to call herself, the queen of cuisine.

"More coffee, gentlemen?" Grace asks.

"No thank you, Grace," says Ceepak. "I'm good."

I slide my mug across the table. "I could use some."

Grace cocks a critical eyebrow. "Late night, Officer Boyle?"

"Yeah."

"I see. Are you and your boon companions still attempting to drink your way into the Guinness book of records?"

I think she means the beer. Grace has known me and my buds a long time. Her restaurant is open twenty-four hours a day. In my misspent youth, 8:00 AM on Sunday was when we used to stumble in for a midnight snack.

"Ceepak and I were on an official run."

"Hmmm." She's not buying it.

"It's true," says Ceepak. "We were on the job until well past midnight."

Grace's scowl immediately morphs into a motherly smile. If Ceepak says it's true, then she knows it must be. I'm granted a full and unconditional refill.

"How was the party at Crazy Janey's last evening?" Grace now asks.

"Crowded," I say then slurp down some Colombian gold.

"Rita and T.J. didn't arrive home until five AM," adds Ceepak.

"I assume she's sleeping in this morning?"

"Yes, ma'am."

"Good. Excuse me, gentlemen."

She takes the coffeepot away to service a sleepy father corralling a family of five. The restaurant is already pretty crowded. Mostly families with young kids—the kind who want pancakes and sausages at 7:00 AM and whine about it until they get them at 8:00.

Ceepak rubs his hands together. "I've been thinking about the mop bucket, Danny."

Of course he has. While I went home and grabbed a couple quick z's on my lumpy pillow, Ceepak went home and thought about mop buckets.

"How did it end up in that corner? Did the other janitor, this Osvaldo Vargas, simply abandon it after his ten PM cleaning? Or did our killer remove it from the maintenance closet prior to shooting Smith because he anticipated the need to clean up his crime scene? Either way, we should be able to see who rolled the bucket out of the closet on the closed-circuit recording, which I'm hoping Slominsky will hand over to us this morning."

Of course. The single security camera. It was aimed toward the snack shop and food court. Precisely where the janitorial supply closet is located! Man, Ceepak's good. I should try this thinking thing when I get home at night instead of, you know, just peeling off my clothes and scratching myself.

The pig bells over the front door jingle. They're like sleigh bells, only the metal balls are molded to look like Porky.

It's Samantha Starky.

And that state trooper. Wilson. The one who knows so much about air bags.

Sam's still in her valet parking pants and red vest. Wilson's in shorts and a pink polo shirt. The shorts show off swollen quads that more or less match his arm muscles. The guy could probably bench-press a Buick.

"Officer Boyle! Officer Ceepak!"

She's up front near the cash register, waving. Practically jumping up and down, flashing us her pearly whites. If this law enforcement thing doesn't work out, Starky need not worry—I figure the Dallas Cowboy cheerleaders are always hiring.

Now the guy named Wilson is waving too. Like we're old pals even though we've only met once.

"Do you know the young man with Officer Starky?" asks Ceepak as the two giddy young kids bound over to join us.

"State trooper. He was at the rest stop Friday night. Knows lots of air bag statistics."

"Indeed?"

I said it to be snarky. Ceepak sounds genuinely interested.

"Hey, you guys!"

Ceepak is standing because basically he's a gentleman and Starky's a lady. I try to get up. My knees bump the table. There goes the coffee creamer. The ones shaped like potbellied pigs are always wobbly.

"I'll get that," says Grace, racing back to the table with a towel to mop up my mess.

"Thank you, Grace," says Ceepak.

"Yeah," I add. "Thanks." As usual, I'm a step or two behind him.

"Just coffee for you two?" Grace now asks Starky and her boy toy.

"No," says Sam. "We're starving!"

"Been up all night," adds Wilson.

"After the party ended at like five or whatever, Wilson picked me up and we went down to the beach and watched the sun rise."

"Some very interesting constellations are visible at that hour," says Wilson. "Venus."

Venus. Goddess of love. Torturer of Danny.

Ceepak is still standing.

"Grace?"

"Yes, John?"

"You have friends and family in Baltimore, correct?"

"Of course. I still consider it my home."

"I was wondering if you knew a Tonya Smith?"

Grace thinks for a second. "No. The name doesn't sound familiar."

"How about Jacquie Smith?"

Grace ponders that one. "No. Sorry. Who are these Smith women?"

"Sisters. They both live in Baltimore. We need to talk to them. However, they don't wish to talk to us."

"I see. They don't trust the police?"

"So it would seem. I was hoping you might reach out to them."

"Are they black, John?"

"Yes."

Now Ceepak gets the scornful lift of an eyebrow. "And you assume we all know each other?"

"No, Grace. I simply assumed these two women might be more willing to talk to you than they were to talk to us."

"Why?"

Ceepak grins. Shows Grace his dimples. "Because you can talk to anyone. You make everyone feel at ease."

Grace sloughs off the compliment. "True. Comes with running a restaurant for thirty years, I suppose. Do you have their phone numbers?"

"No," Ceepak admits, somewhat sheepishly. "The sisters were not inclined to give that information to me."

"John?"

"Yes?"

"While I am typically impressed with your investigative prowess, I must confess—in this instance, you disappoint me. No phone numbers? How am I supposed to contact these ladies? Did you assume that I, at some point in the not too distant past, memorized the entire Baltimore phone book?"

"No, I—"

"We have their numbers," says Starky.

Ceepak finally sits down. "You do?"

"Wilson has 'em, right?"

"Hmmm?" Wilson had been busy—studying the menu. Took all his powers of concentration. In my peripheral vision, I saw him silently sounding out the hard words: *"Bay-kun. Pan-kakes."*

"The Smith sisters," says Starky and, believe it or not, now she shoots me a wink. "You have their phone numbers. Wilson is the one who contacted them down in Baltimore and gave them the bad news about their brother."

Wilson puts down his menu. Nods. I think the guy can only do one thing at a time. Nod or read. Walk or chew gum.

"Always tough duty," says Ceepak.

"Yeah. Then I had to call them again. Gave them the name of a local funeral home."

Ceepak nods. He understands.

"They needed the car back too," Wilson says slowly. "That was my third call."

"Anyway," says Starky, sounding way too hyper and chipper given the recent topic of table talk, "this morning, after we studied Venus and all, he wrote down their phone numbers, because last night, in between parking cars, Danny told me how important it was for you guys to get in touch with Mr. Smith's sisters and then, this morning, I figured, you know, we might find you guys here and you were."

And the girl hasn't even touched her coffee.

"Give Officer Boyle the numbers, Wilson."

I receive another wink.

Ah-hah. Studying astronomy with muscleman? Nothing but a clever ruse to aid me, Ceepak, and the SHPD in our ongoing criminal investigation of the Feenyville Pirates and their theft of Shareef Smith's air bags and CD changer.

"Here you are, sir." Trooper Wilson hands me a business card with two numbers scribbled on the back. On the front, I read his *full* name: William Wilson Goodson, Jr. Yeah. I'd go with "Wilson," too. I hand the card to Ceepak. Ceepak hands the card to Grace. The chain of command is clear.

Grace studies the card. "What do you want me to ask these two ladies?"

"We need to find out more about their brother Shareef's friends. Did he have any in this area? Who do they think it was that he met in the parking lot?"

"And why do you need to know about their brother's friends?"

"We suspect one of them killed Shareef Smith."

"Really?"

"Yes, ma'am."

"Some friend. I'll be in the office."

Ceepak and I watch Starky and Trooper Wilson devour twin towers of flapjacks flanked by the pork sampler plate: bacon, sausage, scrapple, and ham. Sometimes, after I eat breakfast here, I seriously consider switching to a total tofu diet.

It's nearly 9:45. We need to be at King Putt Golf at 10:00. Grace has been back to the table twice with the same news: "No answer. Both numbers."

The pig bells over the front door jangle again, louder than usual.

"Ohmigosh!" says Starky. "It's Senator Worthington!" I think she's gushing.

One of the senator's personal bodyguards must've given the door a hearty shove. The bell strand overhead is still swinging like a piggy piñata.

The senator comes into the restaurant, works the dining room. He's going from table to table, pumping hands. Greeting constituents. About half the folks visiting Sea Haven any given weekend in the summer hail from Philly. Then they go home where they can vote for Worthington every six years.

The senator is in a plaid short-sleeve shirt and khaki pants. The guys on his early-morning security detail are, once again, in dark blue suits. Probably the only suits on the island that aren't swimsuits.

Ceepak stands again. The senator nears our table.

I stand too because I want to check out Worthington's feet.

Yep. He has on the boots.

"Good morning, folks," the senator says, taking Ceepak's hand. Cranking it up and down as if he desperately needs well water for his parched horse.

"An honor to meet you, sir," says Ceepak. "Thank you for all you do for our troops."

The senator squints, crinkles up the corners his eyes. Looks wise and earnest. "Did you serve, son?" He must've noticed Ceepak's hairdo.

"Yes, sir," says Ceepak. "One hundred and first Airborne."

"Iraq?"

"First wave in."

"What's your name, son?"

"Ceepak. John Ceepak."

The senator braces Ceepak's shoulder with his free hand, keeps working the other one up and down. "Well, John Ceepak, thank *you* for all you've done for this country."

Ceepak nods.

The senator finally lets go of Ceepak's hand. Maybe he heard the shoulder joint squeaking. Anyway, he moves around the table, shakes everybody's outstretched hands. I fling mine out there too.

"Good to meet you. How's it going? Enjoying your vacation? Goodness, have fun."

He never pauses long enough to give anybody a chance to answer. If he did, I'd let him know that when I go on vacation, it's usually to Arizona where my folks live in this retirement village where children under the age of eighteen are basically considered illegal.

"Good man," says Ceepak as the senator moves on to other tables and other hands.

"His bodyguards are mostly ex-Marines and stuff," says Starky. "One used to be with Special Forces. Another was a Navy SEAL."

"Really?" I'm amazed Starky knows so much about the senator's staff.

"Yeah. I talked to one of them last night at the party. Mr. Parker."

Starky. With that sweet face, she can ask any guy anything and they'll usually blab their fool heads off just to bask in her smile.

"He also told me that the Department of Defense considers Lieutenant Worthington to be a very valuable recruiting asset. Since he won the Purple Heart and his father is a senator, anywhere he goes, the news cameras follow. *Entertainment Tonight. Access Hollywood. Inside Edition.* The guy goes to a lot of amazing parties to help the Army recruit new soldiers."

Sounds like pretty cool duty.

I might've signed up for it myself if, you know, you didn't have to get wounded first.

*18*

*We get* up from the table because it's time to head over to King
Putt Golf and meet Saul Slominsky.

We hit the sidewalk and see the Mutt and Jeff of the Feenyville Pirates: Nicky Nichols and Mr. Shrimp. They're sitting on one of the
benches Grace has out front for people waiting for a table. There's another tough guy with them. The three of them are yukking it up, smoking cigarettes, flashing gang signs, scaring the tourists.

The new guy is jockey-short with mocha-colored skin. His oily hair
is sheared off in a bowl cut with bangs. His dark eyes dart all over the
place, especially when Ceepak and I come into view. We're not in uniform, but we definitely look like the Law. Well, Ceepak does. I sort of
look like a guy who needs more sleep or coffee or both.

"Gentlemen," says Ceepak when he locks eyes with Nichols and
Shrimp, something that's impossible to do with their young friend—his
eyes don't stay in one place long enough to lock in a target. "Here for
breakfast?"

"Yeah," says Nichols.

"Enjoy," says Ceepak.

"You hassling us?" asks Shrimp.

"Hardly," says Ceepak. "Might I suggest you try the scrapple? It's not to be missed. Have a good one."

"What's that supposed to mean?" Shrimp is up off the bench.

Ceepak gives the little pirate a two-finger salute off the brim of his cap. "Have a good day, gentlemen."

"Who's your new friend?" Before I leave, I have to ask it.

"What?" Shrimp tries to jump in my face, as they say. Except he's too short so he aims his anger up at my chin. "You got a problem?"

"No. No problem. We just like to know who your new recruits are." I figure the Feenyville Pirates are like the U.S. Army—they always need to replenish the ranks.

"Why don't you mind your own beeswax?"

While I pause to ponder how a would-be pirate-gangsta could actually use the term *beeswax,* Nichols, the lumbering giant, finds the strength to tilt back his medicine ball of a head and speak again: "That's Osvaldo Vargas."

"Nicky?"

"What?"

Shrimp takes off his glasses. Rubs his weary eyes. Can't believe he's still working with this dum-dum.

"Vargas?" says Ceepak, suddenly interested in more than exchanging Sunday morning pleasantries. "Osvaldo Vargas?"

The young man's eyes flick back and forth like windshield wipers in a summer thunder boomer.

"Are you currently employed as a member of the custodial staff at the rest area off exit fifty-two on the Garden State Parkway? Do you work for the HMM Host Corporation?"

"Maybe" is his mumbled answer. Of course, seated there on the bench, he's fidgeting like crazy with a frayed baseball cap he keeps twirling around between his knees. When the front spins into view, I read it: *HMM Host.*

"You got a warrant?" says Shrimp.

"Excuse me?" asks Ceepak.

"You got a warrant?"

The other people waiting for tables, the ones with kids and very few visible tattoos, are moving away—checking out the big plastic pig sculpture down at the corner, heading into the bookstore up the block to check out the beach reads and sudoku collections.

"Why would we need a warrant?" asks Ceepak.

"You're cops. You can't ask questions without a warrant!"

"Yes, we can," I say. "We can't *search* without a warrant, but we can ask anybody anything."

"However," adds Ceepak, "you are not compelled to answer our questions. Silence remains your prerogative, should you so choose."

Ceepak? He not only plays by the rules, he makes sure the other side knows them too.

"You heard the man, Osvaldo," says Shrimp. "You don't have to say shit."

"It's a pretty good job," says Nichols. "The janitor gig."

"Jesus, Nicky!"

"He only has to clean the toilets once an hour. I could do that."

Shrimp looks boiled. Guess pirating was easier back in the days before your brother buccaneers fried their brains out with recreational drugs.

Osvaldo sits there. Head down now. Not saying a word. Staring at the hat in his hands.

Ceepak and I mentally file Osvaldo Vargas's connection to the Feenyville Pirates under "Interesting Coincidence?" and head over to King Putt.

We keep the cop car angled against the curb and walk because the miniature golf course is basically across the street from the Pig's Commitment, on Ocean Avenue at Oyster Street.

You can see King Putt's tee-shaped pylon sign from half a mile away. At its base, chained to the pole, is a six-foot-tall resin statue of the chubby Boy King himself—a bratty kid with raccoon-style mascara around the eyes and a floppy pharaoh hat. Instead of the classic staff of Ra, he totes a putter.

We follow the hieroglyphics and make our way into the little hut where you pay to play.

It's early, 10:00 AM. Not many golfers out on the links because all the kids are across the street inhaling pancakes.

The guy behind the counter looks none too happy about coming to work every day in a goofy costume. He's about my age but has to wear a fake bronze breastplate, striped skirt, and King Putt pharaoh hat so it looks like he's wearing an inside-out undershirt where the collar got stuck around the ears before he could yank it all the way off his head.

"Pick your balls," the guy says in a dull monotone. He says it so often, he forgets how funny it sounds.

"We're here to meet someone," says Ceepak. "Police business."

The guy looks up from the Sunday funnies.

"Oh. Hey, Danny."

"Skippy?"

"Yeah."

"You workin' here?"

"Yeah. For the summer."

Skip O'Malley was a part-time summer cop back when I was one too. I think his father owns this miniature golf course. Must be why Skipper is manning the early-morning till in his pharaoh kilt: before he can inherit the family business, he has to learn it from the ground up. Either that, or his old man just loves to humiliate the poor guy.

"How's it going?" I ask, trying to keep my eyes off Skippy's skirt and sandals.

"You know." He gestures with both arms to take in the entirety of his miserable existence. "Same old, same old."

"Yeah. Well, we gotta run. We're meeting this guy out on the links"

"Yeah. He's already here. Didn't pay either. Have a sunny, funderful day." He mumbles Sea Haven's official slogan in our general direction. It's meant for the guests—not the poor schlubs who actually live and work here.

We head out to the course.

"The waterfall is the ninth hole." Ceepak, of course, has been studying the little map printed on the back of the scorecard.

"They call it Victoria Falls," I say as I point at the concrete chute of blue water coursing beside us, "because that's the mighty Nile."

"Educational entertainment," says Ceepak. "Laudable."

Yeah. This is probably why American kids don't know diddly about world geography. We pick it all up playing Putt-Put or going to the Rainforest Cafe.

In truth, King Putt's is a pretty awesome course. Skip's dad spent about a million bucks landscaping its "Sahara Desert" sand traps, fake palm trees, and oasis putting greens. Kids love it here—especially when they're bored with the beach, something that happens, typically, on day number four of your standard seven-day vacation. You can pretend you're shooting your ball down a real crocodile's throat over on Cleopatra's Loop-the-Loop, do battle with a plastic python named Monty on hole four, and try to shoot through the spokes of the spinning chariot wheel on five.

"Danny?" Ceepak must sense my mind drifting back to that summer I hit my first hole in one by going *underneath* the Mummy instead of around it.

He's pointing at this rope-lined set of steps leading up a hill to the cave underneath the waterfall. Inside the half-circle of light, I can see the shadow of a man with a bloated belly. Saul Slominsky.


"Ceepak. Sure. John Ceepak. I remember you. We worked that Tilt-A-Whirl case together. Remember? Me, you, and Boyle. It was the forensics that cracked that baby wide open, am I right?"

Slobbinsky's doing it again. Acting like we're all old chums and this is our annual CSI High reunion.

"So, you're pals with Art Insana? Great cop, Art. One of New Jersey's finest."

I'm guessing Art Insana is one of Ceepak's many friends working with the New Jersey state police. I'm also guessing Insana way outranks anybody from the Burlington County prosecutor's office. If he's Ceepak's friend, he's probably superintendent of something and has gold braids on his hat and a forest of medals on his chest.

Slominsky is holding a rolled-up grocery sack.

"So you guys think we missed some stuff, hunh?"

"Maybe" is all Ceepak offers back.

"Sure. It's possible. In the summer, most of my top guys are off on vacation, you know what I mean? I was working with the B team. Hell, the D team! Bunch of morons. Couldn't lift a fingerprint off a fried chicken bucket!"

He's chuckling. We're not.

"But you work with what they give you, not what you wish you had, you know what I'm saying? These days, anybody with an uncle in Trenton can take a civil service exam and call themselves a crime-scene investigator."

Present company included.

"Anyways, here's how I figure we should work this thing. Since, like I said, I'm more or less short-staffed, I hand this evidence over to you, just like Superintendent Insana suggested, so you can crack that ring of car thieves or whatever you're chasing down. Art has a point. You guys have more free time than I do. You find anything that suggests maybe this thing wasn't a suicide, that maybe this kid Smith got himself murdered, hey, I got no problem. We just tell anybody who's interested how we cracked the case together."

It's quiet in the cave. Outside, you can hear the roaring thunder of chlorinated water tumbling over a fake cliff. In here, all you've got is the occasional plink of a drip losing its grip on the ceiling and hitting the concrete floor.

"So whataya say, Ceepak? We got a deal here or what?"

"What you're suggesting," he says, "constitutes a lie."

"Nah. Not really."

"Yes. Really."

"It's just a slight spin on the situation."

"It's not the truth."

"It's close enough. Jesus, what're we doing here? Debating semantics?"

"This is not an academic debate, Mr. Slominsky."

"Then what is your goddamn problem?"

"I will not tolerate those who lie, cheat, or steal."

"Good for you. I respect that. We should all, you know, obey the Bible, do our duty, and sing 'Kumbaya.' But my job's on the line, here, okay? Art Insana is not my close, personal fucking friend, okay? So I need for you to tell people that I helped you on this thing or I'm not giving you boys jack shit. *Capice?*"

"We can't do that," I say.

"Jesus! You too? Why not? I give you this bagful of evidence, I'm *helping,* am I not?"

Ceepak nods.

"So where's the lie? Just tell the people upstairs I helped out is all I'm asking."

Actually, it sounds more like he's begging.

"What's in the bag?" asks Ceepak.

Slominsky smiles, clutches it to his chest like the guy in the bleachers who just caught the home run ball everybody else wants.

"We got a deal?"

"I will inform anyone who asks that you *helped* us in our investigation."

"That's all I'm saying." Slominsky hands Ceepak the bag.

"Do you have the evidence inventoried?"

"You mean like a list? Nah. List could fall into the wrong hands, you know what I mean."

"What's on the disc?"

"Digital crime-scene photos. I gotta warn you: some are what we call graphic. Rated *G* for 'gory' on account of all the blood and brains splattered everywhere."

Ceepak has already slipped on his evidence gloves. He pulls a sheet of paper out of the rumpled Acme bag.

"Oh," says Slominsky. "That's a memorandum-type deal. One of the young kids in my department, this Stella Boonshoft chick, wasted all day yesterday tracking down what buses might've been on their way to and from Atlantic City Friday night when Shareef shot himself, or, you know, got himself shot. Either way, maybe one of those buses listed there stopped at exit fifty-two."

Ceepak taps the paper. "Yes. Academy bus lines."

"She found one that was there?" Guess Slominsky forgot to read Ms. Boonshoft's memo. "You should look into that. Maybe some of those old farts on the bus heard or saw something."

Ceepak nods. "This is excellent work. Ms. Boonshoft is to be commended for her thoroughness."

"Yeah. I told her to ask around. She followed through pretty good." Slominsky takes back the shopping bag. Rifles through it like it's a sack of dirty socks. Ceepak cringes. "What else we got in here? Oh yeah. Digital tape. From the indoor security camera. You guys got a digital player?"

"Roger that."

"Good. This tape won't play in a standard VCR *or* a DVD."

Why do I think Slobbinsky tried both?

"Oh yeah. Here we go. The dead guy's drug works. We found these in the stall next to his. The handicapped crapper. Anyways, on the floor we found a syringe, spoon, Bic lighter and a 'Hot Stuff' heroin bag."

"Hot Stuff?"

"Yeah, you know—the cartoon devil from the old comic books. Looks like a pointy-headed baby in diapers? Red skin? Curly tail?"

"I've seen the character before," says Ceepak. "Just didn't realize he had a name."

" 'Hot Stuff.' Funny little fuck. When I was a kid, they used to sell his comic books at the drug store on the same rack with Casper and Baby Huey."

Now he holds up a small plastic bag with an even smaller paper envelope inside it. The red devil in diapers is ink-stamped on the front flap.

"You've seen this Hot Stuff smack before, am I right?"

"Yes," says Ceepak.

I've seen the little devil before too.

It's our local brand.

Hot Stuff doesn't come from Iraq or Iran. It's processed and packaged by unknown criminals in Sea Haven. So where did Shareef Smith buy it?

I'm starting to wonder whether Osvaldo Vargas, the young janitor and newest Feenyville Pirate, has a side job as their drug rep down at the exit 52 rest area.

# 19

We dash across the street, hop into our Ford Explorer, and head up Ocean Avenue to the station house.

We've got a digital tape player back at police headquarters and that's the piece of evidence Ceepak says we should examine first. I drive, Ceepak works his cell phone. Calls Grace back at the Pig's Commitment.

"Still no answer? You're trying both numbers? Thank you, Grace. Appreciate it."

He snaps the clamshell shut.

"She thinks the Smith sisters might be at church," he says. "We should swing by the rental house and advise Sergeant Dixon that we're making progress. We might convince him to extend our deadline past seventeen-hundred hours."

That's 5:00 PM. Six hours to go before Dixon and his crew go ballistic and turn into vigilantes like Charles Bronson in that movie on late-night cable: *Death Wish.* Guess taking the law into your own hands was pretty popular back in the seventies. Bronson made like a dozen *Death Wishes.*

"You want to go talk to Dixon first?" I ask as we cruise down Ocean Avenue. Kipper is back in the other direction, north of King Putt Golf.

"Let's hit the house. Study the surveillance tape. See if we are telling the truth when we say we're making progress."

"They were being economical," says Ceepak.

Yeah. I guess they were saving digits. Or tape. Or runs out to Wal-Mart for fresh cassettes. Whoever set the frame rate on the surveillance camera went with the lowest one possible: one-third of a frame per second. About a hundred times choppier than real life. It's like watching the world jitter past on fast-forward. In the top right corner of the screen, there's a spinning time stamp. When we hit the hours we're most interested in, Ceepak asks me to switch to slow motion. I thumb the remote. Now the freeze-frames strobe and blink at us in a stuttering slide show. Snapshots of hungry motorists bopping down the line at Burger King. Popping up to the counter at Starbucks. Bending over in front of vending machines to fish out bags of M&M's. One second a whole group is seated at a table in the food court, the next they're up, and out, and gone. Guess that's what rest areas are all about. In and out. Out and in. All day. Every day.

"I wish we had the exterior tapes," I say, already frustrated by the shoddy footage available from the single interior camera. "The parking lot view could really help us."

"Superintendent Insana is working on it. Apparently, one of the exterior cameras was damaged this weekend and that has caused the delay. However, we should have whatever might be available soon. Maybe today. Perhaps tomorrow. There!"

He jabs his finger at the screen. I hit the pause button.

"Might I have the remote?"

I hand it to him. Ceepak rocks the video back a frame. The digital display reads 21:05:08. Ceepak taps the lower left corner of the screen.

"Do you see him, Danny?"

I lean in. Squint. I see a short, fuzzy blob near another even shorter fuzzy blob.

"Is that a janitor?"

"I believe so. Note the outline of a baseball cap here. And this, we can assume, would be his supplies cart."

"Okay," I say. "Twenty-one-oh-five. Nine-oh-five PM. That would be Osvaldo Vargas."

Ceepak nods. "He signed the clipboard at nine-oh-five."

So he lied. Cheated a little. Didn't actually hit the men's room until, let's say, 9:07.

We skip-frame through the next hour a little more slowly. It's amazing how many people visit the candy shop between 9:00 and 10:00 PM. Everybody's buying something to munch on down the road. This is why they sell snack food in containers that fit in cup holders. Makes it easier to eat and drive.

"There he is again."

Ceepak freezes the frame time-stamped 22:03:47.

"He's a little earlier this hour."

"Indeed," says Ceepak. "We know he will go into the men's room at ten-oh-five."

Ceepak nods. "Let's see if anybody else rolls a mop bucket through this zone prior to Mr. Delgado coming to work at eleven."

Yeah. Because, if they do, it's our guy.

We move through the tape even slower. Minute by minute. Second by second.

"What's that?" I say.

"Mother with baby carriage," says Ceepak.

"Yeah. Sorry."

"Similar configuration. Easy mistake."

We plod on.

Ceepak pauses the tape. Thinks he sees something. No. He was wrong. Shakes his head. "Burger King employee. Emptying trash barrels."

He's right. The BK kid has a different-shaped baseball cap and is pushing a bigger blob.

22:10. Nothing.

22:15. Nothing.

This could be the dullest video ever released—worse than those straight-to-DVD movies they try to flog off at Blockbuster.

"Maybe the killer brought in his own mop bucket," I say, hoping it might tear us away from this very poorly paced movie. This is worse than a black-and-white chick flick in French.

"It's a possibility," says Ceepak. "Definitely a possibility." He's not really listening to me. He's focused, his eyes in a laser lock on the grainy screen.

My eyes drift. I see that Denise Diego, the tech officer who usually works in this room, has a brand new *Lord of the Rings* figurine glued to the top of her computer monitor. Gandalf, I think. The guy with the long white beard. Of course, there were a lot of guys with long white beards in that particular trilogy. Could've called it *Lord of the Whiskers. Bilbo's Bearded Buddies* . . .

"There!" says Ceepak. "Twenty-two-thirty-five and twelve seconds."

My eyes return to the fuzzy screen.

"Unfortunately, the image is quite compressed," says Ceepak. "Limited number of pixels. I can attempt to blow it up. . . ."

The blobs zoom into an assortment of gray squares piled on top of each other like a stack of oddly shaped pizza boxes.

"It's him!" I say. "Osvaldo! The janitor. See? It's the same guy. The same height. There's the baseball cap. The mop handle. That's probably the bucket! You can kind of make out the wheels . . ." I'm tapping the screen in so many places I'm smudging it with fingerprints even Saul Slobbinsky could read. "Is it Vargas?" I ask.

"It's a possibility, Danny."

"He's our guy! I knew it. He's probably running drugs for the Feenyville pirates and sold Smith the Hot Stuff heroin and then went back in to shoot him after he shot up and then, when he saw what a mess he made, he had to go get the mop!"

"Why?"

"Because, like I said, he made a mess."

"Why did he kill Smith?"

"Hunh?"

"Means, opportunity, motive, Danny."

Okay. So far all I've got is opportunity. I think. Maybe. Could just be that other category: coincidence.

"Why would Osvaldo Vargas want Shareef Smith, a visitor from Baltimore, dead?"

"Maybe Smith shorted him on the drug deal. Maybe Vargas and Smith were friends, like his sister said. Maybe Smith made fun of Vargas's mother. I don't know."

"Neither do I. And, until we do, we keep digging."

"Means, opportunity, motive," I mumble. "Mom."

"Hmm?"

"M.O.M. It's how I memorized it for the test at the academy."

"Oh. Interesting. Clever mnemonic device."

Yeah. Now I just have to find all three.


We secure the rest of the evidence. Pack it up properly. We use an official evidence storage carton and toss Slominsky's grocery sack. We also take a quick glance at the crime-scene photos when Ceepak inserts the disk into a computer to make a backup copy of the contents.

The CSI photographer does a much better job of capturing what I sort of caught with my cell phone camera: you can clearly see where somebody slopped a mop across the back wall to cut off the trail of blood trickling down toward the floor. It's three tiles up—right where the stall panel is anchored to its aluminum wall bracket. On the floor, I can see a swirled smudge, most likely the result of a dirty mop head.

Ceepak hits eject.

"Let's go visit Sergeant Dixon. Make our report."

And bargain for a few extra hours to find M.O.M.

# 20

"*You gentlemen* care for a sticky bun?"

Sergeant Dixon looks extremely hung-over. He's sitting on the patio, at the picnic table, smoking a cigar stump and chomping on one of the gigantic wads of fried flour and brown sugar they sell at Crust Station Crumbs, a bakery on Ocean Avenue where they specialize in chocolate chip cookies the size of manhole covers.

"Mickey Mex picked these up fresh, first thing this morning."

Miguel Hernandez is the only other soldier currently at the rental house. He shuffles across the patio with a white bakery bag, its bottom stippled with grease stains. He plops it on the picnic table near Dixon's mug of coffee.

"Dig in," says Dixon. It sounds like an order.

"No, thank you," says Ceepak.

"They're good." Dixon licks a brown wad off his thumb. "Weigh about two tons each. Mickey Mex can pop one in the microwave for you if you want it warmed up, right Mick?"

"We had a big breakfast."

"Oh. Big breakfast. Nice restaurant?"

"Actually, I ate at home. Bran flakes and a banana."

"I see. So that's what you've been doing instead of tracking down the rat bastard who killed one of my men?"

"Negative," says Ceepak. "Since last we spoke, we've amassed a great deal of evidence and are making tremendous progress."

"That so? Good. Excellent. Who's your primary target? These pirates your partner mentioned yesterday? Nichols and Shrimp?"

"Too early to say."

"Really? Well, by my watch it's nearly twelve-hundred hours. As you might recall, Officer Ceepak, I agreed to have my troops stand down until seventeen-hundred. You ask me, it isn't early, it's almost late."

Ceepak changes the subject: "Where are your men?"

"Well, let's see. Mickey Mex is going inside to pour me another cup of java."

Hernandez takes the hint. Heads into the house.

"Handy Andy Prescott and Butt Lips said they were going over to your boardwalk. Wanted to check out the rides so they can puke up all of last night's party food, start the day on an empty stomach."

"And Lieutenant Worthington?"

"Worthless? Who knows—maybe he and his daddy went over to the boardwalk too. Sounds like a good place to show off that Purple fucking Heart."

Ceepak recoils. "The Purple Heart is a very prestigious honor."

Dixon laughs. "Maybe. Depends on how you earned it. You know how Worthless got his?"

"I was told he sustained a leg wound during combat operations."

Dixon laughs again. "Yeah. He sustained some self-inflicted shrapnel in his left toe at a traffic checkpoint."

Ceepak tenses. "Come again?"

"Worthington posted Shareef Smith on guard duty one night. Car stops. Trunk searches. This was up near Yusufiya. Not much traffic. No Hajis passing through wired to blow. Anyway, around three-hundred hours, I hear this single gunshot. Pop! I scramble out of my rack to find out what the hell is going on. I run over to the checkpoint and see

Worthless rolling around in the dirt, screaming his head off. Says a fucking sniper nailed him in his foot when he strolled out of his tent to check up on Smith." Dixon shakes his head in disbelief. "I ask the lieutenant if he has the Haji's coordinates. 'Where is this sonofabitch sniper?' I say. 'I'll personally blast his ass all the way up to paradise and his seventy-two fucking virgins, sir.' "

Dixon chuckles. Needs a second before he can go on.

"Smith points left. Worthless points right. Then, when each one sees what the other guy is doing, they both change their minds and point the other way." Dixon crosses his arms across his chest to point in both directions, looks like a demented version of the scarecrow in *The Wizard of Oz.*

"Poor Worthless. He probably figured he had enough shrapnel in his shoe to win a first-class ticket home. His daddy, however, had other ideas. In case you haven't heard, his old man, Winslow W. Worthington, is going to be our next president. Hey, you know what? Worthless should've sent *those* shoes home to Poppa. Let him walk around Washington in a boot with a hole in the toe!"

Ceepak looks grim. He doesn't like hearing this kind of story. Somebody cheated, then lied to steal something other brave men have given tremendous sacrifices to earn.

"You're telling us that Lieutenant Worthington's war wound was self-inflicted?"

"Nah," says Dixon. "Haven't you heard? Lieutenant Worthington is a war hero. Just ask Shareef Smith. He was out there that night, saw it all. Saw the muzzle flash from over there—no wait, over there." He flails his arms in both directions. Drops them. "Oh. I forgot." He isn't laughing anymore. "You can't ask Shareef Smith anything, can you? Not unless you gentlemen know how to interrogate the dead."

## 21

Now, of course, I'm wondering if the janitor, Osvaldo Vargas, was working for Worthington, a man with a motive.

"Where the hell is my goddamn coffee?" Dixon hauls himself up from the picnic table.

"Sergeant?" Ceepak is probably thinking what I'm thinking. "Are you suggesting Lieutenant Worthington had Shareef Smith killed?"

"No. I'm suggesting Mickey Mex is taking too goddamn long on my refill." He goes over to the sliding patio door, yanks it sideways. "Mickey? Where the hell is my java?"

We're right behind Dixon, staring into the house. The dining room table is covered with half-empty bowls of yesterday's potato chips and piles of playing cards. I see about a dozen empty beer bottles. The bottom of one is loaded with soggy cigarette butts.

"Had to make a fresh pot, sir," Hernandez calls from the kitchen.

I hear the gurgle and drip.

"Come on in, Officers," Dixon says, so we follow him into the rental house.

Man, the place is a mess. Worse than my apartment. Socks and shoes and undershorts and towels and pizza boxes tossed on the floor. Smelly T-shirts draped over lamp shades. Empty vodka jugs crammed under the couch. It looks like an alcoholic teenager's bedroom.

"Sergeant," says Ceepak, "was Lieutenant Worthington here at the house Friday night?"

"You mean when Shareef got shot?"

Ceepak nods.

"Yeah," says Dixon. "He was here. Manning the grill. Makes a mean steak. Marinates it with teriyaki sauce. I think his old man, the senator, had a Japanese pool boy working at his mansion when Worthless was a kid."

"What time did your party start?"

"Officially slated for seventeen-hundred hours but we got started a little early. Four. Maybe five. Worthless was one of the first to arrive."

"When did you get here?"

"Thursday. My uncle met me, opened up the house. Hernandez came early too. Right, Mickey?"

"Yeah."

"I put him on KP duty. Sent him over to that grocery store."

"The Acme," Hernandez offers from the kitchen. He pulls the coffeepot out from under the dripper. Since the machine doesn't have that handy "steal-a-cup" feature, coffee keeps squirting out of the basket and onto the hot plate. He lets it scorch there while he pours Dixon a fresh mug.

"You made a mess, Mickey."

Hernandez hustles back to the counter, dabs at the hot plate with a paper towel.

"Shit!"

Guess he burned his fingers.

"Mickey laid in the food and supplies; stocked the fridge and ice chests. The other guys started showing up, like I said, on Friday afternoon. Except, of course, Corporal Smith. He was coming up from Baltimore. When I called him with the invite, he estimated he could be here by seven."

"Did Smith have friends in this area?"

"Not that I know of. Why?"

Ceepak doesn't answer.

Instead, he asks another question: "Was Lieutenant Worthington here the whole time?"

"Yeah. I think so. Like I said, he rolled in around four or five on Friday. We cooked up some burgers and brats. Around ten or eleven, everybody's hungry again, so Worthless soaks some beefsteaks in this teriyaki and pineapple juice shit he whipped up. Meat tasted awesome. So tender, it was dripping off the bone."

"Did Private Hernandez procure the pineapple juice?" Ceepak asks.

"Come again?" says Dixon.

"Seems a rather exotic item to be included on a basic shopping list." He turns to Hernandez in the kitchen, standing guard next to Mr. Coffee. "Did you purchase pineapple juice when you went to the Acme on Thursday?"

"No, sir. All I bought was orange juice," says Hernandez.

"Makes the vodka go down smoother," offers Dixon.

"Then it's possible Worthington slipped out and went to the grocery store at some point on Friday," says Ceepak, "but you weren't aware of it?"

Dixon shrugs. "Possible. Maybe. Yeah, I guess."

"Sergeant, I need to ask you to extend that deadline," says Ceepak. "Lieutenant Worthington may have met someone when he went out to procure the pineapple juice."

"What? You think he hired a hit man?"

"I think we need more time to investigate this incident. I think we need your word that you will not initiate reckless retribution against individuals who may not even be involved in Smith's death."

"Did you check out the security tapes from the rest area?" Dixon asks.

Ceepak nods. "We are currently in possession of the footage from inside the main building."

"What about the parking lots?"

"We should have those shortly."

Dixon takes a slow sip of coffee.

"I dunno," he says. "I don't like these Feenyville Pirates. Maybe that's who Worthington hired."

I hear the patio door slide open.

"To do what?" It's Worthington. He's with that blonde from the party last night—the one in the skimpy, three-triangles bathing suit. This morning she has a gauzy, see-through beach jacket on top of it. She's playing with a Nextel phone. The bleary-eyed couple is flanked by two of the senator's bodyguards.

"Give me back my phone, Jenny," says Worthington. "Why would I hire someone, Sergeant Dixon?"

"To shine your fucking medals," says Dixon. "Where you been?"

"Out."

"Show me how to see the pictures," says the girl, fidgeting with the phone. Worthington snatches it away.

"Later. I need a beer." He limps over to the fridge. The blonde slinks after him. "Who, pray tell, are the Feenyville Pirates?"

"Local assholes," says Dixon.

"Currently under suspicion for unlawfully breaking into Corporal Smith's automobile," adds Ceepak.

Worthington hands a beer to his girlfriend, grabs another brew for himself.

"You guys want one?" He gestures with the can toward his two bodyguards.

"No, thank you, sir."

"We're good."

They're also on duty.

"My father wants me to work the boardwalk with him this after-noon," says Worthington. "I'll be back at seventeen-hundred hours."

"No need," says Dixon. "Hernandez can man the grill."

"What about the other thing?"

"It's been postponed."

I think we just earned our extension.

Now I hear a cell phone buzzing.

"Excuse me." It's Ceepak's. He steps outside to the patio to take the call.

I stand in the middle of the messy dining room looking into the kitchen. Worthington is leaning on the fridge and draining his beer like he has to finish it in the next thirty seconds or somebody will come and take it away. Probably his dad. The two bodyguards, who look like they buy their shirts at the Big and Thick-necked Store, are in the small dining area. They're both staring at me. I think. It's hard to tell. They're wearing major sunglasses. The girl is yawning. It's probably still last night for her.

"I need another," Worthington says when he finishes his beer. "How about you, Sergeant?"

"Sure. It's five o'clock somewhere."

True. But it's not even noon here in sunny Sea Haven.

"What about me?" Guess the girl's finished her breakfast beer too. It's a wonder how she stays so anorexic.

I look out to the porch. Ceepak holds the cell phone to his ear with one hand and signals to me with the other.

"Excuse me," I say and find a path through the refuse piles, around the bodyguards, and out the door.

"You want a beer, Boyle?" Dixon calls after me.

"No, thanks."

"Breakfast of champions!"

"I'm good." I'm also a cop with a loaded weapon strapped to my hip. This is not exactly Miller Time.

I slide the door shut behind me. Ceepak closes his cell.

"What's up?" I ask.

"We need to go."

"Okay. But what about . . . ?" I gesture toward the house. Worthington. The Man with a Motive and an unaccounted-for chunk of time. A pineapple-sized chunk of it.

"We need to go."

When Ceepak says it like that, I stop asking questions.

# 22

"*Who called?*" I ask when we're inside our patrol car.

"Tonya Smith."

"Great! Grace finally found her?"

"Negative. The sisters are no longer in Baltimore. They had to evacuate their home early this morning."

Uh-oh. "What happened?"

"They suspected they were being watched. Tonya reports that a car, an SUV, was parked in the street outside their home. Two men were sitting up front. The vehicle and the men remained in place all night."

"Like some kind of stakeout?"

"Apparently so. She says the two men 'looked like soldiers.' "

"Do you think it was Rutledge and Handy Andy? Maybe they're not over on the boardwalk like Dixon said. Maybe they drove down to Baltimore last night to harass Smith's sisters. Maybe they're working with Worthington too."

"It's a possibility, Danny. However, as you might recall, the two soldiers were at the party last evening."

Oh. Right. And I was the one who saw them, not Ceepak.

"So what do we do?"

"Fortunately, the sisters slipped out the back door and were able to get to one of their cars undetected. They're driving here even as we speak."

"Here?"

Ceepak nods. "Tonya says they need to talk to me. Said it was urgent. Refused to discuss the matter over the phone."

In case Worthington has wiretaps too! His father's a senator. People in Washington? They wiretap everybody.

"Where are they now?" I ask.

"They just picked up the Atlantic City Expressway off the Turnpike and are headed toward the Garden State Parkway."

Lucky ladies. They get to enjoy all three major toll roads in one trip.

"Tonya insisted that we meet someplace public, in case they're being followed. I suggested the rest area at exit fifty-two."

The scene of the crime.

"They should be there within the hour."


We head across the causeway and follow the signs for the GSP.

Neither one of us is talking. I think we're both, you know, thinking. Piecing together the puzzle. What if Winslow G. Worthington has connections in Sea Haven? A guy with that kind of money from a powerful political family probably has connections everywhere, people who know people to bail you out whenever you need a little assistance. Somebody to mop up your messes—maybe, this time, with an actual mop. People who know how to grease the right skids and eliminate any obstacles in your path. For instance: a fellow soldier who knows how you actually won that Purple Heart the president pinned on your chest.

All of a sudden, this big SUV flies past us in the left-hand lane.

A GMC Denali. License plate: *US SEN 1*, of course. We're doing sixty-five. They've got to be doing ninety.

"Danny?"

"Yeah?"

"Initiate pursuit."

"Shouldn't we—"

"Our primary objective is always the safety of innocent civilians."

I flip on the light bar. Move into the left-hand lane. Give her the gas.

I hear this beeping. Ceepak has switched on the speed gun. Okay. I was wrong. According to the radar, Senator Worthington's vehicle is doing ninety-five. I'm up to eighty.

"Increase speed, Danny. Overtake them."

I push pedal to metal. Well, the floor's actually a rubber mat. All I know is my foot can't push down any farther.

"They're slowing down," Ceepak reports.

Good. Because I'm speeding up. Gaining on them. All the other motorists currently traveling the Garden State Parkway? They're politely getting the hell out of our way, leaving the left-hand lane wide open for high-speed police pursuits only.

*Boom!*

"Oh, shit!"

I say this because I know for certain our front left tire just blew out. I can feel the rubber flopping on the rim. We're riding on metal.

"Grip the wheel, Danny!" Ceepak shouts. "Don't slam on the brakes."

Yeah. I took driver's ed too. Like a decade ago.

"Slowly remove your foot from the gas," Ceepak says as he clutches the overhead handgrip. It comes out choppy, like guttural machine-gun fire because we're riding on the rutted shoulder now. "Reduce speed and ease off the roadway!"

Y'know, it's always good to have an Eagle Scout as your copilot if God is unavailable.

"Turn into the skid."

I'm already doing it.

Doesn't help much. We slide sideways.

"Hang on!" I shout.

We hit a guardrail. Carom off it like a cue ball fired into a billiard cushion.

Our ass swerves out into the roadway. I yank the wheel.

We head off the road and down into the drainage ditch.

Until we hit this rock.

And flip over.

Now we're upside down.

Flipping.

Right side up again.

For a second.

Into another flip.

I slam on the brakes but I don't think it matters since the tires are currently spinning skyward. I hear the light bar and antennae crunch across whatever kind of jagged rocks line this particular gulley.

Now we're the ones who need replacement air bags. There's a big latex balloon holding me in place. It gave me a nasty chest bruise when it exploded open.

We swerve sideways. Slow down. Skidding on your roof down a hardscrabble embankment will do that.

There's a lot less headroom now than when we climbed into the car back on Kipper Street. When Ford built the Explorer for off-roading, I don't think this is what they had in mind.

Finally, we hit something solid, the rear end swings to the right and we shudder to a stop.

"Danny?"

"Yeah?"

"Are you injured?"

I look over. Ceepak is pinned in his seat by the passenger-side air bag and has blood trickling up his forehead. It's going up because, currently, we're both sort of suspended in our shoulder harnesses like the string-wrapped proscuitto and provolone hanging off the ceiling behind the counter at Pizza My Heart. If we weren't wearing our seat belts, I think we'd both be smooshed against the ceiling. Either that or tossed out the window and dead.

"You're bleeding," I say to Ceepak.

"Affirmative. Nothing serious. Minor scrape. You handled that quite well, Danny. Awesome display of driving skills."

Okay. I guess, in this particular instance, winding up upside down in a drainage ditch inside the crushed shell of what used to be a cop car qualifies as a job well done. We're alive and the roller-coaster ride has finally come to a complete stop.

"We need to extricate ourselves from the vehicle," says Ceepak.

"Yeah." I'm all in favor of extrication.

"Close your eyes."

I do.

I hear this "oomph" and then glass shattering.

Ceepak just swiveled right and kicked out the passenger-side window. I'm glad one of us goes to the gym.

I slowly make my way across the front seat. Well, I'm looking up at it. I'm also wondering about the gas tank. And sparks. And all those movies where the car blows up right after the good guys get out. I hope the Ford has the decency to wait.

Now I feel a tug on my right leg.

Ceepak. He's already out the window and helping me.

The man certainly knows how to extricate.

We both rub chunks of safety glass off our shins.

The car doesn't explode. Might look better if it did. Currently, it looks like a lunch box somebody left under a school bus tire.

We move away from the vehicle.

"Are you okay?" a Good Samaritan yells from up on the shoulder of the Parkway.

*Never better,* I want to yell back. Instead I just smile and wave and listen to more safety glass tinkle off my hand. Yes, we've actually become a Springsteen song: "Wreck on the Highway."

"Thank you, sir," Ceepak calls up to the Good Sam. "We are fine. Could you please call nine-one-one? Summon assistance."

I notice that Ceepak's cell phones, both of them, got crushed in our off-road adventure. Mine too. Explains why we can't dial the three digits ourselves.

The guy waves. Runs back to his car to make the call.

Ceepak carefully moves around to the front of our upside-down cop car. It sort of looks like a smooshed turtle some bully flipped over in a hot driveway.

"Which tire was it, Danny?"

"Felt like the front left."

He moves over to it. Nods.

The tire now looks a lot like those truck retreads you see littered all up and down the Interstate every summer, only it's still somewhat attached.

Ceepak reaches into his cargo pants for his magnifying glass. It's not much help. It's shattered too.

So he bends down, slowly rotates what's left of the wobbly wheel. Stops.

"Sabotage," he says.

"What?"

He reaches into another pocket. Pulls out his forceps. Its pincers are bent but still work.

Ceepak plucks at something stuck between the grooved tire treads like a hunk of gravel jammed in the sole of your gym shoes.

He pulls it out. Shows it to me.

It's a razor blade.

# 23

"You sure you guys don't need to go to the hospital?" asks Samantha Starky.

She'd finished breakfast and was hanging out at the station house when the distress call came in: *Officers down.* Yeah. We were down all right—down in a ditch. My buddy George Hansen from Undertow Towing brought his rig to mile marker 55 (that's the one I bent when I went off the road), hooked the crushed cruiser up to his winch, and asked, "So, how'd you do that, man?"

I gave George the abridged version of Mr. Danny's Wild Ride (which, by the way, he considered "totally awesome") then Ceepak and I climbed into Starky's car because we needed to be three miles down the road at the rest stop.

I'm sitting up front. Ceepak is in the back, using gauze from the first aid kit Starky keeps stowed in her wayback to blot at that head scratch. We're sort of cramped inside Starky's personal vehicle. It's a Honda Civic. I think it's one of those hybrids and gets like fifty miles per gallon. Our Ford Explorer used to do fourteen. Now? Well, let's just say its actual mileage days are behind it.

"You guys should know: Chief Baines is totally ticked off," Starky reports. She looks into the rearview mirror so she can address Ceepak. "Did he reach you on your cell phone, sir? He tried like twenty times."

"My cell phones were both incapacitated in the accident," says Ceepak.

Mine too. No more playing that "Mine Sweeper" game on its tiny screen.

"You might want to give the chief a call," suggests Starky.

"Will do," says Ceepak. "As soon as it becomes feasible."

"You want to borrow my cell? All my weekend minutes are free."

"Thank you," says Ceepak. "However, I prefer to wait until after we meet with Shareef Smith's sisters at the rest stop. We're already running late."

"Understood, sir." Now she glances over at me. "You're certain you're uninjured, sir?"

"Yeah." I kind of groan it. Who knew your ribs could hurt every time you tried to breathe?

"I have Advil in the glove box, sir. And I brought along bottled water."

Starky's sort of like Ceepak, a Boy Scout without the Boy part. She's always prepared. I open the glove box. Find the Advil. Starky indicates a cool bottle of Dasani propped in the center island cup holder.

"Thanks," I say.

"No problem, sir. So they put the razor blade between the treads?" she asks Ceepak. "Why didn't they just slash your tires if they wanted to punk you?"

"I don't believe this was intended to be practical joke," says Ceepak. "Whoever sabotaged our tires was attempting to engineer a high-speed blowout that, I presume, they intended to be fatal. It appears that they cut a long and somewhat deep gash between tread ridges, then lodged the razor blade into that groove."

Sort of like you do with a penny to see if you need new tires. If you can see above Abe's head, you do.

"They knew that the blade would work its way into the rubber as the tire compressed under increased acceleration. As we picked up speed, the razor blade pushed itself deeper into the tire until it sliced through. The faster we went, the more severe the cut."

"Wow," I say. "Clever."

"I believe *devious* would be a more appropriate descriptor, Danny. However, their efforts failed. Thanks in no small measure to your excellent driving skills."

Now Starky beams over at me. "Way to go, sir. Awesome. Is that why you like to drive when we work together?"

"Yeah." That and the driver gets to pick the radio station. It's an unwritten rule.

"So who do you think did it?" asks Starky.

I shrug. I don't have a clue. I'm still wondering how come Ceepak knows how to engineer a high-speed blowout. I guess they teach you that kind of commando stuff in the Army.

She looks up into the mirror.

"Sir? Any suspects?"

"Uncertain at this juncture."

"Well," says Starky, who, again like Ceepak, is always attempting to hone her investigative and deductive skills (while I, on the other hand, spend my free time wondering how they paint the tiny word *Advil* on the side of all the gel caps), "I'll bet whoever it was did it while you two were away from the vehicle! Was the car parked in any one place for a long time today?"

"This morning," says Ceepak. "Outside the Pig's Commitment."

"The senator's bodyguards were there!" I say. "Remember? They came in with Senator Worthington. And Nichols and Shrimp! The Feenyville Pirates were on the sidewalk with that janitor when we came out! And what about Slominsky? We were still parked at the Pig when we went over to play putt-putt."

"Sir?" Starky is, of course, confused.

"We discussed evidence related to Corporal Smith's death with Crime Scene Investigator Saul Slominsky this morning," explains Ceepak. "He asked that we meet him at the miniature golf course."

"So," I say, "I'm thinking he suggested we meet him there so one of his other CSI guys would have plenty of time to booby-trap our tires! Those guys know all about tire treads. I've seen it on *CSI: Miami.*"

"You're right!" At least Starky's with me. "Maybe it was his part-ner! The other guy in the bathroom Friday night. The one with all the Chex Mix in his mouth!"

"Yeah!"

Ceepak squirms around in the backseat. I think his chest hurts too—from the air bag impact. Either that or our wild leaps of logic in the front seats are starting to irritate his brain.

"All the individuals you mention are, indeed, potential suspects. However, I would put Senator Worthington's bodyguards at the top of my list."

"How come?" asks Starky.

I know this one: "Because that's who we were chasing when the tire blew!"


Smith's two sisters are standing alongside the Ford Focus when we pull into the rest area parking lot. It's the same car their brother drove to this same parking lot Friday night. I point them out to Starky.

They're parked in a bright-blue–lined handicapped space right near the entrance to the main building. I guess they figured we'd be coming in a cop car so no one would hassle them about parking there without a wheelchair on their license plate. I also figure they wanted to park as close as possible to the front door and all those people streaming in and out. They wanted a public space; they took it.

"Can we park there, sir?" Starky asks. "In the other open slot?"

"Those are reserved for the use of handicapped individuals only," says Ceepak.

"Why don't you drop us off," I suggest. "Hunt down a parking spot. Come back and join us."

"Ten-four, sir."

She stops. Ceepak and I step out. The Civic is lower to the ground than what we're used to so it's a bit of a strain to get up and out. Especially if you recently "extricated" yourself from an upside-down SUV.

"Are you hurt?" Tonya Smith asks. I guess I'm limping a little. Ceepak too.

"Minor mishap this morning," says Ceepak. In his world, that's not a lie. A *major* mishap is riding in a military convoy outside Baghdad and having the Humvee behind you get blown to bits by a roadside bomb. "We're good to go."

Tonya looks at Ceepak warily.

"Show it to him," says Jacquie.

Tonya takes out a folded piece of paper. Hands it to Ceepak.

"I printed it off my computer."

Ceepak works it open.

"Shareef e-mailed it to me a couple years back. When he first went over there."

Ceepak studies the picture. His eyebrows pinch down, like he's trying to figure out how he's seeing what he's seeing.

"The one in the bed? That's Shareef."

Ceepak nods. "I recognize him." He doesn't add: *from the crime scene photographs.*

"Good," says Tonya bravely. "You recognize that other individual? The soldier there, standing beside the bed, shaking Shareef's hand?"

Another nod. "Yes, ma'am."

"That's you. Right? You're John Ceepak? Says so on that business card you handed me yesterday."

"Yes." He still looks puzzled.

"Like I said, it was taken three or four years back. Got the date stamp in the corner there."

"This looks like the American military hospital in Balad."

"That in Iraq? Near Baghdad?" This from Jacquie.

"Yes."

"That's where they took him after."

Ceepak still looks confused. "After?"

"After you dragged him out of that alley. Place called Sadr City. You remember Sadr City?"

Oh, man.

That's where Ceepak won his Bronze Star, where he dragged an unknown soldier to safety under heavy enemy fire.

"That was your brother?"

Tonya nods. I see tears in her eyes. "Yes, sir. You saved Shareef's life. You even came to the hospital to see how he was doing. Remember?"

"I'm sorry—I had forgotten his name. I'd forgotten . . . so much . . ."

"I gave Shareef that digital camera when he first shipped out," Tonya says proudly. "Wanted him to stay in touch. He did. For a little while. For the first year or so, he was always sending me e-mails and snapshots. Last couple of years, he didn't send me anything. Anyway, this was the picture that scared me the most. Seein' him that way."

Since I'm almost up on tippy-toe trying to look over Ceepak's shoulder, he hands me the picture.

I see Shareef Smith lying under blue covers in an Army hospital bed. I can tell it's an Army hospital because a lot of the equipment mounted to the walls is painted olive drab. Shareef is smiling. Laughing. Tubes snake their way into the back of his right hand, anchored in place with surgical tape. He's propped up on pillows in the bed and wears a light-blue hospital gown. The blanket is blue too. Darker. There's a sign hung behind the headboard, near all the IV bags and bottles: *Critical Bed 5*. It's written in red.

And there, standing next to him, shaking Shareef's hand, using his other hand to give the camera his biggest "it's all good" thumbs-up is a grinning John Ceepak. Of course he looks younger and he's wearing his MP uniform. He also has less hair, even more muscles, but you can tell it's him.

"I asked Shareef about you," says Tonya. "When he first e-mailed me this picture. I said, 'Who is that handsome white man visiting you, Shareef?' He said, 'Why, that's Mr. John Ceepak. The bravest soldier I ever met.'"

Ceepak's not saying anything. I see he's working his jaw. The joint is popping out near his ears. His eyes are crimping down tight too—

trying to stay dry. He's back inside that photograph and all that happened beforehand to bring it into existence.

"Shareef followed up on you," says Jacquie. "He asked around at the Army hospital. 'You know this John Ceepak? How come this John Ceepak risked his life to save mine?' "

Tonya smiles softly. "Everybody told him the same thing: You were a brave and honorable man."

"Some of those men told Shareef you were the most honest man to ever wear the uniform," adds Jacquie. "Is that true? You as good as all that?"

"I—" Ceepak stammers. "I—"

"Doesn't really matter," says Tonya. "It's what Shareef thought. What he believed. It's why he drove all the way up here on Friday night."

Ceepak's stunned. Me too.

"Ma'am?"

"He was coming up here to see you, Mr. John Ceepak. Said he had something he needed to show you because you were the only man in the whole world he could trust showing it to."

# 24

"Hi! I'm Samantha Starky. I don't believe we've met."

"I'm Tonya Smith."

"Jacquie."

"I'm very pleased to meet you both. Sorry for your loss."

So Starky found a parking spot. About a half-mile away. Down near the gas station.

"Did I miss much, sir?" she asks me.

"Well . . ."

"Officer Starky?" This from Ceepak. He's squinting. Sees something off in the distance.

Okay. I see it too.

Two Sea Haven PD cop cars cruising down the exit lane off the Garden State Parkway. The one in front is our standard white Crown Vic police interceptor with the pink-and-turquoise stripes and lettering. Bringing up the rear is our one and only Ford Expedition.

The chief's car.

"Could you kindly escort these two ladies inside?" Ceepak says to Starky.

"Ten-four, sir. Would you ladies like some coffee? Maybe a Coke or a yogurt shake? They're awesome at TCBY. . . ."

The cop cars pull into the parking lot.

"Perhaps you ladies could discuss your beverage selection once inside the building?" Ceepak suggests.

"Roger," says Starky. "Ladies?"

She leads Tonya and Jacquie Smith past the outdoor sunglasses carts and into the main building. They disappear into the sea of T-shirts and shorts. Hundreds of weary travelers, stretching their limbs, dislodging their undershorts, heading in to hit the johns and reload on fatty foods.

Since we don't have a police car anymore, Chief Baines has trouble spotting us. He and the other SHPD vehicle cruise up and down the rows of shimmering sheet metal like last-minute shoppers hunting for a parking space at the mall on Christmas eve.

Ceepak waves both arms over his head.

The chief whoops his siren one bleep. The two cop cars crawl over toward the curb. We hold our positions on the concrete sidewalk.

The chief climbs down out of his SUV.

"John. Boyle." He sort of nods and hikes up his neatly pressed pants. Per usual, Chief Buzz Baines is dressed in a starched white shirt and striped tie. His shield is clipped to his Brooks Brothers belt. I get beaned in the eyeball by a reflected sunbeam glinting off his gold badge.

The door on the Crown Vic opens. It's Dylan Murray. He's in uniform. Went with the shorts today because it's a scorcher. Nobody gets out on the passenger side. Guess Murray's flying solo this shift.

"Hey, Danny," he says, pressing back on his sunglasses with an index finger. "Ceepak."

"You two injured?" Chief Baines asks.

"Negative, sir," says Ceepak. "It's all good."

"Except, of course, for your vehicle. I saw it. Back up the road. It didn't look so good."

"Roger that."

"What's going on, guys?"

"We're investigating that burglary I told you about," says Ceepak.

"The Feenyville Pirate thing?"

"Yes, sir."

"This where they broke into the dead man's car?"

Ceepak points toward a lamppost about fifty cars away.

"Over there in that vicinity."

The chief turns. Studies the towering pole. Turns to his left.

"Looks like there's a surveillance camera mounted on that pole there. See it? Up in that black globe."

Ceepak nods.

"Art Insana getting you the tapes?"

"He's working on it."

"I'll give him a call. Tell him to work faster." The chief now focuses fully on me. "So, Officer Boyle, the taxpaying citizens of Sea Haven want to know: how the hell did you total one of their very expensive police vehicles?"

Oh, boy.

"Well, sir, we were pursuing another vehicle. We put the radar on him and he was doing like ninety, ninety-five miles per hour. We were attempting a, you know, a ten-sixty-five."

Baines crosses his arms across his chest. Now I get sun flares off his cuff links.

"Did you happen to notice that the motor vehicle in question belonged to a United States senator?"

"Yes, sir. I saw the tags."

"Okay. Good. So did you think, for maybe just a second, that Senator Worthington was inside that SUV, on his way back to Washington?"

"If so," says Ceepak, "he was traveling at an excessive and dangerous rate of speed."

"It was a motorcade, John! That's what they do. They drive fast. Hell, they speed! Makes it harder for any nut job with a rifle to assassinate him if he flies by in a blur!"

Out of the corner of my eye, I see Dylan Murray looking at his shoes, trying not to laugh.

Ceepak's not mentioning the razor blade jammed into our tire treads so I don't either. Although the way the chief is riding Ceepak's ass, I'm tempted.

"When you two ran off the road," the chief continues, "it was Senator Worthington's driver who first called nine-one-one."

"It's a shame the senator couldn't stop to assist us," says Ceepak. "Perhaps he was late for one of the Sunday morning talk shows." Wow—a surprising and rare display of sarcasm from Ceepak.

The chief ignores it. "So you two left the scene of the wreck to do what? Grab a slice of pizza? Use the facilities?"

I answer so Ceepak doesn't have to lie: "We're talking to witnesses, sir."

"Witnesses? Somebody saw the pirates rip off Smith's vehicle?"

"Not exactly witnesses, sir. . . ."

"People of interest," says Ceepak.

"Solid leads?"

"We think so. We have also uncovered a connection to Hot Stuff heroin."

The chief's eyes widen. "Are the Feenyville Pirates hooked up with that?"

"It's a possibility, sir."

"Good work, John! Now can we, please god, finally, once and for all, locate and destroy their damn drug factory?"

"We're working on it."

"Good. Murray?"

"Sir?"

"You're riding back with me."

"Yes, sir." Murray hands me the keys to the Crown Vic.

The chief cracks a smile. "Try not to wreck it, okay, Boyle? One car a summer is all I intend to tolerate."


Looks like Starky and the Smith sisters went with Starbucks.

They're all sucking frothy frappucinos when Ceepak and I join them at the dining tables near the Hot Dog City counter in the food court.

"Want to hear something interesting?" asks Starky.

"Sure," says Ceepak.

"Somebody messed around in the trunk of their car! The one their brother drove up here Friday night!"

"We know that, Sam," I say. "That's where the CD changer was mounted."

Tonya shakes her head. "They flipped over the carpet."

Ceepak leans forward. Very interested. "How can you tell?"

"There's an oil stain on that rug, on account of the fact that the car is so old and burns too much oil, so I always keep some extra in the trunk. I put the bottle in this cardboard tray I saved off a case of Sprite. But if you hit a pothole, the bottle tips over, and the oil spills out. Leaks right through that cardboard."

Ceepak nods. "Staining the rug underneath."

"Right. So I always keep that tray on the same side. It covers up the spot."

"The greasy splotch," I blurt out. "I saw it Friday night. Sniffed it."

"You could tell it was motor oil?" asks Ceepak.

"Yeah. On account of the smell. The splotch was on the right-hand side."

"That's right," says Tonya. "Only last night, when I parked it over on Mary Dell Road, I noticed the rug was all turned around and backwards."

"The greasy spot was on the *left*!" I say. "Down near the tailgate."

"Exactly."

Ceepak cocks an eyebrow. "Danny?"

"It was that way at the house on Kipper Street. When you asked the ladies if we could look inside the trunk yesterday. The greasy splotch was on the left! I should've realized it'd been switched around."

Ceepak leans back in his chair. "Meaning it was rotated sometime after you saw it here in the parking lot but before we reexamined it at the rental house."

"Somebody was searching for something!" says Starky, her powers of deductive reasoning sharp as cheddar cheese spewing out of a spray can.

"Ms. Smith," Ceepak says to Tonya, "you indicated that Shareef needed to *show* me something."

"That's what he said. When he first got to Baltimore and asked if he could borrow my car."

"Any idea what it was?"

"No, sir. Only that you were the one man he could trust showing it to."

"I'll bet it was Worthington!" I blurt out. "I'll bet he tore up the carpet after the state police towed the car over to Kipper Street! I'll bet he was searching for whatever Shareef Smith brought here to show you!"

"Danny?"

"Yeah?"

"This isn't Atlantic City. We don't bet. We gather information. We investigate. We reach logical conclusions."

"Well said, sir!" This from Starky. Great. They're double-teaming me.

"Sorry."

"Who's this Worthington?" asks Jacquie.

"One of the soldiers from Shareef's unit over in Iraq," explains Ceepak.

"You think he had something to do with what happened here?"

"It's an avenue we're currently exploring."

"Is his father the one everybody says is going to be president? The senator?"

Ceepak nods.

"He's that fool who's always clomping around in his boy's combat boots?"

"Yes, ma'am."

She snorts like a disgusted horse. "Damn man don't fool me. That's just an act. Senator Worthington don't give a damn about our troops. He just wants to move into the White House."

"Shareef didn't like Senator Worthington, either," says Tonya.

"How do you mean?"

"When he was home last week, over at my place for dinner, the news came on. I was in the kitchen. He was sitting in the living room, watching. That Brian Williams was talking to Senator Worthington. 'Effing hypocrite,' Shareef hollered. 'Effing liar.' Only Shareef was using the real *F* word."

"I don't blame him," says Jacquie. "That man's an effing fool."

Tonya plays with her straw. Won't meet anybody's eyes. "Shareef started using all sorts of foul language once he started using the drugs." Now she looks up. Straight at Ceepak. "Oh, yes. We knew all about it. Knew what he was doing."

"Uhm-hmm," seconds Jacquie. "Shareef couldn't fool his big sisters. We raised that boy. Besides, all you had to do was see him in a short-sleeved shirt to know what sort of nonsense he'd been up to."

"He started with the drugs over there in Iraq," says Tonya. "After he was wounded. After you saved his life. I think he was trying to fight the pain."

"Why didn't Shareef come home?" Ceepak asks. "After he was wounded, did they offer him an honorable discharge?"

Tonya shakes her head. "He told us his wound wasn't severe enough. Besides, they needed soldiers." She smiles faintly. "Maybe if you had left him in that alley a little longer, he would've gotten wounded enough to get out."

"Maybe he might be dead too, Tonya!" says Jacquie. "You did the right thing, Mr. Ceepak. We won't ever forget it. So, I'm sorry if, y'know, yesterday, I came off all cranky. It was a long drive up from Baltimore. No air-conditioning. Too many tolls. Besides, I didn't know who you were till we got home and Tonya showed me your business card."

"Understood."

"Shareef reenlisted two times," says Tonya. "Said he didn't want to leave his 'family.' That's what he called the Army, the other soldiers he was over there with. They were more than friends. They were like blood relations. His brothers."

"In your phone conversation Friday evening, Shareef told you a friend was meeting him here. In fact, he hung up when that friend arrived."

"That's right."

"Who were his friends in New Jersey?"

"I don't know," says Tonya. "Who do you think he was talking about?"

"We're also uncertain. However, we intend to find out. Officer Starky?"

"Sir?"

"I don't want these ladies returning home to Baltimore."

"Good," says Jacquie. "Because we aren't going there. Those two fools can sit there all day, waiting for us to come out that front door."

"I know a safe location." Ceepak takes out his notebook and pen. Then he reaches into a pants pocket and pulls out a motel card-key holder and jots down the address printed on it. "It's a Holiday Inn in Avondale. Ask the front desk to put their room on my account."

Ceepak has an account at the Holiday Inn?

He hands the slip of paper with the hotel information to Starky.

"Please call me as soon as the sisters are secure."

"You don't have a cell phone, sir."

"Right. Good point." He thinks for a second. "When the ladies are safely in a room, phone the house and ask the dispatcher to radio us."

"You don't have a police car, either, sir."

"Yes, we do!" I say. "A brand new Crown Victoria."

I just hope no one's been messing with the tires while we were in here with the effing frappucinos.

# 25

The ladies leave.

"You ready to roll?" I ask Ceepak.

"Roger that."

Ceepak rises from the table.

Freezes.

Doesn't say a word.

"Hello, Johnny."

There's this old guy with wild white hair standing about six feet in front of us.

"You're a hard man to find," he says.

He looks like a movie star's DWI mug shot: handsome, rugged face with tight skin except where it's puffed out in saddlebags under his eyes. It's the white stubble on his cheeks and the stringy hair glued into place by a week's worth of grime (or a wind tunnel) that make him look like a drunk.

Ceepak notices the guy is holding a can of Budweiser nestled inside a foam beer koozie. "You cannot carry an open container of alcohol in here," he says.

"I bought the beer holder in the gift shop," the skeezy guy replies. "It's a souvenir. My first trip to Jersey. Wanted to make sure this thing worked." He tilts the can, gulps a slug of beer, and wipes the foam off his lips. "Yep. Nice and cold." Now he looks at me. "This your boy?"

"No."

"I heard you had a son."

Ceepak doesn't answer.

"Heard the kid came with your wife. You're married now, right?"

Still no answer.

"You're smart. Skip the whole dirty diaper deal. Pick up a kid who's already wiping his own ass. Of course, that means your wife must be pretty old. Like buying a used car, Johnny—you're just buying somebody else's trouble."

Now Ceepak takes a half-step forward like he wants to deck this boozehound.

"Hey, Johnny, those people you work with, they're very helpful. Told me exactly where to find you. Said you just smashed up your cop car. You still that shitty of a driver, hunh? Ever since you got your first big-boy bike . . ."

I'm trying to figure out who the hell this guy is and why he's pissing Ceepak off so much. Maybe it's because he's wearing shorts and sandals and you can see where he hasn't washed below the shins since sometime last winter.

"Mind if I sit down?"

Ceepak points to the empty chairs at our table.

"We were just leaving."

The old guy doesn't sit.

"So what's good to eat here, Johnny? Hey—how about that new Burger King deal I heard them talking about on the radio? I've been listening to the radio a lot lately, Johnny. Been on the road for almost a week. Tracking her down. Picking up clues, here and there. Started in Cleveland. Talked to all our old neighbors. Headed out to Indiana. Picked up her trail. I'm a regular detective, huh, Johnny, just like you. You want some advice?"

"No."

"Well, I'll give it to you anyway because, hell, it's my goddamn duty. You should lay off the heroic shit. You solve a major crime or rescue some black kid out of an alley over in Iraq, the newspapers are going to write stories. They love that sappy shit. But, when they write about you, it makes you easier to locate." He smiles. "So, where is she, Johnny? Where's your mother? She in Sea Haven where you work? She having a *sunny, funderful day* like it says on the Web site?"

"I am not at liberty to say."

"Ah-hah! That means you know where she is! Otherwise, you'd just say 'no!' " The drunk staggers a side step forward, addresses me: "He still doing that George Washington bit where he cannot tell a lie?"

I look at Ceepak. Look at the old man.

"I'm not at liberty to say." I figure if it worked for Ceepak, it might work for me.

"Who the hell are you?"

"Danny Boyle."

"You a cop?"

"It's why I'm wearing the badge, sir." I point to it.

"Oh. I see. You're a smart-ass." He balls up his koozie fist. Crushes the can. I've seen arm tendons ripple like that before. My partner flexes the same kind of muscles when he gets mad.

Oh, Jesus.

Now I know who this old drunk is.

"You gonna introduce me, Johnny? Father should meet his son's coworkers. How you doin', Danny Boyle?"

Mr. Ceepak extends his hand. I instinctively take it. It's clammy.

"I'm Joe Ceepak. You can call me Joe Six-pack. All my friends do. You know why?"

I drop his hand and take a wild guess: "You like beer?"

He raises the can in a shaky toast. "Hell—it's five o'clock somewhere!"

So this is Mr. Joseph Ceepak. For a couple years now, I've heard horror stories about Ceepak's father; how the guy loved his booze more than his wife or his two sons. In fact, when Ceepak's little brother Billy was raped by a priest, Mr. Ceepak ragged him about it so much the kid committed suicide. Jammed a pistol in his mouth and pulled the trigger.

Oh, man.

I forgot about that.

I forgot about William Philip Ceepak. Just how hard was it for my partner to look at those crime-scene photographs of Shareef Smith and not see his little brother with his skull blown open? Billy's suicide happened when Ceepak was already in the Army, serving overseas. He wasn't home to protect his kid brother, wasn't able to shield him from their father. I don't think Ceepak has ever forgiven himself for what he once called his "dereliction of duty."

"Kindly leave," says Ceepak.

"Or what?"

"We'll place you under arrest for violating the State of New Jersey's open container ordinance."

"This your jurisdiction?"

"I'll call the state police. They patrol this area quite frequently."

"What if I'm not holding an open container when they get here?" Mr. Ceepak tosses his foam-cuddled empty at a trash barrel. Misses. "Never was any good at basketball. Hell, son—neither were you. Looked like a spaz out there on the court." He flaps his hand up and down and makes what he must think is a funny face. "Hey, remember when 'Santa Claus' brought you that goddamn bicycle?"

Okay. I've heard a few of the Ceepak Family Christmas stories. They'd never make it on the Hallmark Channel unless, you know, they start doing monster movies.

"That was your mother's idea, that goddamn bike. Oh, you wanted one so bad. Whined to her about it all the time. So I had to 'curtail my social life.' That's what your mother called it. Meant I had to give up my beer money so she could go buy you that goddamn red bike at Kmart. Then she made me take you out to that restaurant parking lot first thing Christmas morning to teach you how to ride the damn thing, remember?"

"Yes."

So Mr. Ceepak turns to tell me the story.

"It was early and the restaurant was closed so the parking lot is empty except for this one car. Guess what? Little Johnny Ceepak hit it! Only one goddamn car in the whole fucking parking lot and he hits it! Bent the frame on his brand new bike so bad, every time he goes out to ride, he's reminded how he fucked-up Christmas morning because his handlebars are forever pulling to the right."

Mr. Ceepak is wheezing with laughter.

"Danny?" says Ceepak.

"Sir?" I say it sharply to show Mr. Ceepak how much some people respect his son.

"We need to leave."

"Yes, sir." I practically salute.

"Whoa, whoa, whoa! Wait a goddamn minute. We haven't seen each other in, what, ten, twelve years?"

They're like six inches apart now. Face-to-face.

"Listen, *son*—I'm not leaving New Jersey until I find her. You know where she is. You tell me, I go away."

"Why this sudden urge to locate your ex-wife?"

"That's just it, son—she's not an 'ex' anything. We're Catholics, Johnny, and there's no such thing as 'divorce' in the Catholic Church. Hey, those are the rules. I didn't write them. I did, however, make certain vows in front of God, the priest, and everybody else in that goddamn church and so did she. 'Till death do us part.' Well, Johnny—I'm not dead yet. Neither is she."

"So you heard about her inheritance?"

His father smiles again. "She tell you about that?"

"We talk on a weekly basis."

"Who knew, hunh? Her Aunt Jennifer. No kids. All her sisters and brothers dead. Living all alone in that split-level shack outside Sandusky. Who knew she was sitting on a shitload of stocks and bonds and your mom was her favorite living relative."

"They were close."

"Yeah, yeah. She played it smart, I'll grant her that. Angled her way in, kissed the old lady's ass on a regular basis."

"She read books to her when her eyesight failed. Brought her hot meals."

"Like I said, she played it smart. But what the hell is your mother going to do with two point three million dollars?"

"Move further away from you."

"She's still my wife, Johnny. You ask any priest, they'll tell you. What's hers is mine. In sickness and health, better or worse, richer or poorer. So where the hell is she?"

"I'm not at liberty to say."

"You fucking jarhead moron. Fine. Suit yourself. I'll find her. Of course, if I have to use force to make her keep her vows . . ."

"If you touch her, you'll answer to me."

Mr. Ceepak puffs up his chest. If he ate something besides liquid nourishment, he might still be strong. You can see, despite his best efforts to destroy it, his body is pretty fit.

Ceepak could care less. He eats his vegetables at every meal and could whip his old man with both hands tied behind his back.

"Stay away from my mother," he says.

"Hey, you're such a good son, how come you don't call me every week?"

Ceepak refuses to answer.

"Still pissed off about Billy, hunh? I was just trying to toughen him up, John. Shit, he was a sissy. A pansy. No wonder the priest diddled him. Probably figured Billy was asking for it."

"Danny?"

Ceepak jerks his head to the side. We turn and walk away.

"You should get in on this too, Johnny!" Mr. Ceepak shouts after us. "You earned it. Putting up with your mother's bitching and moaning all these years. Get it while you can, boy. Don't wait for your reward in heaven. Once you die, you're done. You hear me, Johnny? You die, you're done!"

Geeze-o, man.

And I thought *my* dad gave lousy lectures.

# 26

*We make* our way through the mob of tourists emptying chip bags into their mouths.

Our brand new cop car is where Murray parked it: haphazardly angled against the curb.

"Guess we should give Dylan a ticket," I crack, trying to break some of the father-son tension, which has to be higher than the humidity. It's at 98 percent. I know because my shirt just attached itself to my back.

"No need to write up the parking violation, Danny. Police officers are allowed certain leeway in the execution of their official duties."

My partner has officially switched into automaton mode. Ceepak does that sometimes. They say a lot of children of drunks become cops and soldiers so they can finally have some control over their screwy world. After hanging with John Ceepak for a couple years, I know that's where his more robotic moves come from. It's how he stuffs down the rage. He controls his emotions, clips his words, and recites the nearest rule book. Me? I usually pound the steering wheel and scream.

I pull out the keys to the Crown Vic.

"You want to drive?" I ask.

"Haven't you heard? I'm a lousy driver."

"C'mon, that's not true."

"I was making a joke."

"Oh. Cool."

Sometimes with Ceepak, it's hard to hear the punch lines.

I think the Crown Vic Interceptor is brand new. It has that smell all vehicles come with when they roll off the assembly line. Either that or Murray just ran it over to Cap'n Scrubby's Car Wash and had them spritz it with that bottle of "new car scent" instead of the strawberry, which is what I usually go with in my Jeep. Reminds me of this girl I picked up hitchhiking once. Long story.

We're cruising up the Parkway, almost to 62, the exit for Sea Haven. Ceepak checks the time. Twelve forty-five PM. The digital clock is in the techno-looking instrument panel. So are the side-window demisters. We didn't have those in the Explorer. I don't even know what they do. De-mist, I guess. I fidget with a button on the side of my seat. Ah. Lumbar support.

"Vargas is our best lead," says Ceepak.

Guess he's focusing on the case to help him forget he has a father.

"You think the janitor is the one who sold the Hot Stuff heroin to Smith?"

"It's a possibility, Danny. Especially since he appears to be friendly with the Feenyville Pirates, a group that's been on our narcotic-trafficking radar for some time now."

"Yeah. It could've been a drug deal gone bad."

"In any event," says Ceepak, "Osvaldo Vargas is the closest connection we have between contraband known to be processed and packaged in Sea Haven and Shareef Smith, a traveler who had not yet arrived on our island. We have also seen video of a janitor resembling Vargas moving with a mop and bucket through the rest area concourse close to the time we can surmise Smith was shot. Granted, it was a grainy image and positive identification would prove impossible from that single source. . . ."

"But, if he's somehow connected to the Hot Stuff . . ."

"Our chain of circumstantial evidence grows stronger."

"So you and the chief think the Feenyville Pirates are the ones running the drug show in Sea Haven?"

"Yes, Danny."

"That why he gave us a new set of wheels?"

"I believe so. If we can shut down the Hot Stuff drug mill, we will do all of Sea Haven Township a great service." Ceepak reaches for the radio. Takes him a second to figure out how to use it because it's brand new, different from the one we destroyed this morning in our other car. "I need to contact the state police."

"See how they're doing with those parking lot cameras? Maybe they have that tape for us."

"Good point, Danny. I'll ask them about that too."

He twists and turns the appropriate knobs and dials, and is connected to a scratchy voice at the state police.

"This is John Ceepak, Sea Haven PD."

"Go ahead," the radio operator answers back.

"Please be advised that an intoxicated motorist will be leaving the Garden State Parkway rest area at exit fifty-two within the next several minutes."

"We'll send over a trooper. Who are we looking for?"

"Mr. Joseph Ceepak."

"Any relation?"

"He is my father." He says it without a hint of emotion.

"Ten-four."

"He will be driving a 1992 Chevrolet Cavalier RS Sedan. Florida license B-four-two-HFU. Orange County."

Disney World is in Orange County, Florida. I wonder if Mr. Ceepak works there. If he wasn't so tall, he could play one of the Seven Dwarfs: Boozy.

"We'll put this out there," says the state police dispatcher. "Thanks for the tip. Sorry he's family."

"Roger that," says Ceepak. Subtext? *Me too.*

"Is Superintendent Insana available?" Ceepak now asks.

"Negative. He has the day off. However, I've been trying to phone you with a message. . . ."

Man—we so need new cell phones.

". . . the videotapes you requested will be delivered to SHPD headquarters by one PM. A courier is rushing them over to you now."

"Ten-four. Please tell Art thanks when he comes in tomorrow. Appreciate the assist."

"Will do."

"Over and out."

Ceepak slides the mike back into its bracket.

"Let's hit the house, Danny. The outdoor tapes may contain a more solid visual link to Vargas."

I ease into the right-hand lane. "Maybe Vargas will be right there in the picture! In his janitor uniform, selling drugs to Smith."

"Maybe. I sense it was the drug dealer's arrival that prompted Shareef to tell his sister his 'friend' had arrived. And, as you might recall, Smith's vehicle was parked very close to one of those lampposts. The video image should be well-lit."

Meaning we get a crisp, clean shot of whomever brought Shareef Smith his goody bag. Better evidence than a grainy image of a fuzzy blob pushing a fuzzier bucket.

"So," I say, "even though you haven't seen your father in like a dozen years, you know what kind of car he drives and his license plate number?"

"He isn't the only one who knows how to locate someone. I've been keeping tabs on him for a while now. More so this week."

"Is your mom at the Holiday Inn? The one where you had Starky take the Smith sisters?"

"Yes, Danny. Please tell no one."

"Of course not. So, when did she get to town?"

"Very late Friday."

"Ah-hah! That's why you were on the road!"

I earn a nod and small smile. "Apparently, I'm not the only 'detective' in this car."

"Hey, I had a good teacher."

When we hit the house we get word that Starky radioed in to report "her cargo is secure."

"What's that mean?" asks Reggie Pender, our desk sergeant.

"She delivered some items for me," says Ceepak."

"Well, this was delivered for you." He hands Ceepak a digital tape cassette. "Anything good?"

"Porno," I say, just to bust his chops.

"Really?" he busts back. "I thought it might be your recent appearance on Fox TV's *Wildest Police Car Wrecks*."

While Pender and I rev up for round two of our snap-fest, Ceepak's ready to see what's on the tape.

"Danny?"

"Catch you later, Reg."

"Later, Boyle."

Ceepak slips the tape into the player. A black-and-white image fills our twelve-inch monitor. The screen is divided into quadrants.

"This must be the control room tape," says Ceepak.

I do the math: "Must be four cameras in the parking lot."

Ceepak taps the screen. "Two on the southbound side. Two on the north."

"Smith was parked in the northbound lot," I say. "He was coming up to Sea Haven from Baltimore."

"Roger that. Focus on the top two boxes."

"It'll be the upper right-hand corner. That's the light pole next to where he parked."

"Good eye, Danny."

"Should we scroll through? Advance to like ten PM?"

"Agreed."

Ceepak works the remote. Takes us up to 21:50 in the digital time stamp.

We watch.

For ten minutes.

Cars move in and out. Their headlights flare when they hit a bump and bounce a beam directly into the lens. Security cameras can't really handle direct contact with halogens.

Twelve minutes.

More cars. Couple tour buses. People coming out with cardboard trays jammed with French fries and milk shakes. An early midnight snack.

"There!" says Ceepak. I check the time clock: 22:03. Three minutes after 10:00 PM.

Okay. This is creepy. It's the Ford Focus. We watch Shareef Smith's little car pull into the empty parking spot near the base of the towering lamppost.

"That's him," I say, because I have to blurt out something. It's just too weird to know we are sitting here watching what will be the final moments in a young man's life. In less than half an hour, Shareef Smith will be dead.

For five minutes, he just sits there. At one point, the dome light inside his car comes on. Then it snaps back off. Maybe he was reading a map. Maybe that Yahoo! MapQuest deal telling him how to get to the party house. At seven minutes, there's another flash of light inside the Ford Focus. It only lasts for an instant.

"Cigarette," I say.

Ceepak nods but doesn't say anything, his eyes glued to the screen.

"There! Who's that?" 22:09. Nine minutes past ten.

"His friend," says Ceepak.

It's not the janitor. Not Vargas. The guy seen in silhouette is too tall. He also has a limp.

Ceepak says it first: "Lieutenant Worthington."

# 27

The quadrant we're staring at goes black at 22:20—five minutes after Worthington and Smith walked away from the car, heading, we assume, for the men's room.

"What happened?" I ask.

"Seems someone cut the cable."

"Who? The Feenyville Pirates?"

"Perhaps," says Ceepak. "In anticipation of their illegal activities in that sector of the parking lot."

"Breaking into Shareef's car."

He nods. Makes sense. They'd probably been casing the rest stop for a while. Knew which poles had surveillance cameras mounted on them.

"Unfortunately," says Ceepak, "we won't be able to witness the actual burglary."

"But now we know it was Worthington who met Smith at exit fifty-two!"

Suddenly, it all makes sense.

Corporal Shareef Smith was coming up to Sea Haven to see Ceepak. He was bringing along evidence to show the world how the brave son of

Senator Winslow W. Worthington actually won his Purple Heart: he shot his own foot.

Somehow, Lieutenant Worthington found out about it.

"I think Smith was blackmailing Worthington!" I blurt out.

Ceepak cocks an eyebrow. "How so? His sisters tell us Shareef had come up here to speak with me. To show me something."

"Exactly! You were the threat he was using to get to Worthington. Otherwise, if he was really only coming up here to see you, he would've called first. How would he know if you were even in town this weekend? He'd call and say, 'Hi, this is Shareef Smith, the guy you saved in Sadr City. You busy Friday?' "

"Perhaps, Danny. Perhaps."

"Smith knew who Worthington's father was. He also knew that the truth about the Purple Heart might ruin Daddy's chances for becoming president. I'll bet Smith figured he was in line for a big payday—enough money to buy all kinds of dope for the rest of his life. So Worthington left the party on Kipper Street. He snuck out, made sure to pick up that pineapple juice at the Qwick Pick, just in case anybody asked him where he'd been, and drove like a bat out of hell down to the rest area to chat with his old friend Shareef. He probably brought along a peace offering: a dime bag of Hot Stuff heroin, which he bought somewhere here in Sea Haven. I'm figuring he dealt with the Feenyville Pirates and then, while he was making his drug purchase, he inquired about what other services they might provide. You know—arson, murder for hire. I'll bet Worthington paid Osvaldo Vargas, maybe even Nichols and Shrimp, to stage the suicide in the toilet stall and clean up afterwards. Then, they all went out into the parking lot and tore through Smith's car looking for whatever it was he had intended to show you if Worthington didn't pay.

"When they couldn't find it, the Feenyville boys took the air bags and CD changer as consolation prizes. Worthington tried to locate whatever it was he was looking for again—Saturday morning after the state police hauled Smith's car over to the house on Kipper, before the sisters got there to pick it up. He crawled around inside, ripped up the carpet in the trunk, kept searching, still couldn't find what he was looking for, got distracted, and put the carpet back in backwards, which is why the oil stain was on the wrong side! Then he or his father had those bodyguard goons sabotage our tires! If they couldn't get rid of the evidence, they figured they'd get rid of *you*! Me too! Worthington did it! He killed Smith and he almost killed us!"

Okay. I'm exhausted. That'll happen when you crack a case wide open in one fell swoop.

It'll also happen if all you do is rapidly recite everything you'd been thinking about all day.

Ceepak gives my strenuous mental gymnastics a moment of respectful silence.

"Interesting theory, Danny."

"You think I'm right?"

"I think there's a certain logic to what you suggest. However, we need more concrete evidence."

"Like what? We could interrogate Vargas. Find out if Worthington hired him. We could also totally nail those bodyguard dudes. Even that one who's an ex–Navy SEAL. You could handle him, easy!"

"I'd rather concentrate on locating the Hot Stuff heroin drug dealer," says Ceepak. "He, or she, would be able to identify Lieutenant Worthington and considerably tighten our evidence chain."

"Okay. Fine. We could do that. But how do we locate whatever it was Smith was bringing here to show you?"

"Hard to say, Danny. We don't know what it is."

"Maybe it's a sworn affidavit," I suggest. "Some kind of official notarized document. Or the boot!"

"Come again?"

"Maybe Shareef stole the shoe Worthington wore that night knowing ballistics tests could prove the bullet trajectory was only possible if, you know, a guy was aiming down at his own toes."

Once again, Ceepak does me the courtesy of not laughing out loud.

"Let's take this one step at a time, Danny."

The door to the tech room squeaks open.

"Officer Ceepak?"

It's Desk Sergeant Pender.

"Yes?"

"Just got a call from the state police. Apparently, you asked them to arrest your father?"

"Yes."

"Drunk driving?"

"Yes."

Pender stands there with a quizzical expression on his face. I suppose he's waiting for some kind of explanation.

Ceepak doesn't give him one.

Pender glances at the pink slip of paper in his hand. "They said to tell you that they pulled him over, ran the Breathalyzer, but your father only scored a zero point zero five."

Made it by three one-hundredths. The legal limit in Jersey is 0.08.

"The trooper said your dad's driving wasn't noticeably affected by his alcohol intake, so they had to let him go."

"Thank you, sergeant."

"No problem. Hey, will your dad be coming by the house? I'd love to meet him."

"No, Reggie. I don't anticipate a visit."

"He here on vacation?"

"No. Business."

"Really? What line of work is he in?"

"Whatever pays for his next six-pack."

Pender's cheeks sag. I think he finally gets it: There will be no father-son soap box derby at the Ceepak home tonight.

"You want this?" He holds up the pink message slip. In his fist, it looks like a Post-it note.

"No, thank you, Reggie."

"You guys on the book today?"

"Special assignment."

"That drug thing for the chief?"

"Roger that."

"Good luck."

"Thank you."

Pender leaves. Ceepak goes to the desk. Picks up the phone. Presses in a number. I recognize the digits: he's calling home.

"Rita? Fine. No. The front left tire blew out. Danny was behind the wheel, responded accordingly."

Guess Rita heard about our rollover.

"He's fine too. I'll tell him you said so. Rita, I need you to keep an eye on Mom. As anticipated, my father has arrived. Yes. No. He has no way of knowing how to find her. I am currently without a cell phone so if anything happens, if you need to contact me, please call the dispatcher and have him radio us in the field. Right. We will. You stay safe too. Yes. Me too."

The guy's married but he still can't say, "I love you" into a telephone, not in front of any other guys. But, hey—what real man can?

He hangs up.

"Rita says to tell you she's glad you're uninjured."

"Thanks."

Ceepak nods.

"Sorry about that," I say. "Sorry they couldn't take your old man off the streets."

"The law is the law, Danny."

"Has your father always been so, you know, difficult?"

"Yes" is all Ceepak says in reply.

"Guess it's like that Springsteen song. You know—the one he wrote about his dad."

"There are several of those in the Springsteen catalog," says Ceepak.

True. I guess every guy has a boatload of songs to sing about his dad and Dr. Phil or Oprah could fill in any missing lyrics.

" 'Well Papa go to bed now it's getting late. Nothing we can say can change anything now,' " I say, quoting Bruce's "Independence Day." "That's the one I was thinking about. Guess people like your dad never change."

"Some do. In fact, Danny, a recovering alcoholic once told me that all life is change. Growth, however, is optional."

Now Ceepak gets this far-off look in his eye. A lightbulb just clicked on upstairs in a distant corner of the vast warehouse that is his brain.

"Of course," he says. "I'm surprised we didn't think of this sooner!"

Yeah. Me too. And I don't even know what it is he's thinking about.

"Jerry Shapiro," he says.

"Who?"

"You might better remember him as 'Squeegee.' "

## 28

*A couple* summers ago, Squeegee was involved in what we called the Tilt-A-Whirl case.

He was a junkie who used to shoot up heroin near the amusement park ride late at night, after Sunnyside Playland closed. I remember finding all sorts of hypodermic needles in the bushes, more than used to wash up on the beach back in the nineties.

Anyway, Squeegee and his girlfriend Gladys (if you can call any woman over sixty a *girlfriend*) have totally cleaned up their acts and now operate this small health food deli: Veggin' on the Beach. It's very vegan, very earthy. They serve food alive with wellness—says so right on the menu, which, by the way, is printed with biodegradable ink. They bake their bread with nine kinds of grain, flaxseeds, omega-3 fish oil, and maybe dirt. It has a certain crunch.

"We can assume," says Ceepak, "that, given his history of rampant drug usage, Jerry might know who the Hot Stuff heroin dealer is. We've kept in touch. Rita and I frequent their establishment quite often. They make an awesome tofustrami sandwich."

I don't want to know from tofustrami.

"It was Jerry who told me that all life is change when I compli-mented him on how well he had turned his around. I should've spoken to him about Hot Stuff heroin ages ago!"

"Hey, don't *should* on yourself," I say because Ceepak said it to me once. I'm not exactly sure what it means.

"You're right, Danny. We are where we are."

Where we currently are is driving down Ocean Avenue. I take a left at Hickory Street. Veggin' on the Beach is set up in this cottage at the corner of Hickory Street and Beach Lane so it's right across from the dunes and sea grass.

We pull into the parking lot and are immediately greeted by Stan the Vegetable Man—a ten-foot-tall painted plywood portrait of this guy with a smiling pumpkin for a head, a tomato torso, two carrot legs, and corncob feet. There are about a dozen newspaper vending machines lined up in front of the porch because Gladys thinks all newspapers lie but, if you read enough of them every day, you might be able to glean a few nuggets of the actual truth. Jerry and Gladys's dog Henry, a geri-atric German shepherd, is snoozing under the porch as we climb the steps. How do I know this? Some dogs are barkers, others are farters.

We push open the screen door and I'm immediately reminded that even though green moss mixed with Napa cabbage might be good for your pancreas, they're not so great on the nose.

"Good afternoon, Gladys," says Ceepak.

"Give me a minute!" she says as she balances a stinky vegan pizza on a wooden paddle and slowly maneuvers it toward the counter.

Gladys is a small woman—less than five feet tall. The first time I met her, in the lobby of the old Palace Hotel on the north end of the is-land, she was wearing three different skirts and a tie-dyed shirt on top of a goose-down vest. She also had brown paper bags for socks and pushed a shopping cart loaded down with all her earthly possessions. Today she has on Birkenstocks and the official Veggin' on the Beach sleeveless tie-dyed T. They sell them behind the counter along with Stan the Vegetable man baseball caps and buttons that say *I'm Already Against the Next War.*

"Officer Ceepak! Jesus. How the fuck are you?"

Gladys has what my mom might call a potty mouth.

"Fine, thank you."

"Yeah?"

"It's all good Gladys."

"Jesus. How do you manage that? Do you ever read the fucking papers? Do you realize that the United States government is currently watching every move you make? They have your phone records, Ceepak! They know who you're talking to. They know if you're downloading porn in the privacy of your own home!"

"Well, I'm not currently engaged in any such activity."

"You miss my fucking point. It doesn't matter if you're actually *doing* anything wrong. They're in the wires watching you anyway!"

"I see. Is Jerry here?"

"Nah. He's over at the farmer's market. We needed more galanga root for the yin yang fortifier drinks. Beets too."

"We wanted to ask him a few questions."

"What about?"

"Local drug dealers."

"Shit, Ceepak. Jerry's clean. Me too. Eighteen months in August."

"I know. But, I was wondering if, in your past, you might have come across a particular brand of heroin."

"Hey—I never chased the dragon. And Jerry just liked to dip and dab."

Ceepak nods. "He had what one might call a 'baby habit.'"

Gladys grimaces. "You been reading those fucking DEA pamphlets again? Learning druggie slang?"

"Sorry."

She waves her arm and I notice: she still doesn't worry about shaving her pits.

"Jerry's days of firing up speedballs are long gone. Ancient history."

"Yet those who do not remember the past are doomed to repeat it."

"Are you attempting to quote Santayana, Officer Ceepak?"

"Yes, ma'am."

"Santayana also said, 'The world is not respectable; it is mortal, tormented, confused, deluded forever; but it is shot through with beauty, with love, with glints of courage and laughter; and in these, the spirit blooms timidly, and struggles to the light amid the thorns.' But it doesn't fit on a goddamn T-shirt so nobody fucking remembers it, do they?"

"No, ma'am."

Now she wipes her cornmeal-caked hands on her blue jean skirt and gestures for Ceepak to come closer. "Show me what you got."

He hands her a photocopy of the small paper pouch.

"That's Hot Stuff. I didn't know Skeletor was still in business."

"Skeletor?"

"That's his street name. Been working the beach and the boardwalk since Nixon was fucking president. Changed his handle to Skeletor when the corporate running dogs at Mattel warped America's mind with that *Masters of the Universe* crap in the early eighties."

Ceepak arches an eyebrow. He's intrigued.

"Skeletor was He-Man's arch enemy," I say. "Two-Bad was one of his minions."

"See? They warped Boyle. Fucking Mattel. Masters of mind control."

Ceepak tries to get us back on track. "Why the cartoon devil?"

"Skeletor loves comic books. Always has. You ask me, comics are the true opiate of the masses, offering up simplistic and unambiguous moral truths."

"Does the cartoon devil mean anything?"

"Jesus, Ceepak—if it didn't, would he waste his time printing it on tiny little paper envelopes?"

"I suppose not."

"So pay attention. Over the years, Skeletor has operated what you might call a floating drug emporium. He sets up shop in a certain location until he thinks the fuzz are moving in. Guess he hasn't had to move for a couple years. Still operating in the same spot."

"I take it you and Jerry used to purchase Mr. Skeletor's wares?"

"Yeah. Back in the day. Weed. Crystal meth. Coke. Jerry's heroin. Skeletor is a fucking rip-off artist capitalist pig. Charging tourist prices, even to locals. Even in the winter. Long time ago, he was the ticket taker at the Hell Hole. You remember that ride?"

"On the boardwalk?" Ceepak guesses. He came here from Ohio. His local thrill-ride knowledge base only goes back so far.

"Close. Pier Four. It sort of sticks out from the boardwalk. Hey, you're in municipal government. Why the fuck did the pigs close it down? Why'd they fucking fence it off?"

"I'm afraid that was done before my time."

Not mine. The Hell Hole used to be one of the coolest rides on Pier Four, which, like the other three piers, juts off the main boardwalk and runs about three hundred yards out over the beach into ocean—every inch filled with exciting attractions and the thrills of a lifetime. At least that's what the radio ads used to say.

Pier Four had the Sky Coaster, Whacky Wheel, and the Chair-O-Planes. Oh—and Dante's Inferno. That was right next to the Hell Hole and the Devil Dive. Lot of satanic imagery on Pier Four, which made it that much easier for Bruno Mazzilli to convince the town fathers to shut it down. Mazzili, the undisputed baron of the Boardwalk, also happens to own Piers One, Two, and Three. He led the campaign five years back to have Pier Four declared a fire hazard. Today, it's blocked off by a ten-foot-tall chain-link fence with slats of green vinyl slipped through all the slots so nobody can see the dilapidated rides. The Chamber of Commerce hung a sign on the fence: *Pardon Our Dust But Remodel We Must.*

It's been closed for five years. No remodeling. No dust—unless you count the occasional sandstorm when winds whip up the beach in the winter.

"How did this Skeletor become a pusher?" Ceepak asks.

"You rushing me?"

"Sorry. It's just that we're up against a deadline."

"Well slow down and smell the fucking coffee. Jesus, Ceepak. You getting enough B-twelve? I've got gel caps."

"So tell us about Skeletor," I say so Ceepak doesn't have to.

"Like I said, he used to sit on his bony butt on a stool outside the Hell Hole, tearing tickets all day long, leering at the hot chicks in bikinis who wouldn't give him the time of day because he was this skinny-assed bag of bones whose corporate job title was 'stool sitter.' One day, he has a brainstorm. Half the kids in line are toasted. Stoned out of their fucking gourds and they want to go into that big spinning room and see the colored lights streak by and hear weird Meat Loaf music so they can get even dizzier, slide up the wall, feel the floor fall away, and fly like a bat out of hell!"

"I take it this fellow Skeletor soon realized he could make more money selling drugs than tearing tickets?" says Ceepak.

"Exactly. Especially the way he marks up his merchandise. Unbelievable profit margin and return on investment."

I think Gladys and Jerry had to take a couple small business courses before the bank would lend them enough money to open their vegeteria.

"Is he hooked up with the Feenyville Pirates?" I ask.

"You mean Nicky Nichols and that little guy?"

"Mr. Shrimp."

She shakes her head. "No way. Skeletor's been in business since forever. He's got major out-of-town muscle covering his ass."

"The Mob?" asks Ceepak.

"Maybe."

"So the cartoon devil on the drug packet is a nostalgic reminder of his entrée to the drug business?"

"It also tells you where he's currently set up shop."

"Inside the Hell Hole?"

"That crappy fence the city fathers put up? You can do all sorts of dirty deeds behind it. Skeletor's been holed up in there for five fucking years."

# 29

"*Murderers! Death* merchants!"

We're walking up the boardwalk with Gladys and just passed this gigantic, blinking food stand where they sell deep-fried Twinkies, Snickers, and Oreos.

"Why don't they just rip out people's hearts? Jam lard up their arteries?"

As you might imagine, tofustrami and ying yang shakes have never been first choice on the boardwalk stroller's menu, not when there are still more prepackaged snack cakes and candy bars to be dipped in batter and plunged into bubbling oil. I'm thinking a deep-fried Baby Ruth would be delicious, once you got past a name that sounds like a gruesome form of child abuse.

"I'm only narcing on Skeletor because he's a greedy rip-off artist," says Gladys. "Five hundred percent markup . . ."

Ceepak does a hand chop toward the chain-link fence blocking off access to Pier Four.

"How does one gain entrance to the Hell Hole? Scale the fence?"

"Jesus, Ceepak, did somebody deep-fry your brain today? You

think a bunch of junkies are going to climb over a twelve-foot-tall fence? Half of them are flying so high they can't even see their own fucking feet, so how they gonna pull a Spider-Man and scale the wall?"

"I see." Ceepak. The guy never loses his patience, even when dealing with reformed crazy people like Gladys.

"Follow me." She leads us over to one of the concrete ramps that take you from the boardwalk down to the beach.

"There's a secret trapdoor underneath. I think it's where some of the gears that made the room spin used to be." She crouches in the sand and points to the dark shadows between pilings. "It's back in there."

I remember that the Hell Hole was the first attraction on the left when you entered Pier Four, right across from the Chair-O-Planes. I take a step backward and look up. There's a stockade fence decorated with faded clown-face cutouts, but I can see the chipped paint on what used to be the carousel top of that flying-chair ride. Rusty chains dangle down to what are basically swing-set seats with pull-down safety bars you slide across your lap so you could hang on for dear life when that rotor up top sent the chairs flying.

"Unfortunately," says Ceepak, "we really can't investigate Skeletor's lair without a search warrant."

"What?" says Gladys. "You actually pay attention to the Constitution?"

"Particularly the Fourth Amendment. As I'm sure you're aware, all searches are, by definition, an invasion of privacy."

"Even if it's a drug den?" I ask. Maybe I watch Fox news too much.

"Even then, Danny. However, we can, I feel confident, go take a closer look." Ceepak hunkers down and moves into the darkness. I follow.

"Have fun," yells Gladys. "I need to be back at the restaurant. We're doing six-bean chili tonight!"

Beans, beans. The musical fruit.

Ceepak duckwalks forward. "Let's see if we come across something in plain view that might justify a search wider than our wingspans."

We creep forward and come to the entrance: a four-foot square cut into the planks overhead.

"See it, Danny?" Ceepak points to a sticker affixed to the creosote-soaked pillar closest to the entryway: the cute little comic book devil. Hot Stuff himself.

Ceepak sinks back on his haunches. Shakes his head.

"We've probably come too far from the public areas of the beach to justify invoking the plain sight doctrine. Besides, the cartoon sticker, in and of itself, means nothing." He looks bummed. Leans against the piling to think.

It's kind of cramped underneath this end of the pier. Makes me wonder why there are so many songs about romancing your girl on a blanket under the boardwalk while smelling hot dogs and French fries. I think you'd get barnacles on your butt and sand in your eyes from everybody walking overhead.

"Shit!" screams a girl above us. "Shit! Help! Fuck!"

Ceepak springs up. Sticks his head into the entryway.

"Smell of gas fuel," he shouts. "Smoke."

"Fire!" screams the girl. "You stupid fuck!"

Ceepak pops back down.

"Danny?"

"Sir?"

"Call nine-one-one."

Damn. Still no cell phone.

"I'll run up to the boardwalk!"

"Roger that. Summon the fire department. I'll go in. Find the girl. See if anyone else is trapped inside."

"Right."

"Go!" Ceepak hauls himself up into the hole. Now I smell it too. Not French fries and hot dogs but plywood burning and fifty years of carnival-ride paint melting. Then I'm hit with an acrid whiff of that gas they pump into eighteen-wheelers at truck stops. Diesel.

All of a sudden I'm running while thinking about arson because my buddy Mike, who's with the volunteer fire department, told me that sometimes firebugs do this thing where they start a spectacular gasoline fire up high in a structure and a diesel fire down low. The gas fire burns fast, gets everybody's attention. The diesel starts slower but burns hotter. The fire department goes up to put out the gas fire, the one everybody can see. While they're up there, the diesel-fueled blaze kicks in and cuts off their exit, traps the guys up high with no way out or back down.

I fly up that ramp back to the boardwalk.

"Fire!" I scream. "Call nine-one-one! Fire!"

A lot of people are staring at me now. They're licking orange-and-white swirl cones. Nibbling frosted pretzels.

Nobody's whipping out their cell phones.

Except this one guy. He's with his family, buying the wife and two kids, boy and girl, deep-fried Ring Dings or Ho Hos or Moon Pies. He sports a mustache, mirrored sunglasses, and, God bless him, an FDNY baseball cap!

He snaps his cell phone shut.

"Called it in. What's the situation?"

I point toward the fence. Now you can see the smoke, billowing black clouds of it.

"Fire in abandoned ride. Hell Hole."

"Paulie? Gerard?" These two other guys come around the corner nibbling deep-fried wads of doughy chocolate and stringy nougat. Milky Ways, I think. One has on a navy-blue T-shirt, says *Engine 23* on the chest. The other's wearing this fire-engine red tank top. More FDNY apparel.

"What's up, cap?"

"Paulie, grab a can." The captain with the mustache points at a fire extinguisher hanging on the wall inside the food stand, pretty close to the bank of French fryers. Guess grease fires are an occupational hazard in the candy-bar-battering biz.

"Gerard, you got a flashlight?"

"Not on me. In the truck."

"I do!" I say because I always carry a Maglite in my cargo shorts.

"Then, let's roll!" says the captain. We run toward the fence. The firefighter named Gerard grabs a handful of links and shakes it hard. "It's not coming down."

"So we're going over," says the captain.

None of these guys is wearing boots. They're all in sneakers and docksiders.

Paulie's caught up with us. He's lugging the fire extinguisher.

"I'll toss it over!" he yells.

"Guess that means I'll catch it!" says Gerard and he proceeds to haul himself up and over the fence in two swift moves.

"What's your name?" the captain asks me.

"Danny Boyle. Sea Haven PD."

"Dave Morkal. FDNY."

We both start scaling the wall.

"My partner went in from underneath," I say between huffs and puffs. "We heard a girl screaming. Smells like arson."

"Really? What's arson smell like?"

We swing over the top rail.

"Diesel fuel," I say when I land on the other side.

Captain Morkal nods. "You could be right." He looks around. Reminds me of Ceepak assessing a situation. He gestures toward the dangling seats on the Chair-O-Plane ride. "Tear off some safety bars, Paulie. Gerard—yank down a couple chains. Get us about two, three hundred feet."

"On it."

Man, these guys know how to rip and tear stuff apart fast.

I blink twice and Paulie and Captain Morkal come running back from the Chair-O-Plane brandishing these wicked-looking lengths of steel—safety bars they've transformed into wrecking bars. They head over to the boarded-up entrance to the Hell Hole while Gerard tugs down hard on a rusty suspension cable.

"Chain!" he yells and I hear the links clattering into a heap on the boards.

"Boyle?" This from Captain Morkal. He and Paulie are using their poles to pry off the plywood.

"Sir?"

"When we go in, stay low. Air's best near the floor."

"Yes, sir."

"Chain!"

I whip around. Gerard just ripped down another chain. I turn back, look up. There are all sorts of flames shooting up behind the two-story-tall peak of the Hell Hole facade. Smoke is actually shooting out of the nostrils of the humongous demon head looming over the entrance.

I hear the two firefighters rip the plywood sheet covering the doorway free.

"Gerard?"

The third man comes running, dragging a three-hundred-foot steel rope. Looks like he hooked three separate chair strands together to make it.

"All set, sir."

"Boyle? Flashlight."

Captain Morkal leads the way. Paulie is second, hauling the can that he squirts at any flames that flare up around us. I'm the third man in. Gerard's behind me, laying down the chain as we go. I'm not exactly sure why, but I figure he knows what the hell he's doing even if I don't.

"What's your partner's name?" Morkal shouts over his shoulder.

"Ceepak."

We inch our way down the tunnel of terror. Past what's left of the mannequin who used to leap out of the shadows and jab at your butt with a pitchfork. Morkal shines the flashlight up ahead. The tunnel is smoky. Thick with haze. It's like being inside a chimney. My eyes sting.

"Ceepak?" Morkal yells. "Ceepak?"

"Ceepak!" I yell it too.

We reach the end of the corridor. Another door. The sliding entrance to the revolving chamber.

"He in there?"

"I think so."

Without a word, the three firefighters attack the door with their makeshift pry bars.

"Bring the chain in when we enter," says Captain Morkal.

"Roger that."

I swear it's like I'm with three Ceepaks on a mission to rescue Ceepak.

"Come on, you goddamn—" Paulie grunts. Leans into his bar. The door squeaks. He grunts again, it gives.

"Ceepak!" All three of them are screaming it now.

"Over here."

Morkal swings the light.

I see Ceepak. Looks like he's administering first aid to a girl. A skinny blonde. No. *The* blonde. Jenny. The one in the three-triangle bikini. Looks like some of her gauzy beach wrap got burnt.

"He started it!" she screams. "Cooking his shit. Fucking stupid smack junkie idiot!"

The light beam swings where she points.

Lieutenant Worthington. Sprawled on his back. A goofy grin plastered on his face. We may all be about to be deep-fried to a crackly crunch but he's floating off to happy land. I see a thin rubber hose tied off around his upper arm. A syringe, candle, and small square of crinkled aluminum foil—his works—scattered on the ground next to him.

"We need to evacuate!" says Captain Morkal. "Now!"

"Roger that," answers Ceepak.

I see flames shooting up along the curved edges of the circular floor. Licking their way into the room with us.

"However," Ceepak reports calmly, "the trap door exit I came in through is currently inaccessible."

"Paulie?" yells Morkal. "Grab the girl. Gerard—you and me will haul out the drunk."

The three firefighters lumber across the foggy floor. Pick up their charges. Every now and then, Paulie, who has the blonde slung over his shoulder like a laundry bag, shoots a jet of foam at flames attempting to invade his personal space.

"You sure you're okay?" Morkal says to Ceepak.

"Roger that. It's all good."

"Tell you what, I think it'll all be a whole lot better once we're outside. G'head. I've got your back. Boyle? Lead the way!"

I turn around. It's like I'm an airplane one inch below the cloud ceiling, only these clouds are black and boiling mad and full of smoke except where they're hot with fire. I can't see six inches in front of my nose.

"How do we get out? I can't see anything!"

"Bend down, feel the chain, follow it. But, Boyle?"

"Yes, sir?"

"You better haul ass or I guarantee we're gonna be crawling up your butt like a cheap pair of underwear!"

I proceed to haul ass.

The Sea Haven volunteer fire department is hosing down the Hell Hole. The fire is, as they say, contained.

The three guys from FDNY engine 23 shake our hands and head back over the chain-link fence to rejoin their families.

"I thought you were on vacation," Mrs. Morkal busts her husband's chops and hands him a bucket of deep-fried Oreos. Apparently, the firefighters and their families all rented houses pretty close together, over on Oak Street. They invited us to drop by later for a beer if, you know, we aren't too busy.

The anorexic blonde is bundled up in a blanket, sitting in the back of a Sea Haven rescue squad ambulance. She keeps asking for a "fucking cigarette." I would've figured she'd inhaled enough smoke for one day.

Lieutenant Worthington is lying on a rolling gurney. He's still pretty groggy. Stoned, I guess. Probably doesn't even realize that his pant legs got singed.

"We need to cut these off him," says the paramedic. "Check for burns." He pulls out a pair of surgical scissors and starts cutting into the waistband.

"Fucker tried to kill me," Worthington mumbles as the medic snips through his pants pocket.

Ceepak leans down. Strains to understand what the man is mumbling.

"Come again?"

Worthington's eyes go wide. "Find the camera."

"Camera?"

"Shareef," he groans. "He had a camera."

Worthington's eyes flutter shut. He's okay, I think. Just passed out.

"Jesus," says the medic when he cuts through the khakis at the thigh.

"Is that a burn?" I ask.

"No, Danny," says Ceepak. "That appears to be scar tissue from a gunshot wound."

# 30

**Skeletor's drug** operation was so huge he might outrank those other New Jersey pharmaceutical giants: Merck and Pfizer.

After the Sea Haven fire department doused everything down and the Hell Hole looked more like the soggy remnants of a campfire after a downpour—all charred wood and oily puddles—Chief Baines swung by with every cop he could scrape together and some agents from the DEA field office down in Atlantic City. Within the hour, they uncovered approximately five million dollars worth of cocaine, heroin, crystal meth, and marijuana, which, fortunately, never caught fire or we might've all stumbled out of the Hell Hole a little more slowly. Probably would've giggled a lot and raced across the boardwalk to wolf down three-dozen fried Snickers bars and stare at the pretty blinking lights.

After uncovering 675 kilograms of various illegal substances, Chief Baines and the DEA agents posed for pictures and talked to TV cameras. Getting his face in tomorrow morning's newspapers over a caption proclaiming *Operation Crackdown Huge Success* will undoubtedly make our boss extremely happy. We'll probably get to keep our brand-new Crown Vic police cruiser.

Skeletor, of course, was nowhere to be found. The chief sent a state police composite artist over to Veggin' on the Beach to work with Gladys and Jerry and try to sketch a likeness of our legendary pharmacist. I hope the artist likes beet juice and falafel balls. Given the burned-out hippie couple's charcoal-broiled memory banks, the drawing project could take a while.

Once it's drawn and the picture is shown around town, maybe we'll finally nab this guy Skeletor. At least we closed down his Hot Stuff distribution center and shooting gallery, what Ceepak tells me the DEA slang brochures, if no one else, calls a *get off house.* Apparently, you could rent space in the Hell Hole to cook your nickel deck of horse, big Harry, crown crap, dirt, jive-doo-jee, or reindeer dust (the list of slang words for heroin in Ceepak's brochure is, apparently, quite lengthy), get off and then conk out. The blonde told us Worthington started the fire when his hand trembled too much to hold a candle underneath his spoonful of happy dust. Ceepak and me think the gasoline and diesel fuel helped.

The blonde, a model who—by the way—will be on the cover of *Healthy Living* next month, was treated in the back of the ambulance and released. One of her girlfriends, a super-skinny redhead showing off a lot of bony shoulder blade in her tank top, swung by to pick her up and take her back to the city where, I guess, none of the fashionistas ever eat anything besides egg whites and Metamucil.

Meanwhile, Ceepak and I have spent the last two hours sitting in the visitors' lounge at Mainland Medical, the hospital over in Avondale. They operate what's called the regional trauma center. If, while you're on vacation in Sea Haven, an abandoned amusement park ride happens to burn down and you're inside it injecting illicit drugs, this is where they'll bring your sorry, semi-comatose butt.

"We need to talk with Lieutenant Worthington." Ceepak restates the obvious to a passing nurse for the fifth time since we were asked to "kindly wait down the hall," first by this refrigerator-sized orderly armed with an old-fashioned steel bedpan and, then, by the senator's barrel-chested security detail. Two of the guys, the ex–Navy SEAL named Graves and a former Green Beret called Parker, are standing guard outside Worthington's door right now looking like Michael Corleone after his dad, the godfather, got popped.

"The camera Lieutenant Worthington mentioned most likely contains whatever information Shareef Smith intended to show me." Ceepak's saying it out loud not so much for my benefit but to help himself think.

"What do you think was on it?" I figure I might as well ask a dumb question and get in the game.

"That, Danny, is the question."

"Until I saw that bullet hole in his thigh, I would've guessed they were pictures that proved Worthington faked his Purple Heart wound, like Dixon said he did."

Ceepak nods. "The scarring on Worthington's thigh was consistent with a bullet entry wound. It seems he legitimately earned his medal, if not an immediate trip home."

"So why'd Sergeant Dixon lie to us?"

"Perhaps he was covering for one of his other soldiers who did something worse than fake a war wound."

"Well, chasing after Worthington almost got us killed."

"Twice."

"So whoever tore up Smith's car was searching for his camera."

"Such would be my supposition as well."

"That means he has pictures of something bad. Something Dixon or one of the other soldiers did—over there in Iraq. You think one of them was at that prison, Abu Ghraib? You think Rutledge or Dixon or Handy Andy or even Hernandez made a bunch of naked prisoners crawl on top of each other with bags over their heads while Smith snapped pictures?"

"Doubtful. If any of those men had been involved at Abu Ghraib, we would have, most likely, already seen photographic evidence."

Yeah. Okay. So maybe one of the soldiers did something even worse?

"Do you think one of the soldiers killed Smith?"

"It's a possibility."

"But how? None of them was at the rest area. Only Worthington. Maybe they all call him Lieutenant Worthless because they know he's a junkie just like Smith. Maybe the two of them got into a fight in that restroom over their drug stash and one thing led to another. Maybe they were locked inside that toilet stall together, sharing a spoon and a Bic lighter, and one of them had the pistol and got greedy, you know?"

"I don't think that's what happened."

"So somebody else sneaked away from the party?"

"There are other suspects to consider, Danny."

"Who?"

Ceepak makes a subtle head tilt in the direction of the two former special forces soldiers standing guard outside Worthington's room: Graves and Parker.

"Geeze-o, man," I mumble. "The senator's security detail?"

"We already suspect they might've had something to do with sabotaging our vehicle."

The razor blade. We were chasing them when the tire blew.

"But why?" I ask, since Ceepak's the one who schooled me about motive.

"They work for the senator. Perhaps there is something on that camera *he* doesn't want us to see."

Especially if it might prevent Winslow W. Worthington from becoming the next president of these United States.


Four-thirty PM.

Ceepak's been sitting on the couch not saying anything for like fifteen minutes. I stand up, stretch, and fiddle with my radio unit. It's squawking with chatter, mostly stuff about the cleanup going on over at the Hell Hole.

"Hey, they found another twenty kilos of coke," I report when that news flash screeches through the static. Then I hear one of our guys, Dylan Murray I think, report how he just found "a bunch of burnt cable and some kind of detonator."

"Guess that confirms it was arson," I say to Ceepak. "Somebody hotwired the place to burn. Sort of like the Palace Hotel. Remember that?"

He still says nothing.

He's thinking. I should probably shut up. Turn off my radio and my mouth. Maybe go find us both some coffee.

"Danny?"

"Yeah?"

"Do you have a quarter?"

"I think so." I dig in my pockets. Find two.

Ceepak takes them and marches over to the bank of pay phones bolted to the wall. He drops in a coin, presses in the numbers.

"Hello, dear. Yes. We're still at the hospital. Waiting to talk to Lieutenant Worthington. Yes. I think so. Could you please do me a favor? We need to look at all of Shareef Smith's cell phone bills. No. The sisters won't have to go home. With his next of kin's permission, we should be able to obtain the information directly from the service provider. Right. Good. I'm still without a mobile phone so I need to ask a second favor. That's right. You can coordinate with Denise Diego, the tech officer. Right. Thank you, Rita. We will. Me too."

He hangs up.

"Who do you think Smith called?" I ask.

"His friend."

"Worthington?"

"Roger that. We'll also be able to ascertain who, if anybody, called Smith."

"Officer Ceepak?"

Ohmigod. Mount Rushmore himself is striding down the hall. Senator Worthington or, as I now like to call him, suspect number five. Or thirteen. Depends on whether you count him as a single or lump him in with all eight of his bodyguards.

"I want to thank you two gentlemen for rescuing my son."

He sticks out his hand. I shake it. Now it's Ceepak's turn.

He doesn't take it.

"We need to talk to your son, sir."

"I'm afraid that's impossible. He is very heavily sedated."

Yeah. He was that way when we found him too.

Ceepak keeps pushing: "We believe your son has information vital to an ongoing investigation."

"And what is it you're investigating?"

Ceepak pauses.

I jump in: "Somebody stole air bags and a CD player out of Shareef Smith's car!"

"Really?" Man, does that come out icy. The hospital could turn off their central air. "Well, officers, I hope you will understand if I insist that my son be allowed to recuperate a short while longer. I'm certain there is no critical urgency for you to apprehend these petty car thieves."

"There's more to it," says Ceepak.

"Is that so? More? I see. Are you attempting to operate outside the legal limits of your current jurisdiction?"

"We're searching for the truth."

"Always a noble cause. Do we all seek the truth? Of course we do. But can the truth, once found, do more damage than good? Indeed it can, gentlemen, for this country is at war and in dire need of heroes. Does my son's military record serve a higher purpose, no matter what his personal failings? Good heavens, yes. Therefore, in this specific instance, containing what you might consider the 'truth' is, as I'm sure you'll agree, the nobler path for us all to follow."

Ceepak looks annoyed. No, pissed. I don't think he can make his eyes any more intense without popping them out of their sockets.

"We are not interested in exposing the truth about your son's drug addiction—"

"It's not an addiction. A weakness? I suppose one could call it that. A painful and unfortunate habit picked up while he willingly and selflessly served his country on treacherous foreign soil."

I glance down.

Oh, yeah. He's wearing the boots. Might ruin his presidential plans if the press found out the whole truth about the man who wore them first. That guy on *Meet the Press* might ask Senator Worthington if he ever found any tiny bags of white powder hidden inside his boots' hollowed-out heels.

"Your son told us something when we pulled him out of the fire," says Ceepak.

"The ramblings of an incoherent and traumatized victim."

"He mentioned a camera."

"I'm certain he mentioned a great many things in his delirium."

"No, just the one. He urged us to find Corporal Smith's camera."

"Oh, right. The African American. Tragic how he chose to end his life."

"We don't believe it was his choice."

The senator smiles. Holds up a hand to silence Ceepak. "Officer Ceepak, if I were in your position, if I were a beat cop on a small town police force, I would not concern myself with anything my son might have said while, undoubtedly, in an advanced state of shock. My goodness, he was trapped in a fire. Almost died. I would also not waste any more time waiting here to talk to my son because that is simply not going to happen. Do we understand each other?"

Yeah. I think we do.

"Come on, Danny," says Ceepak.

"Good day, gentlemen," says the senator. It sounds like he's gloating. "Oh—and best of luck catching those car thieves."

Ceepak stops. Turns around to face the senator.

He even smiles.

"Thank you, sir. We appreciate your words of support. Oh, by the way," he adds, "we're getting closer all the time. Much closer."

# 31

*We're getting closer all the time?*

Geeze-o, man!

Maybe Ceepak actually did inhale some of that wacky tobacky smoldering back at the Hell Hole. It would explain his warped world-view. How can we be getting closer when he just expanded our suspect list to include all the guys at the party house, Senator Woodrow Worthington, his bodyguards, the entire Department of Defense—not to mention the whole military-industrial complex, which is this thing I heard Gladys rant about one time when I was at Veggin' on the Beach because this girl I was dating was way into energy booster drinks. (PS—we broke up. The girl never wanted to go to bed. Not with me, not with anybody. She basically never slept. I think that booster shot powder they scoop out behind the juice bar is really a tub of pulverized No-Doz tablets.)

So now we're traveling across the causeway, headed back to the island, all set to police our small town and live our insignificant lives so we can dutifully pay our federal income taxes and finance the salaries of the great men doing important things down in Washington.

"Where to next?" I ask Ceepak. I'm driving. He's staring out the window watching seagulls swoop over the bay, maybe wishing he could swap places with them. "You want to head over to Kipper Street? Talk to Sergeant Dixon, ask why he lied about Worthington's war wound? Or maybe we should go up to Feenyville. Talk to the pirates. We never did interrogate that janitor, Osvaldo Vargas."

"I'd like to hit the house first," says Ceepak. "Reexamine those exterior surveillance camera tapes."

"Okay. Sure. What'll we be looking for?"

"A certain black GMC Denali."

"The senator's security detail?"

"I'm thinking someone might've followed Lieutenant Worthington to his rendezvous with Smith. If so, their vehicle might be evident on the tape."

"But, we looked pretty closely," I say. "All we saw was Worthington's car. He greets Smith, the two of them chat, then they head in to the building. Four minutes later, the camera cable gets snipped, probably by our car thieves, or maybe Osvaldo the janitor, working for the crew he knows will be showing up later, and the screen goes black."

"And so, Danny, we look again," says Ceepak. "We look closer. We also pay more attention to the other three cameras."

True. We were more or less focused on the upper right quadrant because that showed where Shareef Smith's car was parked.

"Do you think Senator Worthington set up a Special Forces–type hit on Smith, because Smith knew about his son's drug trouble and, if it came out, it could ruin his chances of being elected to anything except superintendent of sewers?" I ask.

"I think I want to relook at those tapes."

One step at a time. That's Ceepak. Me? I'm forever jumping to conclusions. It's how I wind up flat on my ass so often.

The radio mounted on the dash crackles.

"Unit twelve?"

Ceepak grabs the mike. "This is twelve. Go ahead."

"We need you over at the Acme Supermarket. Ten-thirty-five."

They want us to check out a suspicious person at the grocery store. I wonder what the guy did—fondle too many chicken breasts?

"Sergeant Pender?" says Ceepak. "We are not currently operating in a patrol mode. In fact, as I'm sure the chief has informed you, we are presently involved in an increasingly complicated investigation of—"

"It's your father, Ceepak."

"Come again?"

"The individual misbehaving at the Acme is a Mr. Joseph Ceepak. He told Malloy and Kiger that he's your dad. I just thought, you know . . ."

"Thank you, Sergeant Pender." He slips the mike back into its bracket. "Danny?"

We hit Ocean Avenue and I hang a left. We're on our way to the grocery store with a very short shopping list: deal with Ceepak's old man.


"It's five o'clock somewhere! Hell, son, look at your watch! It's five o'clock right here in New Jersey!"

Mr. Ceepak is standing in the middle of the beer and chips aisle. Judging by the pile of empties near his feet, he is currently on his fourth can of warm suds. Personally, I would've headed one aisle over—to the cold case. Guess Mr. Ceepak has been an alkie so long, he doesn't care if half of what he's drinking is tepid foam.

"You want some chips, Johnny? Salsa?" Now he starts grabbing jumbo bags of Doritos and jars of Chi-Chi's. He tears into the bags with his teeth. Holds out a salsa jar then drops it on the floor where it explodes and splatters out a pattern resembling a squished octopus. Looks like Mr. Ceepak's been doing the salsa-bomb drops for a while now. The linoleum up and down the aisle is blotted with tomato and jalapeño chunks. We definitely need a mop in aisle six.

"Guys?" Ceepak calls to the first officers on the scene: Mark Malloy and Adam Kiger. They're at the far end of the aisle, blocking Mr. Ceepak's retreat. We're at the front end, near the five-gallon buckets of pretzels. "Clear out those civilians behind you. Move them toward the deli counter."

"Ten-four," says Kiger. He heads off to manage crowd control. Malloy stays in position to block the elder Mr. Ceepak's potential escape route.

"What?" laughs Mr. Ceepak. "You gotta move folks out of harm's way, boy? Why? You gonna gun me down?"

"Only if I have to."

"Bullshit! You don't have the balls!"

I hear Velcro rip back. Ceepak's unfastening the flap that secures his Glock inside its holster. I do the same.

"You want a beer, Johnny?" The crazy old bastard tears open another cardboard suitcase of Budweiser.

"No. I want you to kneel on the floor and put your hands behind your back."

"Kneel? You think I'm some kind of altar boy like your faggot brother Billy? Forget it! I'm not kneeling down in front of you, Johnny! No way in hell am I doing that!"

"Do it! Now!"

"Fuck you, Johnny. Okay? Fuck you! Hey, Malloy?" he shouts over his shoulder. "Johnny ever tell you how he bent up the fucking frame on his first bike? One car in the whole goddamn parking lot and he rams right into it. He any better at pistols than he was with bikes? You know what, Malloy? If I were you, I'd get the hell out of Dodge—"

"Kneel on the floor! Do it!"

"Fuck you!" Mr. Ceepak flings the torn cardboard suitcase full of twelve-ounce cans to his left. Some fly free and smash into the lowest shelf, tearing it off its bracket. Snacks get crushed. Nothing serious. Peanut butter cheese crackers, mostly.

"Where the fuck is she, Johnny? Where the hell did you hide my wife?"

Man, are we drawing a crowd. The grocery store is always jammed at 5:00 because everybody's done with the beach for the day and now they're trying to figure out what they're going to eat for supper. So Mr. Ceepak isn't the only one interested in what's on sale in the beer and chips aisle. These people are on vacation. Beer and chips? Down the shore, they're like beef: it's what's for dinner.

"Where the fuck did you hide your goddamn mother?"

"Okay," I say, because, basically, I've had enough. "You heard Officer Ceepak." I walk past my partner. Move down the aisle, march at old man Ceepak. First off, I think the grizzled drunk might actually obey a police officer who isn't his son. Second, he's so tanked, I don't think he can hurt me, even if he takes a swing with another suitcase full of beer cans. I'm guessing if he tries, it'll be high and wide and slow. "Please kneel down on the floor, sir."

"Fuck you, kid."

"Not here. Too many spectators."

"Whaa?" He's blitzed and befuddled.

I place a hand gently yet firmly on his shoulder. "Turn around, sir."

"I thought you wanted me to kneel on the floor?"

"Nah. I changed my mind. Made what we call a situational adjustment."

"Whaat?" I think I'm confusing him. Good. All part of the plan. To tell the truth, I don't expect much resistance. He's totally smashed. Been drinking all day. Probably ready to sleep some of it off. It's how I used to feel after an all-day-and-nighter with my beach buddies. I also think getting arrested is what he wants or he wouldn't have told Kiger and Malloy that he was Ceepak's dad. I think he wants to bunk down in the jail back at police headquarters so he can bug my partner 24-7.

"Just put your hands behind your back and we'll call it a day, okay? You think you can manage that? The turning around bit?"

"Yeah," he mumbles and stumbles into a turn. "Like this?"

"Excellent. Nicely done, sir." I slip a pair of FlexiCuffs over his wrists. "You, of course, have the right to remain silent."

He belches—passing on that particular constitutional privilege.

"Anything you say can and will be used against you in a court of law," I continue. "You have the right to speak to an attorney, and to have an attorney present during any questioning. If you cannot afford a lawyer, one will be provided for you at government expense. Do you understand these rights as I've recited them to you?"

"Yeah. You did it good. Just like on TV."

"Thank you, sir. Let's go book you a bed." I indicate with a light shoulder tap that he should try to start walking forward. He does. It's more of a shuffle, but we're moving in the right direction.

"Can I grab a couple beers for the road?"

"Sorry. No can do."

"Hell, it's cocktail hour."

"I know what you mean," I say as I help him maneuver up the aisle toward his son. "Like you say, it's always five o'clock somewhere."

"You're okay, kid."

"If you say so, sir. Come on. Let's go."

"Is Johnny coming with us?"

"Yeah," I say. "It's his turn to drive."

"Careful, kid. He might wreck the car like he wrecked that damn bike."

"Sounds like good times, sir. Good times."

He looks at me. Dazed now. His few functional brain cells scrambled like scalded eggs in a skillet.

Sometimes I have that effect on people. Even sober people.

# 32

*We lock* up Mr. Ceepak in our holding cell, where he'll spend the night on a drunk and disorderly.

"You handled that well, Danny," says Ceepak.

"I speak 'Drunk.' Besides, if it was my old man, you would've done the same thing."

"Does your father frequently steal warm beer and drink it in the middle of a crowded grocery store while simultaneously destroying snack food items?"

"No. But this one time—I swear I saw him pluck a grape in the produce section and plop it in his mouth."

Ceepak smiles. "Fine. The next time your dad's in town, it'll be my pleasure to arrest him."

"Cool. So let's go look at that tape again."

"Roger that."

He heads up the hall toward the front desk.

All the other cops milling around in the lobby are trying real hard to not make eye contact with Ceepak. Face it, it's pretty embarrassing, having to haul your old man into the slammer so he can sleep off a drunk. Sons are supposed to be the ones out on the street raising hell. Not fathers.

"Excuse me? Sirs? I am *so* glad I found you!"

It's Samantha Starky, bounding through the front door and swinging open the little gate that separates the public from the police.

"The Smith sisters are fine, Rita's looking after them, so I took my mother an iced mocha latte." She's hyped up on adrenaline, maybe latte fumes. "You know that house on Kipper Street? The one where we had to do that ten-forty-three run Friday night, sir? The house that guy Sergeant Dixon said belonged to his uncle?"

"Yeah. Sure." I remember all this but I'm not half as wound up about it as Starky.

"Well, sirs, he was lying!"

Naturally, Ceepak's ears perk up. "How so?"

"My mom? She's a Realtor down at All-A-Shore Realty?"

When Starky's excited, everything comes out sounding like a question.

"They've had one heck of a time renting it this summer."

She hands us each a real estate flyer for 22 Kipper Street. Five bedrooms, three baths, six beach badges, all utilities included. The weekly rental price has, according to the screaming type in an exploding sunburst, been "$eriously $lashed." Guess that's why there's still a *For Rent* sign stuck in the front yard: nobody was biting for the old "$eriously Expen$ive" price.

"My mom says the family that usually rents that house every July for like twenty years all of a sudden at the last minute decided to go to Europe or Disney World."

Maybe they'll just hit Epcot Center and see 'em both.

"You say the owner isn't Sergeant Dixon's uncle?" asks Ceepak.

"No, sir. Mr. Ryan O'Malley owns it. Skip's dad."

Apparently, the O'Malley family took some of their hard-earned King Putt profits and plowed them into real estate ventures.

"And you know what else?" says Starky. "Sergeant Dixon isn't even the one who rented it! Somebody down in Washington did. Called in the middle of last week."

Ceepak's extremely interested now. Me too.

"Is your mother at liberty to divulge the renter's identity?"

Starky shrugs. "I guess so. Even if she isn't, she already told me it was some guy from Senator Worthington's office! I thought that was pretty cool—the senator personally paying for the house so his son and the other soldiers could come up here for a little R and R."

Rest and relaxation.

Or, perhaps, rendezvous and rubout.

"Do you think that's why he rented it?" Starky asks Ceepak. "To say 'thanks' to his son and the other soldiers?"

"I won't speculate on Senator's Worthington's motives at this juncture," says Ceepak.

Me? I speculate that the senator rented the house to lure Smith into uncharted waters so his goon squad—the musclemen with the nice suits, sunglasses, and knockwurst necks—could eliminate a threat to his ambitions for higher elective office. I'm guessing Special Forces Operatives stage suicides all the time. They probably even have a training manual for it.

"What day did the phone call come in?" asks Ceepak.

"Wednesday."

Ceepak marches over to the reception desk, picks up a phone, and presses in a number.

While he waits for someone to answer, I try to remember what movie I saw where the presidential candidate and his mother killed anybody who got their way. It was either *The Manchurian Candidate* or *Big Momma's White House*.

"Room three-fourteen," Ceepak says into the phone.

I figure he's calling that Holiday Inn.

"Tonya? John Ceepak. No, ma'am, but I think we're getting closer. Question: when did Shareef first ask to borrow your car?" Ceepak jots something on a pad of paper. "And he left on Friday?" Another note. "Thank you. No. I think it would be best if you remained at the hotel for the time being." He looks at Starky. "I'm sending Samantha Starky back out to join you."

Starky snaps to attention. Nods an "aye-aye, sir" over to Ceepak. Attempts to make her cute face severely serious. It almost works.

"No," Ceepak says over the phone to Tonya Smith. "I don't anticipate any trouble. I'd just like to have Officer Starky act as my eyes and ears out there since my wife will soon be vacating the premises. Right. Stay inside your room. Stay safe. Thank you."

He hangs up.

"I'm on my way, sir," Starky says to Ceepak.

"Use channel five on your radio if you need to contact us," he says. "Danny? Go to five."

I twist the knob on the walkie-talkie anchored on my belt.

"In case of emergency, also contact the house and request backup. I'll keep my portable tuned to the main frequency."

"Will do, sir."

"Thank you," says Ceepak.

"My pleasure." She turns on her heel, slaps on her sunglasses, and dashes out the door.

"Danny?"

"Yeah?"

"Let's go look at the tape."

"Right."


We concentrate on the time period between 9:30 and 10:30 because we know that Smith and Worthington meet at 10:09 p.m., head into the rest area at 10:16, and the upper right-hand quadrant of the screen goes black at 10:20 when someone snips the surveillance camera cable.

We focus on the upper left-hand frame first, the other camera mounted in the parking lot on the northbound side of the rest area.

We see nothing. A couple SUVs, sure. But no Denalis like the senator's bodyguards tool around in.

"Maybe Worthington pulled in on the other side," I suggest.

"Good point, Danny. He was coming *down* to exit fifty-two from

Sea Haven, transporting the locally distributed drugs. Therefore, he would have entered the lot on the southbound side."

"We don't know what kind of car Worthington drives."

"Inconsequential. We already know he was there. We are most interested in determining if anybody followed him."

So we focus on the bottom right and bottom left boxes.

"No Denalis," I announce when the time code rolls past 10:10. If they were following Worthington, the bodyguards should've shown by now.

"This pickup truck," says Ceepak as he taps the bottom right square. "Why does it look so familiar?"

"It's the pirates'! Remember? They were working on it up in Feenyville when we paid them that visit! What time did it show up?"

Ceepak rocks the video back a minute or two. Tracks the truck's entrance. "Twenty-two-twenty-one."

Ten twenty-one PM.

I glance up at the upper right-hand box. It's already black.

"So the pirates didn't cut the cable."

"Unless," says Ceepak, "they asked Osvaldo Vargas to do that particular job."

"Nope," I say. "Not unless he's the Flash." I tap the screen. "That looks like him right there!"

We watch a short man come out of the rest area building. The lighting is good. Ceepak manipulates the zoom and we get a pretty good look at the janitor as he hops into the back of the pirates' pickup truck. It sure looks like Osvaldo Vargas.

"Apparently," says Ceepak, "Mr. Vargas left work early Friday night." His eyes stay glued on the spinning digital clock. I'm not sure why. It hits 22:22. Twenty-two minutes after ten. The truck starts to move. Vargas is seated in the cargo bay. The vehicle disappears from the lower right square and enters the box on the lower left-hand side as it moves through the southbound-side parking lots. Finally, it crosses that frame and, about thirty seconds later, reappears in the upper left-hand quadrant.

"There they go," I say. "Swinging around to the northbound side."

Ceepak picks up my train of thought as the pickup truck disappears. "Where they will discover Smith's car and remove his air bags and CD changer."

Which they will do unseen in the blacked-out box in the top right corner.

"We need to head back to the hospital," says Ceepak.

"You still want to interrogate Lieutenant Worthington?"

He shakes his head. "No, Danny. His father."

## 33

*We're moving* at a good clip up Ocean Avenue headed, once again, for the causeway that'll take us back to the mainland and the medical center.

"Danny? That vehicle . . ."

Ceepak does a three-finger chop dead ahead.

In front of us, barreling *down* Ocean Avenue, I see a pickup truck. It makes a tire-squealing, axle-tilting, right-hand turn through the currently red traffic light.

"Initiate pursuit," says Ceepak.

"Ten-four."

Here we go again. I just hope nobody jammed a Ginzu knife into our tire treads while we were inside watching videos of—

"The Feenyville Pirates!" I say as I match their speed-demon right turn with a rubber-burning left of my own. "That's their pickup truck!"

"Ten-four," says Ceepak.

I flip on the lights and siren. It's a three-block straight shot to the bridge and I'm hoping I don't set a new Sea Haven PD record by totaling two cop cars in a single day.

"Brakes!" shouts Ceepak.

Good point. The pirates are slamming on their brakes so I better jam on mine—now! Red taillights zoom into full view, my nose nears their cargo bed, and I pray we come to a full and complete stop before their rear bumper offers unwanted assistance.

Missed them by an inch.

This new car? Good antilock brakes.

The three pirates come tumbling out of the pickup cab: Nicky Nichols, Mr. Shrimp, and Osvaldo Vargas.

"We surrender!" shouts Mr. Shrimp. "Arrest us!"

All three of them shoot their hands straight up into the air. The pint-sized Shrimp and the half-pint Vargas flank the big galoot Nichols on the shoulder of the road so he looks like the twelve-year-old second-grader, the slow one who's been held back five or six times.

"It's in the back of the truck," says Mr. Shrimp. "Everything!"

Ceepak and I move closer. Traffic slows down to see what kind of criminals we collar by the side of the road in Sea Haven. We're creating major rubbernecking delays.

"It's all in the box! Everything we ripped off that piece-of-crap Ford." I go up on my toes to take a peek inside the truck bed. I see a corrugated booze box (Captain Morgan rum, of course) loaded with wires and crap. "Lock us up! We did the crime, we're ready to do the time!"

"Typically," says Ceepak, "there's a trial prior to any imposition of a prison sentence."

"Hunh?" Confused, Nichols's SpaghettiO mouth widens.

"You have to hold us in a cell until we post bail," snaps Mr. Shrimp, the crew's legal scholar. "Which we can't do for a couple days. Cash-flow issues."

"Danny?" says Ceepak. "Let's take a look at what's in the box."

I haul myself up and over the sidewalls.

"Gloves," Ceepak reminds me.

So I slip them on and start rummaging around inside the pirates' treasure chest.

"One Kenwood six-CD changer loaded with six CDs," I call down to Ceepak. "A tangle of cables, two speakers with holes punched through the paper cones, the cardboard bottom from a twenty-four-can case of Sprite, plus a bottle of Quaker State five w-twenty motor oil." My evidence gloves are a mess. The oil bottle has brown sludge droplets decorating its neck.

"That's all we took," says Nichols. He sounds like Lurch from the *Addams Family* movies. Harmless.

"What about the air bags?" asks Ceepak.

"They weren't in the trunk," says Shrimp, "so we didn't take them!"

"Somebody did," says Ceepak. He gestures to the three pirates to let them know they don't need to keep their hands raised over their heads.

"It wasn't us!" says Shrimp. "All we got was the crappy CD collection and a half-empty bottle of motor oil before this dude came walking straight at us and we tore the hell out of there!"

"Who was it?"

Nichols squints. Tries to comprehend Ceepak's question. "Who was who?"

"The man approaching the vehicle you were burglarizing?"

"Some dude," says Mr. Shrimp.

"Black, white, Hispanic?"

"Couldn't see. Too dark. We thought he might be the owner so, like I said, we took off."

Ceepak nods. "Taking the contents of Shareef Smith's trunk with you."

"That's right," says Mr. Shrimp. "But I swear on my mother's grave—that's all we took. We didn't even see the damn digital camera, so how could we steal it?"

"Who said anything about a camera?"

"The soldier." Shrimp gestures toward Ceepak. "He sort of looks like you. Only this dude is one mean sonofabitch who says he'll rip off our heads and shove 'em up our butts if we don't give him back the god-damn digital camera he thinks we stole out of his dead buddy's car only like I just told you there weren't no camera in that trunk! Sweet Jesus, how many times do we have to tell you people?" He holds out both wrists, practically begging to be cuffed. "Come on, man. Lock us up!"

"This soldier—does he have a name?"

"Dixon."

I guess Lieutenant Worthington told his buddies about Shareef's camera too.

"Sergeant Dale Dixon visited Feenyville?" Ceepak asks.

"Yeah. Him and his badass Mexican backup. Short little gangbanger in a do-rag. Said they'd be back later tonight. So we took off. Hey, if you want, you can arrest us for speeding and running a red light too!"

"When did you talk to these gentlemen?" asks Ceepak.

"Half-hour ago."

"Did Sergeant Dixon accuse you of being involved in Shareef Smith's death?"

"No. He just wanted the camera and I told him what I'm telling you: there weren't no damn camera in the damn trunk!"

"I understand."

"You believe me?"

"In this instance, yes. Lying would be of no benefit to you. Tell me—the man who came walking toward the car as you were burglarizing it—did he also look like he might be a soldier?"

"Like I said, we couldn't see much on account of it was night and all but I'm pretty sure it wasn't this same asshole Dixon. Wasn't that tall."

"Did the man in the parking lot look like he might be a *former* soldier?" asks Ceepak.

Now Mr. Shrimp looks confused. "I don't know, man. What the hell does a former soldier look like?"

"A little older but still muscular."

And maybe wearing a dark blue suit and sunglasses. Ceepak is describing Senator Worthington's bodyguards.

"All we saw was like a silhouette, you know? On account of that lamppost near the car being so bright."

"He had on a pretty shirt," says Nichols.

"Come again?"

"It had flowers on it. Like they wear in Hawaii."

Shrimp snaps back in disbelief. "You saw his shirt?"

Nichols does a slow bobble-head nod. "It was pretty."

Ceepak turns to me. "Danny, let's radio this in. Have Sergeant Pender send out the tow truck to impound their vehicle. Hand me the box, and I'll stow it in our trunk."

"You're going to arrest us, right?" Mr. Shrimp is begging.

"Yes, sir," Ceepak says as he slips on a pair of evidence gloves so I can hand off the cardboard box.

"We'll wait in your car!" says Shrimp. He and Nichols hurry up the side of the road and practically leap into the backseat of our cruiser. Vargas would probably do the same thing only he can't, because Ceepak is currently blocking his path.

"Mr. Vargas?" says Ceepak.

"Yes?" Poor guy. He sounds scared stiff.

"You left work early on Friday night, is that correct?"

"Yes."

"You went outside, into the south side parking lot, met your two friends."

"Yes."

"You then climbed into the back of this pickup truck."

Vargas looks worried, thinks he's dealing with some kind of psychic mind reader who can see every bad thing that he's ever even thought about doing.

"Yes."

"The last time you entered the men's room was at ten-oh-five PM?"

"I think so. Yes. I signed the clipboard. Left work."

"You didn't clean the men's room?"

"No. I left it for the old man. Señor Delgado. He doesn't think I clean so good so what difference does it make if I clean it at ten o'clock or not?"

"Did you close off the right-hand side?"

"No."

"You didn't pull the tape across to shut off access to the toilets on the right?"

"No!"

"How tall are you, Mr. Vargas?"

The little janitor looks as startled by the new question as I am.

"Five-two," Vargas answers.

"Five-one," shouts Shrimp from the backseat. I guess he's determined to be the taller of the two dwarfs.

A look of grim comprehension crosses Ceepak's face.

"Of course," he says, sort of to himself. "Thank you, Mr. Vargas. Please join the others."

The little janitor scurries up to our car. As soon as he's in, Mr. Shrimp, who got the hump seat, reaches over and slams the door shut. I read his lips: "Lock it! Lock it!"

I hand the box down to Ceepak. He takes it and I hop out of the truck bed.

"Danny?"

"Yes, sir?"

"Do you remember when you received the ten-forty-three call on Friday night?" he asks.

"A little before one AM."

"And do you remember who the complaint came from?"

"A neighbor, I think."

"Were you advised which neighbor?"

"No. We were on patrol. The call came across the radio. We took it. Headed over to Kipper and Beach Lane."

"Were the soldiers rowdy when you arrived?"

"Oh, yeah. They were whooping it up. Chanting. Blasting heavy metal music."

"Was your one AM run in response to the first complaint of the evening?"

"I think so. The dispatcher didn't, you know, say, 'It's that house again, we warned them once,' or anything like that."

"What time do you presume Sergeant Dixon and his men started drinking on Friday?"

I try to remember my first encounter with Sergeant Dixon. "Can't say for certain, but I remember he said Smith was late, that the party was slated to start at nineteen-hundred hours. Seven PM."

"But," says Ceepak, "Dixon told us most of the men arrived earlier.

Do you think they waited until nineteen-hundred to begin imbibing alcoholic beverages?"

"No." I remember our trips to the house yesterday and earlier today. "They seem to start the day with beer for breakfast. I'd say these guys probably get loud a little after lunch every day. So how come nobody complained about Dixon and his buddies' party earlier in the day on Friday?"

"I have a theory."

"Care to share it?"

"Not yet, Danny. Soon."

This is classic Ceepak. He won't offer up his opinion until he's placed the last piece into his jigsaw puzzle. However, judging from the look in his eyes, I'd say he's finished most of it—not just the straight-edged border my mom taught us to always do first.

"Before proffering any theory as to what might have happened," says Ceepak, "we must first determine *why* it happened."

"We need to find that camera," I say. "That's why Shareef was killed."

Ceepak nods his agreement.

"So where do we look?"

"Where no one else has."

We haul the pirates back to the police station.

Our two jail cells are getting pretty crowded. Ceepak's dad is currently bunking with the drool bucket: Nicky Nichols. Maybe they can swap recipes. Become real roomies.

"Should I put the box in the evidence room?" I ask Ceepak.

"Hmmm?"

Ceepak is in one of his deep-think fogs: he's physically here in the lobby with me but his brain is somewhere else, searching for that camera.

"I'll be right back," I say and turn up the hall with the cardboard box.

Behind me, I hear the front doors swing open.

"Lieutenant Ceepak?" asks this deep, rumbling voice.

Odd. Ceepak's not a lieutenant in the SHPD. He's not even a sergeant. I turn around to see who just waltzed in.

One of the senator's bodyguards.

The towering black guy named Parker who, we've been told, is former Army. Special Ops. Green Beret. All six feet, six inches, and three hundred pounds of him.

"Sorry to intrude, sir," he says in a low voice that could rattle rafters. "Is there some place quiet we could talk?"

34

All of a sudden I feel like I'm in one of those movies where the bad guys send over a knight under a white flag and we let him into our castle and then the whole "I come in peace" deal turns out to be a trick and a billion savage barbarians storm the gates because we forgot to lower the drawbridge after we let in the evil ambassador.

I'm pretty sure this bald black dude in the sunglasses and suit is one of the bad guys who hid that razor blade inside our front left tire. When that didn't work, he and his pals tried to incinerate us inside the Hell Hole.

Frankly, I'm none too pleased that Ceepak and I are currently walking up the hall with one of Senator Worthington's hit men.

"Officer Ceepak?"

It's Denise Diego, sticking her head out of the door to the tech room. She's our top computer geek and came in on her day off to help us track down and analyze Corporal Smith's cell phone records.

"I just checked out the first fax from Verizon Wireless," she says.

"Anything interesting?" asks Ceepak.

"I need to find a few more numbers."

"About who Smith called?"

"Nah. Those are printed right on the bill. It's the incoming calls we're still working on. A Verizon guy is helping me i.d. the callers."

Ceepak gives a sideways glance at our guest and chooses his words carefully.

"When do you expect to receive that information?"

We hear a phone jangle in the darkened room behind her.

"Right about now."

Diego disappears into her den of glowing screens, blinking LEDs, and *Lord of the Rings* paraphernalia. Meanwhile, Ceepak and I continue up the hall with our uninvited guest to the interrogation room.

"We can talk in here," Ceepak says.

"Good. Anybody on the other side?" Parker whips off his sunglasses and checks out the sheen of his bald head in the one-way mirror covering one wall.

"No."

"Good."

Of course he doesn't want anybody eavesdropping. He's most likely planning a sneak attack and doesn't want someone on our team watching when he whips out his weapon and mows down me and Ceepak. Maybe I watch too many movies but I'm thinking we should've frisked this guy or had him walk through a metal detector like they have at airports and big-city courtrooms whenever Michael Jackson goes on trial—the same kind we don't have at SHPD headquarters because we're peace officers with a beachy kind of 'tude.

"My name is Cyrus Parker," our visitor announces. "You were with the one-oh-first out of Fort Campbell?"

"Yes."

"Me too. Fifth Special Forces Group."

Ceepak nods. "I was with the Third MP Group. CID."

"And you went over to the sandbox as a lieutenant during Operation Iraqi Freedom," says Parker. "I was there for the first go-round. Desert Storm."

I can tell Ceepak's had enough with the swapping of war stories. "Why are you here, Mr. Parker?"

"You know what's the best part of being ex-military?" he asks. "If you don't like your orders, you don't have to follow them. You can just quit."

"Have you recently left the senator's employ?"

"No. Not yet. But I think he's going to fire me. Probably some of the other guys I put together for the crew too."

"Why?"

Parker grins. "Because, Lieutenant Ceepak, a few of my men and I have decided to disobey an order we consider to be blatantly illegal."

"And what order is that?"

"Senator Worthington has ordered us to kill you, sir." Now he smiles at me. "You too. You're Danny Boyle, right?"

"Yeah," I say. "But how come you all of a sudden decided to disobey the same orders you've been following all day?"

"Come again?"

"You guys already tried to kill us twice today. First, you sabotaged the tires on our Ford Explorer."

"Negative."

"Come on, pal," I say—and Ceepak lets me. "You rigged up that razor blade so it'd slash through our steel-belted radial when we initiated a high-speed pursuit of *your* Denali."

"No sir," says Parker. "We did no such thing. In fact, I'm the one who called nine-one-one."

"Why didn't you stop and offer assistance?" asks Ceepak.

"Because Senator Worthington would not permit me to do so. He had informed us he'd been urgently recalled to Washington for a crucial vote. We assumed it was another one of those Terri Schiavo situations and the president needed all like-minded senators back in town on a Sunday to pass a special law for somebody."

"Come on," I say. "You expect us to buy that?"

"You should. It's the truth."

"So why didn't you continue to D.C.?" asks Ceepak.

"About twenty miles down the road, the senator received a phone call—or so he says. I, of course, didn't hear anything. Must've had his cell unit set on vibrate." He says it like he doesn't believe it. "When he said, 'so long' to whoever he was pretending to be talking to, he told us the vote had been canceled and we could return to Sea Haven, where he hoped to spend more time with his son."

Yeah—frying him inside an abandoned amusement park ride.

"Well what about the Hell Hole?" I ask.

"The fire?"

"Yeah. Who organized that little weenie roast?"

"Again, my men and I had nothing to do with that incident."

"And I'm supposed to believe you because it's 'the truth' again, right?"

"Yes, Officer Boyle. Besides, if any of us *had* been involved in or-chestrating that conflagration, you would not be sitting here. You'd be lying in the morgue."

I snort a chuckle. "Because you guys are that good, right?"

"Yes, sir. We most assuredly are. If you don't believe me, I suggest you to talk to certain members of Saddam Hussein's Republican Guard who in 1991 were bivouacked south of Baghdad near the Tigris River. Their bunker burned down the night before our tanks rolled north out of Kuwait City."

Ceepak props his elbows on the table, locks his hands together—I guess so he can glare more steadily at Parker.

"This order to kill Officer Boyle and myself—it's recent?"

"Affirmative. Came down about an hour ago. The senator pulled me and Graves off guard duty at the hospital so we could join the others in their pursuit and apprehension of you two. Apparently, you gentlemen represent a dire threat to national security. But, seeing how my men and I are independent contractors and, therefore, no longer sworn to obey the orders of the President of the United States or the orders of the offi-cers appointed over us, we are currently at liberty to decide that the or-ders as given are basically total bullshit. Graves and I left the hospital as instructed but came over here instead of the rally point."

"And why does Senator Worthington consider us to be a threat to national security?" asks Ceepak.

"He claims you are currently in possession of certain documenta-tion that could severely compromise America's ongoing war efforts.

Apparently, you two have located some extremely sensitive photographs."

Here we go again: Shareef Smith's damn digital camera.

"The senator says the pictures in question are classified satellite images detailing the military installation in central Baghdad known as the Green Zone. Furthermore, the senator advises us that if you two were to turn said photographs over to Sunni or Shi'ite insurgents—or even the wrong reporters at the *New York Times*—you would seriously jeopardize the safety of all those currently operating behind the zone's blast walls."

"Bullshit," I say.

The ex-soldier's grin grows wider. "Roger that." He rocks his wrist, checks his watch. "I believe the senator's story is just that. Sheer, unadulterated, high-test bullshit. Therefore, gentlemen, might I suggest that we proceed over to the Holiday Inn in Avondale to retrieve the Smith sisters? They'll be safer here inside police headquarters."

"How do you know where they're currently located?"

"The senator told us. Apparently, one of the young ladies has her cell phone turned on. When you're the chairman of the Senate Select Committee on Intelligence you can ask your friends over at the NSA to track just about anyone you want, provided, of course, they have their cell phone powered up. You two gentlemen, on the other hand, have been somewhat harder for the senator to track."

Guess smashing one's cell phone has its advantages.

"Are Smith's sisters in danger?" asks Ceepak.

"I would suspect so."

"Why?"

He shrugs. "Why else would Senator Worthington be tracking them?"

"Let's roll," says Ceepak. We move toward the door. Parker follows us.

"We'll follow behind you guys in our vehicle," he says.

"No need," says Ceepak.

"You might require backup."

"If so, we'll summon the state police."

"Lieutenant Ceepak, given the nature of Senator Worthington's recent order and his unlimited resources within the DOD, I'm suggesting you might need *serious* backup."

Why do I think this guy has some kind of major canon strapped underneath his suit jacket and hand grenades stuffed inside every one of his pockets?

Ceepak fixes his gaze on Parker's eyes. "Why your sudden interest to assist the local police force?"

"Because I suspect Senator Worthington has been lying to me for some time and that, sir, is something I simply can not abide. When I was at West Point, we had an honor code—"

"I'm quite familiar with the academy's code, Mr. Parker."

"Then you already know I have zero tolerance for lies, liars, bullshit, and bullshitters."

"Then we should get along just fine." Ceepak says it like he's still not sure what side of the line Parker really falls on. "Where is the senator?"

"The rally point."

"Which is where?"

"The radio lady's mansion."

"Mr. Parker," says Ceepak, "I appreciate your offer of assistance. However, we do not require nor can we encourage civilian involvement in ongoing police investigations."

"Fine. Graves and I will just follow you. I trust there's no law against a couple civilians taking a Sunday drive even if they happen to be following a police vehicle for the duration of said drive?"

Ceepak thinks about that for a second. Wonders whether he can trust this man. "Not that I'm aware of."

"Then we're good to go."

Ceepak holds open the door, lets Parker head down the hall.

Tech officer Diego comes into the hallway. She's holding a rolled-up tube of paper.

"You can wait for us out front," Ceepak says to Parker.

"Will do."

Ceepak waits until he is gone. Then he waits another couple seconds to make sure he's *really* gone.

"What's up?" he finally says to Diego as we follow her into the computer room.

"Heard back from Verizon. Wrote up a topline summary." She hands the paper to Ceepak. "In the past week, Shareef Smith called Washington, D.C., a dozen different times. Same number."

"Any idea who he was attempting to reach?"

"Yeah. That was the easy part. Took like ten seconds."

"And?"

"He made numerous short phone calls to the office of Pennsylvania Senator Winslow W. Worthington. The last call to D.C. was on Wednesday morning under a usage type coded U."

"What does that mean?" I ask so Ceepak doesn't have to.

"*U,* for whatever reason, is Verizon's code for 'data.' So, I'm guessing he sent the senator a text message or a picture or something."

A picture. A photograph.

"Excellent work, Officer Diego," says Ceepak.

"Wait," she says. "There's more." She taps near the bottom of the page. "Incoming calls. Most came from a Tonya Smith."

"His sister," I say.

"But on Thursday and Friday, Smith's cell phone received several calls from another Winslow Worthington. Winslow *G.* Worthington. Any relation to the senator?"

"Yeah," I say. "His son."

# 35

*Once again,* we're traveling across the causeway, headed for the Holiday Inn in Avondale.

I'm driving; Ceepak is in the passenger seat, working the radio, checking in with Samantha Starky, who's currently on-site at the motel in Avondale.

"Please ask Rita to immediately transport my mother to the backup location. Over."

"Yes, sir," says Starky on the other end. "Will she know where that is, sir? Over."

"Roger that. Over."

Starky is the one who started in with the "overs" at the end of every sentence to indicate that she's ready for Ceepak to talk again because that's what the official ham radio etiquette handbooks say you should do.

"The state police are already on scene," Starky continues.

"Come again?" Oops. Ceepak talked before she said, "over" or "Mother may I?"

"I contacted Wilson," Starky chirps on. "You met him this morning, at the Pig's Commitment? Remember?"

She's rat-a-tat-tatting so fast, this leg of the radio transmission may never be over.

"He swung by with his partner. Terry O'Loughlin. Nice lady. They're both here now. It's a slow day and they were just basically cruising the Parkway, writing speeding tickets and stuff when I caught Wilson on his cell and explained our security situation here and how I thought, you know, it may not be totally safe, seeing how I'm unarmed and people have been trying to kill you two guys all day long." Finally, a pause. "Over."

"Well done, Officer Starky," says Ceepak. "You showed tremendous personal initiative in summoning support. We're on our way. Estimated arrival time—five minutes. Over."

"Roger. Over."

I glance up into the rearview mirror. They're still back there. Special Ops Parker and Navy SEAL Graves.

"You trust those guys?" I ask Ceepak.

"Well, Danny, as Springsteen says, 'In your heart you must trust.' "

"Yeah, but in that other song, he says 'I don't know who to trust.' "

"That would be 'Devils and Dust.' "

Duh. *Dust* rhymes with *trust*. I should've nailed that one.

"So what does your heart say?" I ask. "Trust or not?"

In my peripheral vision, I notice Ceepak glancing into the passenger side mirror. Checking out the Darth Vader mobile following behind us. Are Parker and Graves evil Imperial Storm Troopers or scrappy Rebel Alliance X-Wing Pilots?

"Parker is a graduate of West Point. Said all the right words."

"But, what if he's lying about not lying?"

Ceepak sighs. Our brand new tires whine. So far, I don't hear the clickety-clack of another stainless-steel razor blade.

"You raise a good point, Danny. He may simply be saying what he knows we want to hear. Putting the proper spin on his words. So much of this investigation has already resembled an unrelenting carnival ride." Ceepak sinks back into his seat. "When I was a boy, my mother took me to the Warren County fair."

Yep, we're off on a random tangent, but what the hey—it beats listening to Starky say "over" over and over again.

"That in Ohio?" I ask.

"Yes. Near Lebanon. They had a ride similar to Sea Haven's Hell Hole. The Gravitron. I remember it looked like a flying saucer racked on the back of a fifty-foot trailer so the proprietor could transport it from fair to fair. You boarded the ship through a sliding door much like you might see in a science-fiction movie about Martians."

Who knew Ceepak watched those?

"The Gravitron had been designed to simulate NASA's astronaut experiments using centrifugal force to generate the gravitational pull encountered during blastoff and space travel."

"Same with the Hell Hole," I say, remembering my queasy spin before they shut it down.

We cross underneath the Garden State Parkway overpass and keep heading west. Avondale is about three miles up the road so we have time for Ceepak to reminisce, although I'm curious how he's going to make the logic leap from g-forces to our current investigation into Shareef Smith's staged suicide.

"Do you recall how you felt when the room began to rotate?" he asks.

"Sure. Like your head was locked in a neck brace."

"An apt description, Danny. As the speed increases, you barely realize you're moving because everything you can see is moving with you. You can't turn your head from side to side. All you can see is whatever's right in front of your eyes."

In the Hell Hole, it was the guy in the devil horns pushing buttons in the booth at the circle's center.

"Such has been the ride Corporal Smith's killer has sent us on. We have only seen what he wanted us to see."

"How do you mean?"

"He put the tissue paper ring around Smith's neck to stop anyone from seeing blood on the floor, orchestrating a delay of the body's discovery."

"But some blood trickled down the back wall and he had to come back to mop it up."

"Again, he was concerned with what would be seen and when it would become visible."

"So what else did he want us to see?"

"For one, the cartoon devil on the Hot Stuff heroin packet."

"He left that there on purpose?"

"I believe so. Remember, the packet was only one piece of the drug paraphernalia found scattered in the adjoining stall. Clearly, the killer wanted us to know that Shareef Smith abused drugs. It would help justify the apparent suicide."

True. Slominsky came in, saw a suicide, saw the drugs, case closed.

"But, wait—then we started investigating the Hot Stuff heroin."

"And, the killer was clearly aware of our efforts. Knew that the trail of clues would eventually lead us to a boarded-up ride on a fenced-off pier. By seeing only what the killer intended for us to see, we ended up exactly where he wanted us."

Well, almost. I think he actually wanted us in body bags.

"Danny, why do you suppose Shareef Smith had a MapQuest printout tucked into his shirt pocket? Why did he even need a map to find his way to the party house if he was meeting Lieutenant Worthington at the rest stop?"

"Yeah. I wondered about that. Earlier. Honest."

"I'm sure you did. More specifically, why did Smith need to write down Lieutenant Worthington's cell phone number when we know he already had it captured in his own phone? Why was that number written where the police were certain to see it?"

"Because whoever did this wanted the state troopers to call the house on Kipper Street when they found the body?"

"Exactly. They also wanted someone from the Sea Haven police department to witness that incoming call."

Geeze-o, man. The killer wanted me, or some other cop, to see the soldiers partying it up at 1:00 AM, to give whoever did it an alibi.

"So many beers . . ." I mumble.

"Come again?"

"That's why there were so many empty beer bottles heaped in the recycling bin when Starky and I got there Friday night."

Ceepak nods. "Exactly. Evidence that they had all been at the house drinking all night long."

"Even if one of them had actually run down to the rest area to meet up with Worthington and Shareef," I say. "But wait—Smith's toilet stall was locked. The janitor had to use his pocket knife to flip the latch up."

Ceepak nods. He's obviously already considered this. "Do you remember the layout of Smith's stall?"

"Yeah. Sure. I mean the toilet stalls in every men's room in the world are basically the same. You go in the door, there's a wall behind the toilet, some kind of panels on both sides."

"And how high off the floor are those two side walls?"

"About a foot. Maybe more."

"Do you think you could crawl underneath them?"

"On the wet floor of a public toilet?"

"Think like a killer."

"Yeah. Okay. If there was a dead guy sitting on top of the toilet with half his brain splattered against the rear wall, yeah, I could crawl under that side panel pretty fast."

"The locked door was just another item the killer wanted us to see. To make Smith's death look like it *had* to be a suicide."

"Well, where the hell was Smith's drug buddy Worthington while all this was going on?"

"We'll discuss that later," says Ceepak, avoiding my question because, like he told me earlier, he has his theory but not the motive. "Pull in here."

I turn into the Holiday Inn's parking lot and glance up into the rearview mirror again.

They're right behind me.

Good. Maybe these two are legit. I hope so. I'm starting to think we might need a small army to go up against the clever bastard who took out Smith and almost nailed me and Ceepak—twice!

# 36

*Okay, this* is seriously spooky.

As I'm sliding the transmission up into park, I see a flurry of activity in the parking space beside us. The big man, Cyrus Parker, comes flying out of the shimmering black SUV like a twinkle-toed hippopotamus. His buddy, Graves, comes around the front bumper of their vehicle and tramples a flower bed. Both bodyguards are swiveling their heads side to side like they're tank turrets, scanning the horizon, scoping out potential threats.

"Clear!" Parker yells.

"Clear!" Graves agrees.

Ceepak and I haven't even opened our doors yet. The two men in the dark suits are flanking both sides of our cruiser. I feel like the president climbing out of his limo or Justin Timberlake arriving at the MTV awards. Parker is staring at the building in front of us. All I see are some shrubs, a motel lobby, and four stories of brick, glass, and rubber-backed curtains.

Graves is staring the other way. Toward the highway and the Holiday Inn sign where the reader board welcomes all the guests celebrating Chuck and Charlotte Gudorp's 30th Wedding Anniversary.

I look over at Ceepak in the passenger seat.

I notice he's checking his weapon. I do the same.

We step out of the vehicle. Now Ceepak is the one scanning the horizon. I do the same. I don't see any trouble. Just some guy wrestling suitcases out of his trunk while his wife watches and tells him how he could do it better.

"Thank you, gentlemen," Ceepak says to Parker. "We'll take it from here." He steps onto the sidewalk that leads up a small slope to the canopied driveway in front of the main lobby. I follow.

"One second, sir," says Parker. "Bravo team, report." This he says to his sleeve.

I hear sound leak out of his earpiece like somebody playing their iPod too loud: "Clear, sir." Now I see a triple flash of headlights up the hill, another colossal SUV in the parking lot on the far side of the sheltered entryway. It's parked alongside an empty state police cruiser. I'm wondering who's guarding the two Worthingtons since half the D.C. crew seems to be on Danny and Ceepak duty today.

"The advance team indicates you're good to go," Parker reports.

"Roger that," says Ceepak.

Wow. They sent an advance team and Starky got us state troopers? Forget Justin Timberlake. We're Brad Pitt.

Ceepak and I continue up the curving concrete pathway.

"Don't you think this is kind of overkill?" I whisper while we walk.

"Perhaps," Ceepak whispers back. "Or perhaps Parker and his team know who and what we're up against. At this point in time, I welcome any and all assistance to insure the safety of Smith's sisters."

"What about your mom?"

"She and Rita have already evacuated to a more secure location."

"Will I get to meet her later?"

"Sorry, Danny. Given my father's arrival, I feel it best to limit knowledge of her whereabouts to immediate family members only."

"I'll bet she's a great lady."

"That she is. Springsteen could've written a song about her similar to the one he wrote for his own mother."

I can't believe this. We're strolling up a sidewalk under the watchful eye of bodyguards in case some unseen enemy tries to kill us for the third time in one day and we're still swapping Springsteen trivia.

"Which song?" I ask, mostly so I don't think about what an easy target I am right now.

"'The Wish.' You'll find it on the *Tracks* album."

"Any specific lyrics?"

"We should probably discuss that later, Danny." He gestures toward the double doors.

I see what he sees: Samantha Starky, frantically waving both arms over her head like she's lining up an F-14 Tomcat for a landing on an aircraft carrier. Inside the glass walls of the lobby, she has her own personal bodyguards: William Wilson Goodson, Jr. and a female trooper with some serious New Jersey–authorized firepower strapped to her hip.

"We're in here, sir!" The glass muffles Starky's shout.

Ceepak motions for Starky to stay where she is. She retreats a half step. Now I can see Tonya and Jacquie Smith behind her. They step backwards too. We enter the lobby. We are not greeted by a hail of bullets.

"Good evening, officers," Ceepak says to the troopers.

"Good to see you again, sir," says Wilson.

"Any trouble?" Ceepak asks.

"No, sir."

"Except the towels," says Jacquie. "We needed more hand towels but I guess somebody forgot to send any up." She says it loud enough for the terrified woman in the blue blazer behind the front desk to hear.

"We have plenty of fresh towels at police headquarters," says Ceepak. "We also have a shower in the women's locker room."

"What's going on?" asks Tonya.

"You're coming back to Sea Haven with us."

"You arresting us?" demands Jacquie.

"No. We simply want to insure your continued safety by transferring you to the most secure location we know."

"What?" asks Tonya. "Why?"

"This location has been compromised."

There's a whoosh of hot outdoor air behind us. I spin around. Expect to see the enemy. It's Parker.

"We need to move, sir," he says to Ceepak. "Now."

"Who's he?" snaps Jacquie.

"A friend," says Ceepak.

"Whose friend?"

"Yours," says Parker. "I'm sorry for your loss, ladies." He's not directly addressing the two sisters because his head is too busy swinging back and forth looking for trouble.

"Ladies?" Ceepak gestures toward the door. "You'll ride with Officer Boyle and myself. Troopers? Could you please follow behind us and transport Officer Starky back to base?"

"Will do." says the one named O'Loughlin. I figure she likes to drive. Fast.

"We'll lead the way," says Parker. "Smith sisters on the move," he says into his sleeve.

"Clear," leaks out of his left ear again.

Parker pushes open the door and all the armed individuals form this phalanx around the two scared sisters and the one weaponless part-time summer cop—all following a six-foot-six bear in a dark-blue suit and sunglasses.

I just hope we don't scare off any of the Gudorps' party guests.


We make it back to police headquarters in Sea Haven at 7:15 PM without incident.

No roadside bombs. No tire blowouts. No drive-by shootings. But I think I just got a small idea of how it must've felt for Ceepak when he was over in Iraq, driving in a convoy, just waiting for all hell to break loose on an innocent-looking stretch of road. I have never been so glad to pull into our own parking lot. We're in the Green Zone again. Behind the wire where the bad guys can't get us. At least I don't think they can. Inside, we have shotguns and stuff. Tear gas too.

Ceepak asks me to escort the Smith sisters to the interrogation room. He moves over to a quiet corner behind the front desk to have a quick word with Parker. As I walk the two women up the hall, I look over my shoulder and see Parker nodding. Ceepak shakes his hand and

Parker hurries out the front door, talking to his sleeve, ready to do whatever Ceepak just asked him to do—that is, if he's really on our team and
not just pretending.

"Would you ladies like a soft drink?" Ceepak asks when he joins us at
the conference table. "Coffee?"

"No, thank you," says Tonya.

"You got a Sprite?" asks Jacquie.

"I think we can arrange that."

I start up from the table because, as the junior partner, I'm usually
the soft-drink-fetcher. Ceepak gestures for me to sit back down. Then
he nods toward the mirrored wall.

"Officer Starky will handle the refreshments."

Guess Ceepak wants me in here with him. Cool.

"Ms. Smith?" Ceepak says to Tonya. "Do you know where we might
find your brother's digital camera? We suspect it contains photographs
he intended to show to me."

She shakes her head. "No. I don't even know if he still has it. We
gave it to him before he shipped overseas that first time. But, like I told
you before, he hasn't e-mailed us any pictures all year. I think he
may've lost it over there—"

"He broke it," says Jacquie.

"In Iraq?" asks Ceepak.

"No. My place. Last week."

Tonya looks surprised to hear it. "Jacquie?"

"He came over for dinner. He was stoned again."

"When?" asks Tonya.

"Wednesday. You had to work the late shift, remember?"

Tonya nods. "Shareef dropped me off at the hospital. Borrowed the
car. That was in the afternoon. Three PM. He wasn't high or I swear I
would not have given him the keys."

"Well, sister, he was ring-dang-doo ripped when he came by my
place. Almost drove through my garage door. I ran out to see what happened after I heard him hit my garbage cans. I was carrying my Kodak

because I wanted to get a picture of Shareef looking sharp in his uniform before he shipped back, only he wasn't wearing it."

"And it was on Wednesday that he told you about damaging his own camera?" asks Ceepak.

"Oh, he didn't tell me. He saw my camera and started screaming how cameras don't do nothing but give you nightmares. Then he reached into that car, practically crawled through the window, and came out with the Sony we gave him all clutched up in his fist."

Tonya lowers her head.

"All of a sudden," Jacquie continues, "Shareef cocks back his arm and winds up like he's pitching for the Orioles and hurls that little camera right up against the side of my house. I heard it hit the brick and break but that wasn't enough for Shareef because, like I said, the poor boy was on some kind of drugs that made him mean and nasty. So first he lets loose with a string of the foulest language I ever did hear and then kicks that little camera out into the street. I say, 'Shareef, you know how much that Sony cost your sister and me?' He doesn't answer. Just stands there staring at that camera lying in the middle of the road. I yell at him, tell him to go fetch it, and maybe we can take it in and have it fixed but it's like he's asleep and can't hear a word I'm saying."

I hear Tonya sob. Hell, if this keeps up, I might join her.

"Then," says Jacquie, sadness creeping into her voice too, "this big ol' truck came rumbling up the road. Garbage truck. One of those big demolition company ones. Had a dirty teddy bear strapped to the front grille. We both heard it crush Shareef's camera. Heard the metal snap, the lens crunch. That's when Shareef finally turned around to face me. You know what he said?"

Ceepak shakes his head.

"He said, 'What's for dinner, sis?'"

# 37

The digital camera everybody's been trying to find? It doesn't exist.

Shareef didn't have it in his car when he drove up to see Ceepak or meet Worthington or do whatever it was he meant to do when he headed north on the Garden State Parkway Friday night. Whatever was recorded on its memory stick has been forever erased by a dump truck.

Starky brought Jacquie her Sprite but Jacquie didn't drink any of it. She also offered to bring them dinner but neither sister was hungry.

"If you change your minds," said Ceepak, "just let Officer Starky know. She'll get you anything you want."

Starky sat down at the table, right next to Jacquie. Then she reached out her hand. "I'm so sorry," she said. Jacquie looked up. Took Starky's hand. Truth be told, there are some things Officer Samantha Starky can do a whole lot better than I'll ever be able to.


Ceepak and I head across the hall to the tech room.

"Should I go get the CD player so Tonya can identify it?"

"Not now, Danny. Let's give the sisters some time."

"Sure."

"I'd like to look at the crime-scene photographs. The CSI team's and yours."

"The ones I took with the cell phone?"

"Roger that."

"They're on the Web."

I feel like a walking advertisement for Verizon's PixPlace. *Lose your cell phone in a near fatal car wreck? Don't worry—you don't have to lose your pictures when you almost lose your life!*

Ceepak halts at the tech room door, his hand frozen on the knob.

"We're missing something, Danny."

"Yeah. The motive. Shareef Smith's pictures."

"Something else. Something that's not right in front of our faces. Something the killer didn't want us to see."

He's riding the Gravitron again. Trying to wrench his head away from the wall and look to his left or right and see what's right there where no one wants him looking.

"Well, let's go find it!" I say, probably sounding way too gung-ho for anybody except Ceepak.

"Roger that!"

He pushes open the tech room door with renewed vigor. Ceepak rallies faster than anybody I know. However, his surge of energy nearly evaporates when we hear the tender strains of a love song wafting out of Denise Diego's computer speakers.

And then it cuts out because Diego just heard us walk in.

"Sorry for the mushy music, guys," she says, one hand on her computer keyboard, the other buried wrist-deep in a bag of cool ranch Doritos. "I'm cutting together a slide show for my friends' wedding. Casey and Michele. It's a *This Is Your Life* type deal set to music to embarrass the hell out of 'em both at the rehearsal dinner."

On the computer screen I see a young boy, about six, with a baseball bat propped on his shoulder, his Cubs cap cocked sideways like only a Sears portrait photographer would do. I guess when your name is Casey your folks are required to have at least one photo with you at the bat.

Diego pushes a few buttons, the hard drive grinds, and the screen goes blank.

"I was killing time till you guys told me what we needed to do next." She swipes her palms together, rubs away the Dorito crumbs. "What's up?"

"The crime-scene photographs provided by Saul Slominsky," says Ceepak. "We need to take another look."

"No problem." Diego punches a couple keys. "I scanned them all in earlier. Makes it easier to access and manipulate the imagery."

Now instead of a cute kid named Casey at the bat, we are presented with the gruesome image of the recently deceased Shareef Smith, dried blood streaming down in thick rivulets out of both nostrils, that grisly paintball splatter of gray-and-red just above and to the left of his wrenched-back head.

"What about the floor?" says Ceepak.

Diego moves her cursor across a row of thumbnails. Finds the close-up shot of the floor where it connects to the rear wall.

"Here we go."

She clicks and we once again see the smear where somebody wiped off the drizzle from the bottommost row of tiles.

Ceepak rubs his temples. He's not seeing anything new. We already know this part of the story.

"What about the picture Danny took with his cell phone?"

"It's not very good," I remind him. "Low resolution. The camera phone only has about two pixels."

"I realize that," says Ceepak. "Still, I'd like to reexamine it."

"Hang on."

A couple grinds and whirrs later, we're viewing my online photo album. Diego moves her mouse and clicks.

Great.

It's the stupid snapshot of Saul Slominsky standing like a smiling bozo in front of the sinks—posing for the keepsake portrait he thought I wanted when I first pulled out my cell phone and powered up the camera.

"Uh, not that one," I say. "The next shot shows the crime scene."

Ceepak raises a hand.

"Just a second."

He leans in. Studies the screen.

"Can you enlarge it, Officer Diego?"

"The whole thing?"

"No. I'm most interested in this area." He taps the screen.

"Behind him?"

"Right. The mirror."

"Pretty big flash burst is all I see," she says, "but you want it, you got it."

More keys click and clack.

"How's that?"

"Can you sharpen it?"

"Yeah. Hang on. Here we go." Click.

"Adjust contrast."

Click.

"Good. Excellent. Who are they, Danny?"

"Who?"

"There. From the reflection in the mirror I see what appear to be two men hunched over in the stall immediately next to the one where Smith's body was found."

Now it's my turn to lean in and stare.

"Oh, yeah. Two CSI guys. They were in there collecting the drug paraphernalia off the floor."

"Both of them?"

"Yeah. It's the handicapped stall so, you know, it's bigger than the other ones."

Ceepak smiles.

I'm not exactly sure why. Maybe he thinks it's funny: two grown men on their hands and knees, scooting across the grungy floor of a public bathroom, bagging and tagging evidence off tiles smudged gray by shoe dirt mixed with urine. No. Wait. Ceepak wouldn't find that funny. It's what he'd do.

The smile means something else.

"What's up?" I ask.

"It's the final piece of the puzzle, Danny. It's how they did it."

The smile just grew wider.

"*They?*" I say.

Ceepak nods but doesn't say anything because his big brain just figured out something else too. I can tell. It's in his eyes.

"Officer Diego?"

"Sir?"

"When you attend this wedding, how will you transport your musical slide show?"

"How do you mean?"

"Well, do you transfer everything to a portable computer, then take that unit with you?"

"I could, but the wedding's in Chicago and I don't like to fly with my laptop, so I'll just burn a disk. The restaurant will hook me up with a computer and projector on the other end."

Ceepak nods. "Danny?"

"Sir?"

"Now would be a good time to retrieve Tonya Smith's CD changer. More specifically, I'd like you to bring in the magazine holding its six music disks."

38

*All six* slots of the disk changer are filled.

Drowning Pool's *Desensitized.*

An Echo Company home mix—the CD with Quiet Riot's "Cum on Feel the Noize" burned into it. Most of the music on that particular playlist is heavy metal because, I guess, that's what war sounds like. Steel ripping. Hot iron screeching. Rage thrashing through your brain.

CD number three is a gospel collection. A dozen songs entreating the Almighty to have mercy on the singer's soul and not let him be forsaken in the Valley of The Shadow of Death, which could be another name for Iraq.

Smith also seemed to like rap. He has *Big Boi and Dre Present Out-Kast* featuring their hit "B.O.B" (Bombs Over Baghdad).

And then there's the one disc without any music.

A data-only CD.

Shareef Smith's slide show, we presume.

We also presume he wasn't intending on taking it to a friend's wedding in Chicago. He was coming to Sea Haven to share it with John Ceepak.

That disk had been slipped into the fourth slot, so it would be camouflaged by the music-filled CDs on either side.

Ceepak pulls on his evidence gloves and extracts the disk.

"I suspect he sent a photo or two from this disk to Senator Worthington," he says.

"E-mail?" asks Diego.

"Negative. I surmise he transferred the data to his cell phone."

"Sure," says Diego. "You can do that."

"It would explain the data call on his phone bill," I add, because I'm always the guy stating the obvious.

Ceepak rotates the slim CD and it catches a flare from a halogen work lamp. On the less shiny side, Smith had written a crude label with a black Sharpie marker: AL HAHMUDIYAH—NOV. 19.

"Who's Al Hahmudiyah?" I ask.

"It's a place, Danny. A small village about fifteen kilometers southwest of Baghdad in an area often referred to as the triangle of death."

Geeze-o, man. This is going to be bad, I know it.

"Can we look at this on your computer?" he asks Diego, who's staring at the CD as if it's toxic—which it probably is.

"Yeah. Sure. Hang on."

She depresses the eject button and the computer's disk tray slides out.

"Just lay it down in there," she says to Ceepak.

He does.

The door slides shut.

"If they're 'jpg' or 'tiff' pictures, I can open them with Adobe Photoshop."

Ceepak just nods.

"Maybe I should make a backup of the whole file first," Diego now suggests. "It's my standard protocol."

"Is there some risk that Photoshop will irreparably damage the images?"

"No," Diego admits. "Not really." She was just stalling. Hey, I don't blame her. We're about to see what kind of digital photographs can get a man killed.

"Let's view the photos first, make the backup later." Ceepak's voice is steady, his eyes riveted on the screen.

Diego clicks on the icon for Adobe's Photoshop program.

It takes a moment to load and then its browser presents us with all the readable files currently residing on Diego's computer. She ignores the folder labeled *C&M Wedding* and clicks on the round icon for Smith's CD.

Now the two-dozen photos line up like a miniaturized Sunday-morning comic strip of half-inch boxes—six columns across, four rows deep. Staring over Diego's shoulder, my first impression is a sea of brown: desert dust, adobe buildings, and chocolate-chip-camo battle fatigues.

"Start at image one," says Ceepak. "Enlarge it."

She does.

It's a full-framed shot of some sort of sign. Maybe a T-shirt stretched across a square of plywood. The shirt is desert-camo tan and sports a grinning skull and crossbones, sort of like a Jolly Roger, only the skull is wearing a helmet and the crossbones are automatic weapons, probably M16 assault rifles. Above the helmet, in a curving headline, is written *ECHO COMPANY*. On one side of the skull: *MESS WITH THE BEST*. On the other: *DIE LIKE THE REST*.

"Next picture."

Diego clicks forward.

It's all of them. Dixon, Handy Andy, Rutledge, Worthington, Smith, and Hernandez. The six men scowl like angry rappers on an album cover and are wearing olive drab T-shirts with the left sleeves rolled up to expose something they've inked on their upper arms in the same spot where triathletes scrawl their numbers.

"Can you zoom in on one of those arms?" Ceepak asks.

"Yes, sir."

She does it and we're tight on a pixilated pair of letters: *J.S.*

"What does it means?" Ceepak asks the room, which is stone-cold silent except for the fan motor buzzing inside Diego's computer.

"*J.S.* could be John Sullivan," I say. "He was a soldier with Echo Company who was killed by an improvised explosive device. Dixon told Starky and me about it on the drive down to the rest area."

I figure the *J.S.* temporarily tattooed on their shoulders is some sort of memorial for a fallen brother. I glance at Smith in the group photograph. He looks like I've never seen him before. Angry and fully alert. He doesn't appear to be on any kind of drug other than raw hate.

"I wonder who took the picture?" asks Diego.

"They could've done it with the camera's auto-timer," I suggest.

"Inconsequential," says Ceepak. "So far they're simply soldiers posing for a group portrait. Let's view the next image, please."

Diego clicks forward.

The nightmare begins.

Shareef Smith is no longer in the shot. He's behind the camera. Recording the horror for posterity.

It's Sergeant Dixon in full battle gear. Helmet strapped on tight. Goggles down. His assault rifle is aimed at an old man in a wheelchair. The old man has his hands up. He's surrendering. He's begging for his life. Dixon is smirking.

"Next photo."

Dixon blew the old man's head off. His white robes and what's left of his white beard are now black with blood. His wheelchair is lying on its side, like somebody kicked it over. Dixon mugs for the camera, a cigar clamped between his teeth. In the background, I can see three elderly women in black burkas. They're kneeling on the ground, screaming, pleading with two other soldiers. Handy Andy and Rutledge, I think.

"Next."

The camera is tighter on the other two now. Rutledge is brandishing his weapon over the wailing women. Handy Andy is rigging up wires to the oldest one's hands, wrapping bare copper around her wrists, making her look like Jesus praying in the garden. I see a car battery sitting in the rocky sand near his left boot.

"Next."

The two soldiers pose triumphant over the three dead bodies. They both have their rifles resting against their hips, their fists raised high like they just brought the noize.

"Next."

Handy Andy dumped the car battery's acid on one elderly woman's face. You can see the burn marks where it scorched the fabric around the eye slit on her headpiece.

"Next." Ceepak is barely audible.

Lieutenant Worthington. He's shoving a young girl, a teenager, down to the dirt floor inside a small hovel. I see other girls, their clothing ripped off, their faces bruised and battered, trying to cover their breasts.

Ceepak doesn't say anything. Diego clicks on.

Worthington rapes the teenager. Beside him, maybe waiting his turn, is Miguel Hernandez—his M16 aimed at the young girl's head.

Click.

A group shot. The soldiers posed near naked bodies stacked like cordwood in the middle of the same room.

Jesus. This is worse than Abu Ghraib. Worse than Haditha. Worse than anything I ever thought human beings could do to each other.

Diego is clicking faster. The photos stream by, a string of unrelenting savagery. Dixon and his men look like they're enjoying themselves immensely. Smith too. Occasionally, he steps out from behind the camera to join in on the fun.

We see Hernandez and Rutledge, taking turns kicking another old man, this one clutching a Koran. In the distance, you can make out the dome and minarets of a mosque. Maybe the man was a mullah.

The six-member strike team moves through Al Hahmudiyah like a well-oiled killing machine. Each man appears to have his individual assignment. Handy Andy, Hernandez, and Rutledge round up a group of targets. Dixon, Worthington, and Smith gun them down.

Maybe Echo Company wiped out the whole village that November 19. Maybe they burned it down because in one picture, Handy Andy empties a can of kerosene on top of a pile of dead bodies while Rutledge stands by, ready to ignite it with the glowing stub of his cigar.

I'm thinking after November 19 is when Shareef Smith started fighting "the pain" with heroin. He had journeyed into the valley of the shadow of death and discovered that he was the one casting the shadow.

"Enough," says Ceepak. "Enough."

Diego nods. She can't speak. Neither can I.

"Please print a copy of the thumbnails. We need to take that with us."

Diego swivels in her chair, puts photo paper in the printer. The mechanical motions give her something to do besides remember what we've just seen.

"Then go ahead and make that backup copy of the disk. Put it in the safe. I'll ask Sergeant Pender to station an armed guard outside the evidence room."

"Okay," says Diego.

"We have our motive," I mumble. "We know why they killed Smith."

Ceepak nods. "We also know how they did it."

"We do?"

He nods again. "The same way, Danny. They brought Al Hahmudiyah home with them."

# 39

*I need* a shower. Mouthwash. A time machine. Something to make it all go away.

Instead, we press on.

Ceepak and I head up the hall toward the front desk. Starky is there, juggling a couple cans of Sprite and chip bags from the vending machine.

"The sisters got thirsty," she says. "And hungry."

Ceepak nods. She sees his grim face.

"Everything okay, sir?"

Ceepak's eyelids look about as heavy as mine. For the first time in a long while, he doesn't paste on his jaunty smile and tell the world, *"It's all good."*

"We found Smith's photographs."

He need say no more. Starky can tell: it's all bad.

"You guys heading back out?"

Ceepak nods. "I need to make a phone call first. . . ."

"Rita?"

"No. Cyrus Parker."

"Wait a sec . . ." Starky unclips the cell phone from her belt. "I'm going to be here all night with the Smith sisters. If I need a phone, I can use one of the landlines so you guys can take this since, you know, yours don't work anymore."

Starky's cell is wrapped up inside a pink leatherette holder that looks like my mother's old cigarette case, but Ceepak takes it anyway.

"Thank you."

"No problem, sir."

Starky bops up the hall with her snack food items.

Ceepak flips open the clamshell. Finds a scrap of paper in his top pocket: Parker's mobile number.

"Cyrus? John Ceepak. I wanted you to know—we found Smith's photographs." His eyes narrow. "Worse. Right. How are things at your end? Appreciate it. Roger that." He closes up the phone, clips it to his belt.

"You still trust Parker?" I ask.

"I do. And soon, we'll discover whether that trust is warranted."

"I don't know—those guys in the pictures. They're all soldiers too."

"Which makes what they did even worse. Let's roll."

"Where to?"

"The house on Kipper Street. It's time for the men of Echo Company to answer for at least one of their crimes."


When we come down the front steps of police headquarters, Parker's partner Graves is standing on the sidewalk waiting for us.

He's with one of the senator's other bodyguards—a white guy almost as big around as Parker. It's nearly 8:30, the sun has slipped down over the bay, but these two still have on their sunglasses and, judging by the bulges beneath the breast flaps of their suit coats, I'd say they're also wearing their weapons. I notice the big guy checking out Ceepak's belt. Guess he saw the pink princess phone. Hope he saw the Glock too.

"Officers?" says Graves, as he gives us the palm of his hand.

"Yes?" says Ceepak.

"Did you locate Smith's photographs?"

Ceepak pauses for just an instant. Hey, us finding Smith's photographs is none of his damn business unless, of course, all this major-league cooperation from Parker and the rest of Senator Worthington's crew was only given in order that we would find what they couldn't.

I knew Parker was a bad guy. But Ceepak trusted him. Trusted the Code. Which, by the way, also means my partner will now feel compelled to tell this other thug the truth.

"Did you find the photographs?"

Ceepak nods.

"Excellent. The senator will be happy to hear it. This way." He gestures toward the SUV illegally parked at the curb—another black GMC, a Yukon, I think.

"We have our own vehicle." Ceepak takes a step up the sidewalk. Graves moves to block him.

"The senator needs to speak to you."

"Tell him to call during normal business hours and we'll set something up."

Another step, another block.

"He needs to speak with you now."

"*Now* doesn't work for me."

"Me, neither," I chime in.

"Get in the car."

It's my turn to take a step to my left and the other tough guy's turn to block me.

Then I hear Graves's earpiece cackle.

"Target acquired" leaks out of it.

I look over at Ceepak. There's a red dot holding steady in the center of his forehead—somebody playing with a laser pointer or a sniper lining up a shot from yet another SUV.

"Maybe we should go with them," I suggest.

Grudgingly, Ceepak agrees.


They confiscate our weapons, promising that we'll get them back after we have our little meeting with the senator.

"Sorry we need to do it this way," says Graves from the front seat. He's on the passenger side. Gigantor is behind the wheel. A GMC Denali with tinted windows is tailing us. My guess? Parker. The liar who lied about not tolerating liars.

We're headed south. Down to the golden tip of Sea Haven where the rich folk live.

"Where are you taking us?" asks Ceepak.

"The radio lady's mansion. The senator thinks her house will afford the privacy required to discuss pressing matters of national security."

I see. Wiping out the village of Al Hahmudiyah? A very important part of the ongoing war against global terrorism.


We're escorted into Crazy Janey's mansion. The living room, I guess. The ceilings are at least thirty feet high. The walls at the far end are actually windows looking out on the pool and the ocean beyond. The furniture is all white.

Our two escorts bar the front door behind us.

The guys in the other SUV? They didn't get out of their vehicle when we pulled into the driveway. Like good executioners everywhere, they're remaining anonymous. Instead of putting on black hoods, they've rolled around to the backyard where they can cover our asses through Crazy Janey's big plate glass windows. I expect to see the red light of a sniper sight dancing over my heart any second now.

Senator Worthington sweeps in from the kitchen. He's sipping something brown out of a crystal tumbler. He swirls it casually. Ice cubes clink.

"Officers! Good to see you." He says this as if we're all in the clubhouse at his country club. "Thank you so much for coming down today."

"Did we have a choice?" I say because I'm the wise ass on the team.

Worthington ignores me. "Please take a seat, take a seat."

Ceepak stands where he is. Me too.

"Fine," says Worthington. "We can stand if you like. Where are your sidearms?"

"We removed them, sir," says Graves from behind me.

"Really? That wasn't necessary. Officer Ceepak is ex-military. He knows what's at stake here."

"No," says Ceepak, who never likes it when somebody makes up his mind for him. "I do not."

"I'm referring to the incident in Al Hahmudiyah," Senator Worthington continues, crinkling his brow, playing the wise grandfather to Ceepak's petulant child. "A military action that might be misconstrued if viewed out of context by the wrong individuals."

Yeah—people with at least one functioning eyeball.

"Is it a concern? Of course it is. Do these things happen in the fog of war? Heavens, yes. As you know, Lieutenant Ceepak, they are a necessary part of war, especially when dealing with a brutal counterinsurgency— shadowy dead-enders and suicide bombers with no respect for human life."

"The same might be said about the men of Echo Company," says Ceepak.

"No. Not really. But then again, there are extenuating circumstances that I, unfortunately, am not at liberty to discuss. But, surely, as a former student of strategy and tactics, you know it has always been necessary to present the locals in an occupied land with a choice: we can be your best friend or your worst enemy. It's up to them."

"These people were not presented with a choice," Ceepak says back. "They were brutally slain to avenge the death of John Sullivan, a member of Echo Company killed by an insurgent's roadside bomb."

"If what you say is true, the military authorities will mete out the appropriate punishment. However, we must not let this incident become fodder for public debate, where it has the power to deplete already sagging morale."

Or ruin somebody's presidential campaign.

"So you had Shareef Smith murdered?" asks Ceepak. "To cover up the truth?"

"Heavens no. That young man committed suicide. I'm afraid it was a clear case of post-traumatic stress disorder aggravated by an unfortunate intake of narcotics. Something that, as you now know, has plagued my own family."

Now Worthington is giving us his noble father look, artificial concern for his junkie son ridging his furrowed brow.

"My son is a good man," Worthington continues. "Up until the incident today, he had been clean and sober for nearly a year. Was it easy for him? Of course not. Did he reach out to other addicts still in the grip of their addictions? You bet he did. That's what brought him down to that rest area off the Garden State Parkway on Friday night. To tell the truth, it's the whole reason I rented the beach house in Sea Haven for the boys: to help facilitate Corporal Smith's recovery."

Ceepak arches an eyebrow higher than I've ever seen him arch one.

"You rented the house on Kipper Street last Wednesday," Ceepak says. "One day after Shareef Smith text-messaged images from the Al Hahmudiyah massacre from his cell phone to your e-mail address."

"Exactly," says Worthington. "When I received that photograph, I realized just how much mental anguish this brave young soldier was battling."

Geeze-o, man. No wonder the guy made it all the way to senator. He lies better than anyone in Washington, and that's saying something.

"Did you bring the photographs with you?" he asks

Ceepak slowly unclasps the envelope. Lays the contact sheets on Crazy Janey's very classy glass-topped table. Surrounded by all this clean whiteness, the pictures look even bloodier.

"And the originals? Were they on a disk of some sort?"

"Yes."

Senator Worthington motions for the envelope, like Ceepak should hand it over.

So he does.

Because there ain't no disk in it.

"Where is the disk?"

"In a secure location."

"I suppose you made a backup?"

"It's our standard protocol," I say because I can make it sound more sarcastic than Ceepak could.

"We'll need to go back to police headquarters," Worthington says.

"We'll retrieve the original, as well as any and all copies you may have made."

"We can't do that," says Ceepak.

"Excuse me?"

"The disk contains evidence pertinent to an ongoing investigation."

"Didn't I just say that?" the senator asks the universe. "We need to turn the evidence over to the appropriate military authorities so they can investigate this incident without causing undue collateral damage to our brave troops still on the battlefield."

"The Burlington County prosecutor's office needs the evidence as well," says Ceepak.

"Who? For Heaven's sake—I'm talking about the Department of Defense and the global war on terrorism. . . ."

"The Burlington County prosecutor is the woman who will represent the State of New Jersey and Shareef Smith in the murder trial of Dale Dixon, Andrew Prescott, Stephen Rutledge, Miguel Hernandez, and your son, Woodrow G. Worthington."

"Jesus," says a voice behind us. "Once an MP, always an MP."

It's Dixon and everybody from Echo Company except the senator's son.

They're all cradling beers. They don't look armed; guess the senator's bodyguards have that angle covered. They do, however, look totally tanked.

"You want to arrest *all* of us?" Dixon scoffs. "You know what that tells me, Ceepak?"

"No."

"You're on a fishing expedition. You don't know jack shit."

Ceepak grins back at him. "That's where you're wrong, Sergeant Dixon. I know everything."

# 40

*There's* a red dot dancing on Ceepak's chest.

I look down at my own shirt. Looks like they're targeting the bottom button on my polo's two-button collar.

Now the pink cell phone clipped to Ceepak's belt starts to chirp. Starky has a pretty obnoxious ringtone: Keith Urban's "Tonight I Wanna Cry."

"Don't answer that!" snaps Senator Worthington.

Ceepak reaches for the belt. I hear Graves behind us lever back the trigger on whatever kind of hand cannon he is currently aiming at our heads. For good measure, the laser dot swings up to a spot right between Ceepak's eyes. I look down again. No dot on the button. I can't see between my eyes but I'm guessing my executioner has adjusted his aim too.

The phone keeps plunking out its mellow bass line while some kind of synthesized trumpet takes the melancholy melody.

"Do not answer that!" the senator reiterates his position.

"Don't even fucking touch it!" adds Dixon, slurring a few of the words, then taking another long pull off his beer.

Ceepak raises both hands. He will remain in full compliance with the senator's request. Another bar of bad electronic mush blares from his belt. As requested, he does not answer it.

The senator looks annoyed, but he lets the ringtone do its thing.

Of course, this annoying cell phone interruption tells me something: the senator didn't do the GPS-chip cellular-phone-tracking stuff on the Smith sisters himself because he doesn't realize that somebody might be tracking Starky's phone right now and the longer it rings, the better his or her chances of pinpointing our current position.

I'm betting on Tech Officer Denise Diego. She saw the slide show and knows what kind of people we're dealing with. She also knows people over at Verizon. Maybe she guessed why we're not currently responding to any and all radio calls. Maybe, when she ran to the store for a quick Doritos refill, she noticed that our vehicle was still parked in the lot.

Yes, I'm hoping it's Diego pinging us for a GPS location. I'm also praying it's not one of Starky's girlfriends calling for makeup tips.

The synthetic song finally stops.

"So, Officer Ceepak," says Dixon, "tell us what you think happened to the poor little pussy. Tell us how we killed Shareef Smith."

The other men surrounding Dixon swig their beers. Prescott. Rutledge.

But not Hernandez. He looks sick to his stomach.

"Come on!" Now I know for sure Dixon has been drinking all day. He's in one of those pissy troughs that come between beer buzzes. "I want to hear what this hot shit cop from a two-bit tourist trap thinks happened in that goddamn crapper."

"What you are requesting will serve no purpose, Sergeant," says Senator Worthington. "We need to go retrieve that disk."

"That can wait."

"No, Dale. It can not wait."

"Relax, Winny. You're not president yet. I want to hear Ceepak's theories. Might provide us with just cause. Always a good thing for a soldier to have before he kills a man."

"It may take some time," says Ceepak, unfazed by Dixon's threat. "You orchestrated quite a plan, Sergeant. Your men moved as they did in Al Hahmudiyah. Employed the same combat team tactics."

"Hey, take your fucking time. The fridge is fully stocked. Tell us what you think you know. But, choose your words carefully. If we don't like what you say, we'll ask those two gentlemen outside to blow your fucking brains all over Crazy Janey's clean white carpet."

"Honestly, Dale," the senator protests.

"Shut the fuck up, Winny, and sit down."

"Might I remind you that my men are the ones with weapons?"

"Corporal Graves wants to hear this too," says Dixon. "Right, Graves?"

"Roger that," says Graves. I turn my head just enough to see him swing his weapon over to Senator Worthington's general vicinity.

"Graves was Navy," says Dixon. "He, like me, will gladly kill anybody you order us to, provided, of course, you give us a justifiable reason to do so!"

So it's the senator's turn to throw up his hands in defeat. He sits on the sofa.

"Fine," he says. "Hurry up."

"It's a long story," says Ceepak. "A complex plan. Ingenious, actually." He's taking his time. I think he figured out that potential cell-phone-tracking deal six synthesized trumpet bleats before me. He's buying the cavalry riding to our rescue a little more riding time.

"Come on, Ceepak," says Dixon. "Show me what you got!" He settles back into that chair like he's ready to watch a good baseball game.

And so Ceepak begins.

"For some time, Shareef Smith felt remorse over the actions of Echo Company on nineteen November in the Iraqi village of Al Hahmudiyah. The rape and murder of the locals was, in my estimation, undertaken as an act of revenge for the death of John Sullivan, a member of Echo Company who was a casualty of an insurgent's roadside bomb."

"The fucking cowards blew his legs off!" snarls Dixon. "Set it off with a cell phone."

Ceepak nods. He's been there. Seen that.

"Months earlier," he continues and turns to face the senator, "your own son had been the target of an Iraqi sniper. A wound that deservedly earned him the Purple Heart and should've warranted him a ticket home. However, I sense that you, sir, had other priorities and requested that he remain in country to shore up your political ambitions."

"Come on, Ceepak," says Dixon. "This is ancient history. Get to the good stuff so the men outside can kill you with a clean conscience."

Ceepak nods again. He's being very amiable.

Buying more time.

"Last week, while on leave in Baltimore, Corporal Smith attempted to make contact with Senator Worthington. He called your office several times because he believed what you say on TV: that you're the American soldier's best friend in Washington."

"Hernandez?" Dixon yells. "I need another beer here."

Hernandez slogs off to the kitchen to fetch it.

"Go on, Ceepak. I'm enjoying this."

Ceepak faces Senator Worthington. "Frustrated by your refusal to accept his calls, Smith sent you an e-mail with evidence of the atrocities attached."

"Watch your choice of words, son," warns the senator. "*Atrocity* is an inappropriate descriptor for the execution of a time-honored counterinsurgency tactic."

"When you still refused to talk to him, Smith decided to come see me."

Funny. No one's disputing this.

"Meanwhile," Ceepak continues, "you ordered your son to call Smith and find out what he intended to do with his photographs. When he mentioned my name, your son volunteered to help Smith deliver the evidence. I suspect you forced your son into performing this task, Senator. I believe your son to be an honorable man."

Meaning, of course, the father isn't.

"You then had your staff use their contacts within the D.O.D. to locate me. Easy enough to accomplish. I keep current on any and all requests for personal data that come in from the Army."

Of course he does.

"When you discovered that I was currently employed by the Sea Haven police department, you had your office rent one of the few beach houses still available on the island. The house at twenty-two Kipper Street where my partner first met Sergeant Dixon and the others."

Ceepak gestures in my general direction. Doesn't matter. My out-door sniper already knows who I am.

"Your son was apparently quite persuasive. He convinced Smith to delay contacting me until after they had both attended an Echo Company party at the Jersey shore. Maybe your son further enticed Smith with an invitation to the gala to be held here on Saturday night. Maybe he promised Smith that he would finally get to meet you. Have a face-to-face conversation about his concerns. I'm not sure how he persuaded Smith; I just know he was successful. Otherwise, I'm certain, Smith would've called to tell me he was coming."

Hernandez returns to the living room with a whole six-pack of beer. He yanks a can out of the plastic rings and tosses it to Dixon. Handy Andy and Rutledge reach out and grab cans too. Ceepak presses on.

"Smith and your son made arrangements to meet at the exit fifty-two rest area where they'd further discuss their plans for bringing the Al Hahmudiyah massacre to your attention. Smith promised to bring his photographic evidence. Lieutenant Worthington would then escort Shareef to the party house because, as he no doubt explained, all the beach houses up and down our island look pretty similar. A map wouldn't do Smith much good."

"So why the hell did he have one in his damn pocket?" asks a very drunk Dixon.

"Because you put it there where the police could easily find it."

"You found fingerprints?"

"No."

"Like I said, soldier: you got shit."

Ceepak continues: "Sergeant Dixon and private Hernandez arrived in Sea Haven on Thursday—a day earlier than the others so they could do reconnaissance work at the rest area. In fact, when we subpoena Thursday's tapes from the indoor security camera, I'm quite confident we'll see you two."

"Doing what?"

"Several things. First, of course, locating the interior camera, noting its coverage area. You also paid special attention to the men's room, where I'm certain you examined the posted cleaning schedule. You also observed the night janitor, Mr. Osvaldo Vargas, and noted that he was a close physical match for your man, Mr. Miguel Hernandez. They're both Hispanic. They're both short. What are you? Five-one? Five-two?"

Hernandez doesn't answer. But his eye twitches.

"I suspect we will also see you two roaming through the parking lots, identifying the exterior surveillance cameras. You were most concerned with the two on the northbound side because you knew that's where Lieutenant Worthington would meet Smith."

Now Ceepak gestures toward Handy Andy. "On Friday night, you were, initially, the outside man."

"What? This is such bullshit."

"Your job was to snip the security camera's cable. You're quite good with video equipment. I understand you arranged for free cable at the rental house on Kipper."

"You gonna arrest him for it?" asks Dixon. "Because you still have no proof on this other fairy tale you're telling."

"Sergeant Dixon?" says the senator. "Can we wrap this up? We need to go secure that disk."

"Of course," Ceepak butts in, "he was given very specific instructions as to *when* to snip the cable."

"Oh, really?" Now Senator Worthington is pretending to be bored. "And when would that be?"

"Right after your son showed up. After he and Smith walked together into the rest stop."

Worthington attempts a laugh. "Heavens to Betsy! Sergeant Dixon is right. You have no actual evidence. You're making this up. Concocting lies out of whole cloth."

"No, Senator. We have seen your son and Smith together in the parking lot just after ten PM. Sergeant Dixon made certain to leave an evidence trail that would clearly implicate your son should anyone choose to investigate this incident further."

The senator's glare swings over to Dixon now.

Once again, it's my turn to state the obvious: "Guess if your son was arrested for murder, it could cost you a few million votes, hunh?"

## 41

*I think* they're all going to shut up now.

I think they're going to quit interrupting Ceepak so they can scowl at each other instead. So far, Rutledge is the only one Ceepak hasn't mentioned, but I have a funny feeling the big moose's turn is coming up.

"Shareef Smith arrived at the rest area at twenty-two-oh-three. Three minutes after ten PM. At approximately ten-ten, Hernandez, Rutledge, and Dixon entered the men's room, having seen the night janitor, Osvaldo Vargas, exit after completing his hourly cleaning.

"They set to work. Rutledge and Dixon took up their position in the furthest toilet. The handicapped stall. They had the Russian-made PB/6P9 pistol with them, a war souvenir brought home illegally from Iraq. They attached a full silencer, even though they know the PB/6P9 is quieter than most conventional firearms even without the additional tubing screwed onto its muzzle.

"Mr. Hernandez, disguised as a member of the janitorial staff— something quite easy to accomplish with an appropriately colored polo shirt, baseball cap, and a pair of khakis—proceeded to shut off the right-hand side of the men's room by spooling out the 'closed for maintenance' retracta-belt tape. He also activated the Tornado floor blower to cover any noises that might be made during the coming execution of Corporal Smith.

"Lieutenant Worthington arrived at nine minutes after ten and detained Shareef Smith in the parking lot until he received the go signal from Handy Andy, who was stationed in a vehicle near the security camera stanchion. I note that you gentlemen as well as Lieutenant Worthington all carry Nextel cellular units. The walkie-talkie function comes in quite handy in certain situations, doesn't it?

"Worthington proceeded to lure Smith into the men's room with the promise of a free high. He had procured what is known as Hot Stuff heroin from a Sea Haven drug dealer who has operated undetected for years out of the abandoned Hell Hole ride on Pier Four. Purchasing the illegal substance locally was another attempt by Sergeant Dixon to leave a trail of evidence traceable to Lieutenant Worthington, a man with a known history of drug addiction.

"Worthington escorted Smith into the rest area careful, of course, to avoid the one internal security camera's line of sight. He suggested that they slip into the closed-off section of the men's room to shoot up. He gave Smith the works kit and heroin packet, directed him to what I will label stall number three—the second to last from the wall. I suspect your son then entered what I will label stall number two, where he pretended to inject drugs as well."

Ceepak gestures toward Rutledge and Dixon.

"You gentlemen used the handicapped stall, the oversized unit closest to the wall, as your prep area. You carried in a small gym bag or suitcase holding the silenced pistol as well as some sort of cheap plastic ponchos, which, by the way, are quite easy to obtain at any gift shop here on the island. You've killed up close before, so you knew there would be residual splatter, that your clothing would become spotted with Smith's blood. I'm quite certain the old man you killed in the wheelchair taught you that lesson. But a simple plastic rain poncho was the only precaution you needed to take because you knew a public bathroom would be a forensic field rife with fingerprints, footprints, hair samples, and the DNA of a thousand different strangers. You really didn't have to worry about leaving clues. There were too many already on the floor, the doors, and the walls for any investigator to single out yours. It's probably why you chose the men's room at a rest area as your killing field in the first place.

"Once cloaked in your makeshift aprons, you did a weapons check and bided your time until you heard Worthington and Smith enter. Perhaps they carried on a brief conversation between stalls, commenting on the quality of the local drugs. When you were satisfied that Smith had, indeed, infused the opiate into his veins, you waited a little while longer—knowing that, by now, Handy Andy and Hernandez had effectively closed off the entrance to the rest room.

"Hernandez, in his guise as a member of the custodial crew, was stationed at the main door to the men's room, informing the few travelers seeking the facilities at that hour, that the bathroom was temporarily closed for maintenance. I suspect that Handy Andy, posing as a frustrated tourist, came into the building to help spread the word of the men's room's temporary closure. It's why he was wearing a flowered Hawaiian shirt that night, as witnesses will attest. His costume was a bit of cliché, perhaps, but his back-and-forth dialogue with Hernandez at the entryway undoubtedly had the desired effect. Temporary crowd control.

"I admit that this last bit is conjecture on my part. But, before we bring you gentlemen to trial, we will interview the passengers on the Academy bus that left the Taj Mahal Casino in Atlantic City at nine-twenty-two PM on Friday night. We know they stopped at the exit fifty-two rest area during the hours in question and, although we haven't yet had sufficient time to interview them, I'm quite certain some of the male passengers who were inconvenienced will be happy to identify you, Mr. Hernandez, as the janitor who told them the men's room was temporarily closed. I further suspect they will recognize you, Mr. Prescott. As will the Feenyville Pirates."

"Who?" asks Handy Andy.

"The men who were breaking into the trunk of Shareef Smith's vehicle when you returned to the parking lot to initiate the search for his digital camera. You weren't in the parking lot the whole time; otherwise you never would've let the pirates rifle through Smith's trunk before you had a chance to search it yourself."

Handy Andy says nothing in reply.

"Back inside the men's room, the designated killers stormed into stall three. Smith at that point would, of course, have been docile, already under the influence of what, I'm quite certain, was a heavier-than-usual dose of heroin. One of you gentlemen then lowered the latch on the stall, locking the door from the inside to help paint the suicide picture.

"I suspect you were the one who forced the silenced pistol into Smith's hand," Ceepak says to Rutledge. The muscle. "Did you pull Smith's finger to squeeze back on the trigger or did Sergeant Dixon assume that task himself? Yes, I think it was probably Dixon."

Ceepak paces over toward Dixon's chair.

"I suspect it was also Sergeant Dixon who had the misguided notion to ring Smith's neck with the sanitary seat covers, hoping that the thick stack of tissue would stanch any blood streaming out of Smith's head wound before it dripped down to the floor. To set up your group alibi, you needed to insure that a certain amount of time elapsed before Smith's body was discovered because your entire team had to hurry back to the rental house on Kipper Street. You knew you had nearly an hour before a real janitor returned to the men's room on his rounds and discovered that one side had been inexplicably closed off. Plenty of time for you to return to Sea Haven and wait for whatever public authorities were summoned to the scene to telephone you.

"Of course, you knew they would call. That's why you left the map with Lieutenant Worthington's cell phone number scribbled on it in Smith's pocket.

"Then, Dixon and Rutledge crawled under the side walls of the stall and rejoined Lieutenant Worthington. You walkie-talkied Hernandez, who signaled back that the coast was clear. Hernandez walked away first, so if anyone saw you three gentlemen exiting the men's room, carrying your zipped-up gym bag, where I'm certain you stowed the blood-stained ponchos, they would have simply assumed that the janitor had finished his work and you were the first ones in and out of the reopened facilities. You left the 'closed for maintenance' retracta-belt up to close off the right-hand side as long as possible. You also kept the floor dryer blowing to stop any incoming guests from venturing into the roped-off area for fear of slipping on a freshly mopped floor.

"You then nonchalantly waltzed out of the building and into the parking lot, where you helped Andrew Prescott finish ransacking Smith's car, tearing out the air bags to make the burglary look legitimate. Frustrated in your search but unable to waste more time looking for the camera, you climbed into your vehicles, knowing that Handy Andy has disabled the pertinent surveillance camera that might record your rapid departure. Fifteen or twenty minutes later, you were in Sea Haven, where you pretended to have been partying all night.

"You also needed a witness for your alibi. The best witness, of course, would be someone whose word could not be easily impugned. A police officer, for instance. So, once you had returned to the house on Kipper Street, you cranked up the volume on your stereo system, created as much noise as you could, you even began chanting running cadences—everything you could think of to disturb the peace and incite your neighbors to call nine-one-one. Perhaps one of you gentlemen even called in the noise complaint yourself.

"Officer Boyle and his partner arrived on the scene. They noticed, as you had hoped they would, the curbside recycling bins brimming with empty containers. You knew the state police would probably discover the body sometime after eleven PM and make contact with you after midnight. You couldn't control the precise moment of discovery so you arranged for a van full of strippers to show up, just in case you needed further delaying tactics. Danny and Officer Starky arrived on the scene, the state police called, and you had your alibi. Everything went off as planned. You executed your stratagem with military precision. Unfortunately, you made one mistake. Back in the bathroom. Isn't that right, Mr. Hernandez?"

Hernandez squirms a little at his end of the sofa.

Ceepak moves closer.

"You had the last job. One final sweep of the men's room to make certain no one would notice anything except Shareef Smith's shoes.

Most visitors to the restroom at that hour would suspect that a man in a toilet stall in the closed-off section was doing something lewd or untoward—especially if they were observant enough to notice that his pants weren't rolled down. Afraid to get involved, they'd simply do their own business in the open side and be on their way. However, all that would change, if they saw what you saw when you made that final sweep. Wouldn't it?"

Hernandez doesn't answer but he sure looks squirrelly.

"You saw blood dripping down the back wall. You saw it trickling to the floor. You knew that in short order it would form a noticeable pool. So, being a quick-thinking Airborne Ranger, you showed initiative. You took matters into your own hands and ventured outside the parameters of the approved plan.

"Without hesitation or, if I may say so, thinking, you dashed all the way to the janitor closet on the far side of the food court, where you found a mop and rolling bucket. You were going to clean up Sergeant Dixon's mess again, weren't you? Just like when he makes you fetch his coffee before it's finished brewing and it spills all over the coffeemaker.

"You forgot about the security camera aimed toward the gift shop and food court, didn't you, Private Hernandez? Forgot that it would record your image as you pushed the mop bucket back toward the men's room."

Hernandez bristles but doesn't respond.

"Of course, I admit, when we first viewed the tape, we assumed you were Osvaldo Vargas, the real night-shift janitor. The image was grainy and, as I've already indicated, you two are very similar in build and coloring. However, we recently learned that Mr. Vargas left work early Friday night. In fact, we have his departure on tape. Therefore, the short man with the mop and bucket could not be Osvaldo Vargas. It has to be you.

"You returned to the men's room and, without opening the locked stall door, which you knew to be an important element in the suicide scenario, you attempted to swab away the gathering blood. You poked your mop under the door and thrust it into the stall. You went at it from the sides and left behind the faint streak marks that first indicated to us that the truth behind Smith's death was something besides what we were meant to see. One of your mop shoves accidentally knocked Smith's drug paraphernalia into the adjoining stall. Maybe you didn't see it slide over there. Maybe somebody came into the men's room and you panicked.

"Whatever the reason, Mr. Hernandez, you ruined the master plan. You quickly dumped your dirty water into one of the toilets, flushed it away. You parked the empty bucket in the corner, and hightailed it back to Kipper Street to rejoin the others.

"So tell me, Miguel. The mop? It wasn't in the bucket. Is it still in the backseat of your car?"

# 41

"*All right.* Enough."

Senator Worthington is up and off the couch.

Ceepak keeps going: "I will now tell you how these same soldiers twice attempted to kill my partner and me. The first incident, involving a technique of inserting razor blades—"

"I said enough, Officer Ceepak. Jesus H. Christ, are you retarded?"

"No, sir. I'm in full command of my mental faculties."

"Really? I don't think so. Do you think that I, or any loyal member of the United States government, can stand by and allow you to disseminate misinformation about the war effort? Of course we can't. You're a threat to national security. This sort of negative talk not only undermines the morale of our troops, it serves to embolden our enemies. Mr. Graves?"

Up near the front door, the senator's bodyguard is looking kind of stunned. Guess he was paying attention.

"Sir?"

"You men need to detain these two individuals." The senator points at Ceepak and me.

"What charges, sir?"

"Charges? Goodness, we don't have time for formal charges! This will be a preventive detention as outlined under the Patriot Act."

Graves looks confused. "Preventive detention?"

"The Patriot Act clearly states that we can hold American citizens precisely *because* we do not have sufficient evidence to prove that said citizens have committed a crime meriting detention. Do I wish I had the evidence prior to arresting Ceepak and Boyle? Of course I do. Do I have the time to pursue it while allowing these two individuals to continue spreading their terrorist claptrap? Of course not. September eleventh changed everything."

Graves still doesn't look convinced. In fact, he looks even more confused.

"Besides, what these soldiers did in Al Hahmudiyah was a justified act of war. Goodness, the Romans used the same tactic when battling barbarians! Did you know, Officer Ceepak, that there have been no further attacks out of Al Hahmudiyah since these brave men went in and did what had to be done on nineteen November?"

"What these soldiers did was wrong. In Al Hahmudiyah and at exit fifty-two."

"What do you know about any of this?" says Dixon. "You got out while the getting was good. You cut and ran, Ceepak. Took a nice, cushy job down the shore where you can play MP with the beach babes. Meanwhile, my men are over there, tour after tour, playing 'bend over, here it comes again,' and we're supposed to play nice with the dune niggers after they fuck up one of my best men? You *are* fucking retarded. You pretend to follow the West Point code, even though you could never hack it at the Academy? Fine. Play soldier all you want, you sanctimonious piece of shit, but here's the real code, the only fucking code that counts: I will not tolerate any man who jeopardizes the life of a single member of my unit. Whether it's some old fucking mullah, a crybaby turncoat like Shareef Smith, or a rear-echelon motherfucker like you!"

He turns to Graves.

"Sailor?"

"Sir?"

"Shoot these two individuals. Shoot them now!"

"I don't know. . . ."

Dixon pivots and screams at the other bodyguard blocking the door. The white giant. "Call it in! Tell your snipers to take their shots!"

"Do it!" Senator Worthington says from the couch.

The giant hesitates.

The senator insists: "Do it on my authority!"

The giant's arm starts moving up toward his mouth.

I look down at my shirt.

The red dot is gone.

I check out Ceepak. His is missing too.

I look back at the bodyguard who's just about ready to radio in the strike command. I can't tell who's going to get shot when he does. Then I notice a red dot targeting *his* heart.

"Take them down!" he barks into his sleeve.

I close my eyes. Cringe.

Shots are not fired.

"Take them down!" he orders again.

Still no gunfire.

"Do it yourself!" the senator screams.

The giant whips out what looks like machine gun and I hear glass crack.

"Fuck!"

The giant drops his weapon and shakes his right fist to fling away some of the pain.

Now the front door swings open.

It's another bodyguard, weapon drawn. He's swiveling at the hips, surveiling the situation, aiming his automatic at everybody in the room, and trying to see if anybody is aiming one back at him.

They aren't.

"We're clear," the new guy shouts into his wrist. "Everybody stay where you are!" he yells into the room. "Acquire secondary targets!" This goes back to the wrist.

I check my chest again. I'm clear. Guess I didn't make the "secondary" list.

Senator Worthington, however, did. I see a red dot dancing up and down against his fluffy white hair. Dixon has earned one too.

The glass door leading out to the patio slides open.

Cyrus Parker steps into the living room. He brings his sniper rifle with him.

"Sorry to be late," he says. Now he turns to the giant moaning on the floor up near the front door. "Jesus, Chalhoub—you bought the senator's bullshit?"

Chalhoub the giant, is curled up in a fetal ball the size of a Volkswagen and just keeps groaning, "fuck, fuck, fuck" over and over.

"And you, Graves. This that urgent errand you had to run?"

"Sorry, Cyrus," mumbles Graves.

"Roger that," says Parker, shaking his head. "You are one sorry piece of shit, son."

About six of our cops sweep into the room followed by two more men in blue suits and earpieces. Guess we had four of the senator's former bodyguards on our team; they had four on theirs. It was all even-Steven. Two nervous paramedics run in to take care of Chalhoub.

Now Sam Starky steps through the door.

"Danny? Are you okay?"

"Yeah," I say, "I'm fine."

She's unarmed, so I call out, "Step back, Sam."

Her smile grows broader. "Yes, sir." She moves back to the poolside of the patio door. Then, she wiggles her fingers in a little wave to let me know she's glad I'm alive. I go ahead and wave back. What the hell— she's pretty cute and I'm not dead.

Parker, who is heavily armed and has already demonstrated that he's not afraid to open fire if presented with what Sergeant Dixon might call "just cause," moves through the room.

"Lieutenant Ceepak, how you holding up, sir?"

"It's all good."

"Excellent," says Parker. "Anybody call while I was out?"

"Affirmative. Unfortunately, I was unable to answer my cell phone."

"Maybe they left a message." Now Parker gestures with his rifle.

"Took that shot at Mr. Alex Chalhoub's trigger finger from a hundred yards out. I still got it, don't I?"

"Roger that," says Ceepak, smiling for the first time all day.

"I hear *you* can pierce Roosevelt's ear on a dime."

"I never said that."

"I didn't say it was you who told it to me."

"Cyrus?" This from Senator Worthington.

"Good evening, Senator Worthington," says Parker.

"Are you aiding and abetting known threats to national security?"

"You mean Officers Ceepak and Boyle?"

The senator nods.

"Aw, relax. America can handle anything these two dish out. It's *you* she needs to worry about."

The senator looks livid.

Parker shrugs. "I'm just saying, is all."

"Mr. Parker, I no longer require your services. Your employment contract is hereby terminated."

"Excellent news, sir," says Parker, his voice booming. "Because I certainly wouldn't want to work for any man who tried to fry his own son."

"I have no earthly idea what you're talking about."

"Sure you do. That fire at the Hell Hole, the one that came this close to cremating your boy, you had these gentlemen from Echo Company set it for you. Now, now—don't deny it, sir. You're just ambitious, is all. Hell, you'd probably back a truck over your own mother if it helped you become president. And don't try lying to me, sir. Graves here might buy it but I've been sniffing your bullshit up close for way too long to continue buying any of it. It was arson. And Dixon's crew here—they were your arsonists."

My guess? Handy Andy took the lead. He is, as his nickname implies, handy. Plus, he's the one we saw dousing dead Iraqis with a can of kerosene during the slide show.

"Don't be preposterous, Cyrus! Your suggestion is absolutely laughable."

"Your son didn't think it was all that funny. Officer Ceepak was good enough to hook me up with a member of the FDNY who accompanied me to the hospital where he explained to your son exactly what happened. Said you had these gentlemen set one of those gasoline-upstairs, diesel-fuel-downstairs deals that typically insures that everybody inside the building comes out dead. You son would be here right now to personally tell you to go fuck yourself but, well, the doctors told him he couldn't leave the hospital just yet."

Now Parker reaches into his suit coat pocket.

"He did, however, ask me to show you this."

He pulls out a cell phone.

"It's Nextel's Motorola i-eight-sixty. Has a little video camera in it. Isn't that something? I've already seen the main feature. The clip's only about ten seconds long, shorter than that cell phone footage of Saddam Hussein's necktie party, and the image is kind of shaky, because your son had to hold the camera up over his head and point it down like this." Parker demonstrates. Stretches his arm over his head, wiggles the camera. "It was the only way he could capture what was going on in the toilet stall next to his." Now Parker gestures toward Dixon and Rutledge. "These two? They were too busy jamming a pistol into that sleepy young brother's mouth to look up and notice they were on candid camera. This one? He's the son of a bitch who squeezed the trigger."

Ceepak was right.

It was Dixon.

# 43

*After that,* things really started to deteriorate.

The all-for-one, one-for-all Airborne Rangers started turning on each other.

Handy Andy Prescott swore he had no idea what the other guys were doing inside the men's room. He thought it was all some kind of prank. He just cut a couple video cables out in the parking lot and wore a Hawaiian shirt. He was surprised when he heard that Shareef Smith was dead.

Miguel "Mickey Mex" Hernandez let loose with a string of what I can only assume were extremely foul Spanish words and went into a tirade about how he wasn't the one who screwed up, that he was only cleaning up Sergeant Dixon's mess again, that he knew the stupid tissue papers wouldn't work.

Stephen "Butt Lips" Rutledge? He didn't say much. He was one of the featured stars in Woodrow G. Worthington's homemade YouTube video.

We let the other cops haul Dixon and the rest of Echo Company back to the house—after we made sure the Smith sisters had a suite at one of our better bed-and-breakfasts. Looks like Ceepak's dad will have even more bunk mates this evening.

Senator Worthington? He made a few phone calls. I think the attorney general is a friend. The F.B.I. will arrest him tomorrow morning in one of those "surrendered himself to authorities" type deals.

Ceepak, Parker, Starky and I headed over to the rental house on Oak Street to say thanks to Captain Morkal and the other FDNY guys. First they saved our lives. Then they helped persuade the younger Winslow Worthington that he didn't have to live up to his nickname, he didn't have to remain Lieutenant Worthless. He could do something honorable and decent by telling us the truth about what happened to Shareef Smith in that restroom off the Garden State Parkway.

It was 11:00 when we arrived at Captain Morkal's rental house. Nobody was chanting or "hoo-hahing." Mostly it was just a bunch of guys sitting around sipping beers, listening to the ocean waves off in the distance, nibbling honey-roasted cashew nuts, and swapping stories.

Starky and I grabbed a beer then shared a bench together over at the picnic table while everybody else hung out in the deck chairs closer to the cooler.

"I came out with Mr. Parker because the GPS deal in my cell phone only told them your general vicinity but when I saw the neighborhood Diego and her Verizon buddy were pinging you in I had a pretty good idea it might be Crazy Janey's place on account of last night, at the party, she told me she was going up to the city today and the house would be empty and would I mind swinging by at some point during the day to make sure nobody broke in or anything since she knew that I was also a cop and not just a valet parking attendant only I couldn't remember the exact address so I hopped in Parker's SUV and showed him where to find you."

Starky is extremely attractive as she hyperventilates.

"Thanks," I say.

"No problem, sir. It's what partners do. We back each other up."

True. However, as we all learned in class today, it's what soldiers do too—sometimes when they probably shouldn't. So I guess the whole protect-your-comrades-at-all-costs concept might be one of those

"good thing–bad thing" situations. I'll have to ask my philosophy pro-
fessor, Dr. Ceepak, about it the next time things are extremely slow on
the job and I'm about to fall asleep anyway.

"Sir?" says Starky, sounding sort of nervous.

"Yeah?"

"Is it against departmental regulations for partners to fraternize?"

"Nah. I don't think so. Ceepak and I do it sometimes. Cookouts and
stuff. You and I are basically fraternizing right now."

She takes in a deep breath. "I was hoping for something more official. Would you like to have dinner together sometime? I make an awesome pork tenderloin."

"Sure. That'd be great. And then we could go see a movie."

"A movie would be awesome, sir."

Perhaps. But only if Sam Starky remembers my first name isn't
"Sir."


Starky headed home around midnight.

The firefighters regaled us with stories about their adventures in
New York City. Told us about the rich lady who parked in the no-
parking zone in front of their firehouse on West Fifty-eighth Street one
weekend and when somebody came out to tell her it was illegal she
said, "But it's Sunday. I thought you were closed."

We all laughed. Maybe too loud.

One of Captain Morkal's kids came out to the patio in his pj's. A boy
about six or seven. Guess we woke him up.

The captain propped his son up on his knee and told him not to
worry. That Ceepak and I were police officers and, even though we
were off duty, if anybody made too much noise again, we'd arrest them.

His son smiled and leaned against his father's chest while captain
Morkal hugged him tight.


It's time to call it a night. We're all just about unwound. All it took was
one beer to remind me that I'm totally wiped out.

"Gentlemen." It's all Cyrus Parker says as he stands up.

It's all he needs to say.

He extends his hand. Ceepak takes it first.

"Thank you, Cyrus."

"Hell, I'm an Airborne Ranger. Still livin' that life of guts and danger. Boyle."

He takes my hand. His is the size of a catcher's mitt.

"Tell me, Boyle—is Ceepak as good a shot as everybody down in Fort Campbell says he is?"

"Roger that," I say.

"Danny's quite good himself," says Ceepak.

Parker rumbles a laugh. "Well, seeing how I am currently unemployed, maybe I should stick around town. We could find us a range, make a friendly wager."

"Definitely," says Ceepak. "We could use the target range over at the state police training facilities."

"The state police, hunh? I wonder if they're hiring."

"I'm certain they can always use another good man, Colonel Parker." Parker seems surprised that Ceepak knows his former rank. Ceepak explains: "I still have a *few* friends in the military."

Parker takes off.

Captain Morkal's son has fallen asleep in his lap.

"We should go too," says Ceepak.

"Yeah. Thanks for the beer, guys."

We say our good-byes and climb into our cruiser.

"You want me to drop you off at your place?" I ask.

"Negative. I feel I should swing by the jail, first. Check in on my father. Make certain he's not causing the night shift any undue grief."

"I'll go with you."

Hey, Ceepak's old man listened to me once—maybe my "special skills" will be required again.

———

We walk into the police station.

The desk sergeant tells us that Mr. Ceepak is currently being held in the interrogation room.

"There's a lock on the door so we rolled in a cot and set him up for the night. He was aggravating all the other prisoners."

Ceepak was right. His old man is nothing but trouble.

"Sorry about that," he says. "We'll go have a word with him."

"Yeah," I say, "I'll tell him to behave or he gets zero aspirins when his hangover kicks in."

We head up the hall. Ceepak uses his master key to unlock the IR door.

When we walk in, Mr. Ceepak isn't in the cot they've set up for him. He's sitting at the far end of the conference table.

Smiling.

"Well, hello, Johnny. I hear you two boys had a very busy day today."

Ceepak clenches his jaw.

"When I was in the back, I had a nice little chat with those Army morons you arrested. So they staged it, hunh? Killed one of their own guys and made it look like a suicide?"

"That's right."

Mr. Ceepak leans back in his chair. "I gotta tell you, son, I'm surprised you caught them. Guess you weren't too busy overseas this time, off in Germany being a hot-shit soldier. They do the bit with the pistol jammed up the kid's mouth?"

Ceepak nods.

"Just like your little brother Billy, hunh? And it took, what? All five of them to pull it off? Jesus. I always told you I'm better than any of you pissants in the Army." He taps the side of his bony skull. "Smarter too."

Ceepak's eyes narrow. "Are you suggesting Billy's suicide wasn't?"

"You figure it out, hotshot. You figure it out."


I have a feeling Ceepak will be heading home to Ohio soon. There is no statute of limitations on murder.

At least his mother will be safe: I think Mr. Ceepak said enough to keep him locked up while the State of Ohio puts together its case for a decades-old crime. They don't usually let you post bail when you're a murder suspect.

I'm sorry I didn't get to meet Ceepak's mom. I have a feeling she's the main reason John Ceepak turned out the way he did and became one of those "glints of courage" that Gladys-the-veggie told us about, struggling "to the light amid the thorns."

When I got home to my apartment, I shuffled through my iPod and found that Springsteen song Ceepak mentioned when he and I were discussing his mother. The one called "The Wish." The one Bruce wrote for his own mom.

I think these are the lyrics Ceepak wanted me to hear:

*If pa's eyes were windows*
*Into a world so deadly and true*
*You couldn't stop me from looking*
*But you kept me from crawlin' through*

Don't worry, Mrs. Ceepak. Your son might've looked into that deadly darkness, but he didn't crawl through.

And I won't, either.

We'll just head out to Ohio and piece together another puzzle.

You'll see, Mr. Ceepak. We'll figure it out.

Well—your son definitely will.